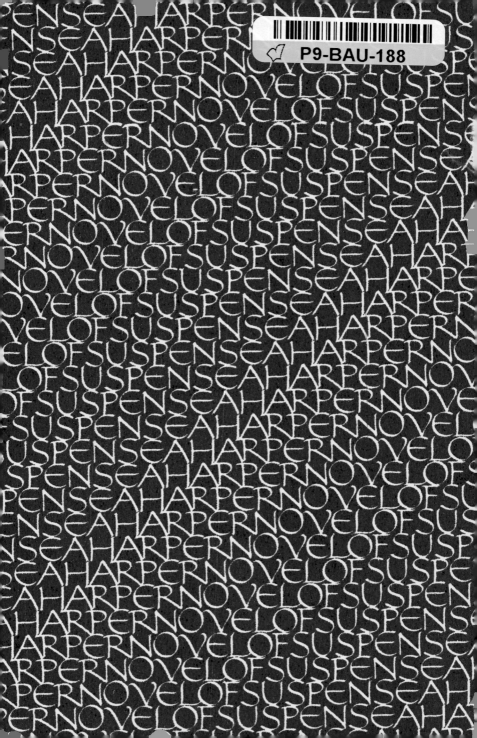

RIPOFF

• • • • • • • • •

Books by Arthur Maling

RIPOFF

BENT MAN

DINGDONG

THE SNOWMAN

LOOPHOLE

GO-BETWEEN

DECOY

RIPOFF

· · · · · · · · ·

Arthur Maling

HARPER & ROW, PUBLISHERS
New York, Evanston, San Francisco, London

A HARPER NOVEL OF SUSPENSE

FIRST EDITION

Designed by C. Linda Dingler

Library of Congress Cataloging in Publication Data

Maling, Arthur.
  Ripoff.
  I. Title.
PZ4.M25Ri   [PS3563.A4313]   813'.5'4   75-25091
ISBN 0-06-012809-7

76 77 78 79 10 9 8 7 6 5 4 3 2 1

For
Faith Baldwin,
with affection and gratitude

RIPOFF

• • • • • • • • •

● ● ● ● ● ● ● ●

I don't like anonymous telephone calls. Especially when they come through at one o'clock in the morning. And when the caller is drunk.

But I've learned not to disregard them. Under any circumstances.

"I want to talk to Brockton Potter," the man said, slurring the words.

"This is Brockton Potter," I said.

"I want to talk to Potter—Brockton Potter."

"That's me. What's on your mind?"

"I want to talk to Potter," he said again. "I know something."

The girl beside me sat up and pulled the sheet around her. Her name was Monica. We'd met for the first time earlier in the evening. She pushed her hair back from her face and reached for a cigarette.

"I *am* Potter," I said impatiently. "Who are you? What are you trying to say?"

"I've got some information. About Interlake General."

"Who are you?" The matches were on the table at my side of the bed. I struck one for Monica.

"I work for Interlake and I know something."

"What's your name?"

There was a silence. Finally the man said, "They're crooks."

"Who are you, and what's your job?" I asked.

There was another silence.

Monica exhaled smoke. "What's going on?"

I shrugged.

"Screw you," the man said. "The only one I'll talk to is Brockton Potter." And he hung up.

I frowned at the telephone, then put it down. "Give me a drag," I said to Monica.

She handed me the cigarette. She had lovely shoulders. "Do your friends often call at this hour?"

"That was just a drunk." I inhaled and offered her the cigarette.

"Keep it," she said. "I have to be going."

"So soon?" I was disappointed. I'd expected her to stay the night.

"I have to work in the morning."

"Artists don't keep regular hours." She'd told me she was a sculptor.

"This one does." She moved to the other side of the bed and got out.

It wasn't only her shoulders that were lovely.

She started to dress. She paused to examine the pile of reports on the table beside the chair on which she'd put her clothes. "Are you in the insurance business?"

"Not exactly. But I do research on insurance companies, among other things." I stubbed out the cigarette. "I'll drive you home."

"Don't bother. I can take a cab." She hooked her brassiere and stepped into her slacks.

She'd have stayed, I thought, if the telephone hadn't rung. "What are you doing tomorrow night?"

"Going to Long Island." She zipped the slacks and pulled the sweater over her head. Then as she arranged her hair she looked around the room. She noticed the Picasso drawing. "Is that an original?"

"Yes."

She eyed me. "Research," she said thoughtfully.

"I'd like to see you again. What about Sunday night?"

"I'll still be on Long Island."

"What's your last name? I'll call you."

She smiled. "You're a researcher. Do some research."

"Come on now, Monica."

"Don't get up. I'll find my way out." She left the bedroom.

I put on a robe and went after her. "Monica!"

She was out the front door before I could stop her. I watched her as she walked briskly toward Fifth Avenue. A taxi went by. She signaled. The driver stopped.

I closed the door and went upstairs. They arrest people for drunken driving, I thought; they ought to arrest them for drunken telephoning too.

But later in the day the same man called again. And this time he was sober.

2

● ● ● ● ● ● ● ●

I'd had breakfast with Dr. David Chang. As a favor to Jim Berry.

Jim was with the Mason Growth Fund. He was my friend as well as my client. He'd been told about Chang by Allen Winston, a competitor of mine, and wanted me to give him my opinion. Chang, a Chinese-American from Boston, was an eye doctor. He'd come up with a new kind of plastic for contact lenses. It enabled the wearer to keep them in his eyes longer than lenses made from any other material and with less danger of infection. He'd formed a company to manufacture the lenses and needed money. Allen's firm was going to float a stock issue. He was urging Jim to buy a large jag of the shares.

Chang and I ate in his suite at the Regency and talked for two hours. I don't know anything about contact lenses but I do know how to interpret figures, and the figures Chang showed me looked good. Furthermore, he struck me as level-headed and bright. I came away from the meeting in a cheerful mood. Not only could I recommend that Jim buy the stock, but I could put some of my other clients into it as well.

It was noon when I got home. And the telephone rang almost immediately. I hurried to answer it, thinking that the caller was Jim Berry. It wasn't, however. It was Tom Petacque. I have two partners. Tom is the likable one.

"How about a workout this afternoon?" he asked.

I hesitated. Tom and I often played squash on Saturday afternoons. Both of us enjoyed the game. But I had vague thoughts of going back to the bar where I'd met Monica and finding out who she was.

"How did it go with the doctor?" Tom asked.

"Fine. I think he's on to something."

"Great. I want to hear about it. Come on up to the club. We'll play a few games, then we can talk."

I let myself be persuaded and agreed to meet him at three o'clock.

I sat down at my desk and began to write up the notes I'd made during the session with Chang. The squeal of brakes startled me. I went to the window and looked out. A taxi had almost hit a car. The cabby was shouting at the driver of the car. I sighed. I'd half known when I bought the house that I was buying an illusion; that while West Eleventh Street has a tranquil nineteenth-century air, in reality it trembles with the same anger as the rest of twentieth-century Manhattan. But I still didn't like to be reminded of that fact.

The taxi skirted the car and went on its way.

My telephone rang.

"Mr. Potter?"

"Yes." He sounded like the man who'd called the night before, but I wasn't sure. "Who is this?"

"I can't give you my name, but I have some information that'll be of interest to you."

"Did you call me last night?"

"I might have."

"You said something about Interlake General."

"I guess I did call then, because that's what I want to talk to you about."

"I'd take you more seriously if you'd give me your name."

"I can't, Mr. Potter. They'd kill me if they knew I was talking to you."

5

A disgruntled employee, I thought. "Then perhaps it'd be better if you didn't talk to me."

"I'm telling the truth, Mr. Potter. I'm in danger. If the facts about Interlake come out, it'll be as big a scandal as Yankee Clipper."

I felt a prickling at the back of my neck. It was the feeling I'd been getting recently whenever anyone mentioned Yankee Clipper. Almost thirty million dollars' worth of policies had been sold at a discount by the Yankee Clipper Life Insurance Society to other insurance companies—on people who didn't exist. And I was the one who'd exposed the fraud.

Lightning doesn't strike twice in the same place, I thought. For the facts about Yankee Clipper had come to my attention in exactly the same way: by an anonymous telephone call from one of the employees of the company. "From what I know of Interlake," I said, "it doesn't sell its policies to reinsurers."

"I'm not talking about that. I'm talking about the assets."

"What about them?"

"Some of them aren't there."

"What!"

"They've been stolen."

Another kook? As a result of the publicity I'd received in connection with Yankee Clipper, a number of oddballs had managed to get in touch with me. One kept insisting that Lloyds of London was a front for Palestinian terrorists.

"That's impossible," I said.

"It's not impossible. It's happened."

"I don't believe you. The Insurance Commission examiners—"

"Mr. Potter, twenty-three million dollars' worth of securities have been stolen. I have a list of them."

"Then I suggest you show it to the Insurance Commission and let them investigate."

"I intend to. But I'd like you to see it first."

Whoever he was, he'd read all about the Yankee Clipper case. The man who'd blown the whistle on that company had taken the same precaution: he'd informed me and then the Insurance Commission and told each of us that he'd told the other. "All right," I said after a moment. "Send it to me. I'll take a look."

"Without an explanation the list wouldn't mean anything."

A kook—no. Someone with a chip on his shoulder—yes. I said nothing.

"Mr. Potter, if it comes out that I tried to tell you and you wouldn't listen—"

"Don't threaten me. I don't like it."

"I'm not threatening you. I just want to tell you what's going on. Please!" Desperation crept into his voice.

I felt a stirring of uneasiness. Suppose he'd stumbled across a lesser irregularity and misunderstood it. It still might bear looking into. On the other hand, the fact that I'd exposed one crooked insurance company didn't make me a policeman for the entire industry. "All I am is a securities analyst," I said.

"Please! I can't leave town without people getting suspicious, but you can come here. You can—"

"Wait a minute. Where's 'here'?"

"Chicago."

I should have known. Interlake General was a Chicago-based company. Yet I'd assumed that the man was calling from New York. I was surprised—and glad to have an out. "Sorry," I said. "I don't take trips to meet people who won't give me their name."

His voice grew even more desperate. *"Please,* Mr. Potter! I *can't* give you my name. Not *now.* It's too *dangerous.* But *don't* say no. At least *think* about it. I'll call you back tomorrow. Maybe by then you'll change your mind. *Please!"*

He didn't give me a chance to refuse again. He hung up.

3

My backhand has always been the weakest part of my game. Usually I'm able to compensate for it with speed and with tricky shots that hit the front wall like two inches above the floor and then drop. But today the compensatory abilities weren't working. Tom had won the first game 21–14, the second game 21–12 and was winning the third game 15–6. In addition to having been run ragged, I'd been hit twice by the ball, simply because I hadn't got out of the way fast enough.

It was my serve. I paused to catch my breath, then lobbed the ball gently. It bounced back from the wall and all but landed on Tom's racket. He aimed a shot at the right front corner. I reached the ball easily and slammed it hard enough to send it ricocheting from the front wall to the back one. Tom got to it before it touched the floor and swatted it. It struck the front wall high and arced toward the rear left-hand corner of the court—my perennial nemesis. I raced for it, swung, misjudged, hit the wall with my racket, lost my balance and crashed into the wall.

I wasn't hurt, but I was momentarily stunned.

Tom came over. "Are you O.K.?"

"Yes."

"Are you sure?"

"Yes."

I picked up my racket and we resumed the game. Tom eased

off, but even that didn't do me any good. He won the next five points and was about to win the game when I careened into the wall again—the back wall this time—and broke my racket.

"What the hell," he said. "We'd better quit."

I nodded, and the two of us trudged off to the locker room. We showered and dressed in silence.

"Something on your mind?" Tom asked finally.

I shrugged.

"Well, in case you haven't noticed, your shirt is buttoned cockeyed."

I looked. It was. I rebuttoned it.

"Come on," he said. "I'll buy you a drink."

We went down to the bar. He asked me about Chang. I gave him my opinion, rather disjointedly.

"Something *is* bugging you," he said after a while.

I was reluctant to tell him. I knew he'd overreact. I decided I'd better, though. "A man called me last night and again this afternoon. He seems to want me to expose another insurance company."

He did overreact. He put his drink down very slowly. Some of the color left his face. His expression became guarded. And with Tom that was a bad sign. His manner was normally breezy and candid. He didn't act cautious unless he was genuinely upset.

"What did *you* say?"

"I brushed him off. But he didn't want to be brushed off. He said he's going to call again tomorrow."

Tom examined his fingernails and frowned. "I have a hangnail," he said.

I watched him. We'd been friends for ten years and partners for four of them. I was as close to him as I was to anyone. I understood him. He'd grown up in a military environment. His father was a retired general. His brother had chosen an army career, and his sister had married a graduate of West Point. Courage had been stressed throughout his childhood. It was dif-

9

ficult for him to admit that he was scared. And yet he scared easily. I'd learned that during the Yankee Clipper turmoil. He was a great securities salesman and a beautiful human being—kind, sincere, conscientious, honest, generous. But it didn't take much to make him panic inside, and he knew it. So he tried extra hard to appear cool.

"Chances are the guy's a nut or an alcoholic," I said reassuringly. "The first time he called he was drunk as a skunk."

Tom fiddled with the hangnail. "Another Yankee Clipper situation could put us out of business, Brock."

"It wouldn't do us any good, I agree. But look at it the other way: suppose the man's right, even a little bit, and it eventually gets around that he tried to tell us and we ignored him. What would happen to our reputation then?"

The hangnail got the better of him. He made an attempt to bite it off and failed. Then made another attempt and succeeded. He dropped his hand and stared at the tabletop. "I think," he said, "that we'd better have a directors' meeting. As soon as possible. Do you want to call Mark, or shall I?"

I sighed. Telling him had been the right thing to do, and Mark was certainly entitled to the information also. But a directors' meeting hardly seemed necessary. "Nothing's happened yet, Tom," I said. "Just a couple of phone calls. Let's wait and see."

"No, Brock. Nothing's happened yet, but something might. And I don't want it to. And if you go off half cocked—"

"I'm not going off half cocked, for Christ's sake! All I did was answer the telephone."

"Nevertheless, I think the three of us ought to talk it over. Do you want to call Mark, or shall I?"

"You call him. You're the one who wants the meeting."

He got up from the table and left the room.

I was annoyed. At myself for having mentioned the matter. And at Tom for insisting on a meeting. He was the one who was going off half cocked, not I.

He returned shortly. "He's leaving for Southampton in a few minutes," he reported. "It's his father-in-law's birthday. But he agreed to come back in the morning. We're going to get together at your place at eleven."

"Great," I said without enthusiasm.

He looked more cheerful. Sharing the problem with Mark seemed to have eased the internal pressure.

But my own mood had deteriorated to the point where I began to see the dark side of things, and I was glad, after just one drink, to get away from him.

4

The name of our firm is Price, Potter and Petacque, and some wag once called us three peas in a pod. But he was totally wrong. We don't look alike and we don't think alike. The only unanimous decision we ever reached was the decision to go into business together. Everything after that was a matter of disagreement and compromise.

Tom and I had worked for the same brokerage house. He'd been in sales and I'd been one of the securities analysts. We'd known and liked each other. Mark had been an outsider. What had attracted us to him had been his money, not his personality.

It was a continual source of surprise to me that people like Mark Price still existed. He was straight out of the world of F. Scott Fitzgerald. Updated perhaps, but only to a limited degree. Groton, Yale, Southampton, a duplex on Fifth Avenue—the whole bit. With the casual arrogance, the cool good manners and the strange eccentricities that can be produced by that sort of background.

For a number of years he'd worked for his father, who was a senior partner in Price, Underhill, the investment bankers. But he and the old man hadn't got along, so he'd left the company, bought his own seat on the New York Stock Exchange and at the time Tom and I became acquainted with him was trading for his own account. Fortunately for Tom and me, the idea of forming a brokerage house of our own appealed to him.

In spite of the problems that most stockbrokers were having, we'd done well. Perhaps because we were a specialty house. We didn't deal much with the general public. Our customers were the funds.

Doing business with the funds has become less profitable now that it's legal for them to negotiate the commission rates on the large blocks of securities they buy and sell. You can still make out, though—and we did. By negotiating commissions, but only up to a point. What we had to offer was personal service. That included research. Which was where I came in. I'd built one of the best little research teams on Wall Street. Cheapest isn't best, our firm argued; if you want our service you have to pay for it. And some of the biggest funds were willing to do so.

Tom, Mark and I were equal partners. While I handled the research, Tom was in charge of sales and Mark ran the office. Tom was one of the best securities salesmen I'd ever known. Besides understanding stocks and bonds, he had a knack for making friends. He'd managed to build up close relationships with money managers all over the country.

And to give him his due, Mark was good at his thing too. He was meticulous and thorough and worked like hell. The trouble with him was his temperament.

Not the arrogance—that was more or less offset by the good manners—but the eccentricities. For despite his wealth, he was one of the stingiest men I'd ever met. At least in small things. He did own a ten-room duplex on Fifth Avenue. And a sixty-foot schooner. And a five-acre spread in Greenwich, Connecticut. But he and his wife served drugstore hard candies to their guests, and the cigarettes in their cigarette urns had been there so long that they fell apart when you picked them up, and Mark had been wearing the same raincoat for as long as I'd known him. Furthermore, he believed that everyone was out to cheat him.

I didn't mind getting up hungry from the dinner table at his house, but I did object to the difficulties he created at the office. He checked expense accounts to such a point that several of our best people had resigned in protest. The switchboard operators were always complaining that he drove them crazy, questioning them about the monthly telephone bills. And he suspected our suppliers and customers alike of trying to put something over on us.

Yet when I'd got us into trouble over the Yankee Clipper situation, Mark had stood by me more staunchly than Tom had.

It was odd how my efforts had backfired. To the public I was a white knight. Dauntless securities analyst exposes huge fraud. Persistent researcher topples giant insurance company. The Lone Ranger rides again!

Since our firm doesn't depend upon the public, however, public approval wasn't important. And the people we do depend upon saw the matter in an entirely different light.

The Securities and Exchange Commission, for example. The folks there were sore as the devil, because I'd tipped them off after I'd tipped off our customers. I'd been too excited at the time to realize that I was doing anything wrong, but the SEC didn't approve of my actions and the SEC runs the show. It censured us. And almost gave us a thirty-day suspension.

Then there were the customers themselves. I couldn't warn all of them simultaneously, so each one accused me of warning the others first. Yankee Clipper stock went from fifty-eight to twenty-one in a week, and I simply couldn't convince anyone that he'd got out at the right time. As a result, we lost business.

And finally I became a pariah among insurance men. Outwardly they treated me with more respect than ever before. Presidents and chairmen of the board were suddenly delighted to take me to lunch. But they'd become afraid of me and behind my back they passed the word to their underlings: "Watch out for Potter; he's a troublemaker." Even the companies that had been bilked by Yankee Clipper and should have been grateful to me grew cautious when I was around. I eventually came to the conclusion that they preferred being bilked to being shown up in public as suckers. In any event, information became hard to get.

None of which was fatal. All of which hurt. And made me less than eager to be a popular hero for the second time.

Mark arrived first. In his motoring outfit: jeans and torn sneakers.

The birthday party had been very nice, he said. Two orchestras, a hundred and fifty guests. He'd given his father-in-law a meerschaum pipe.

"Now, what's the rhubarb about?" he asked presently. "Rhubarb" was one of his favorite words. He used it to mean anything that disturbed the even tenor of life.

I started to tell him, but before I could get into it Tom arrived.

I made some Bloody Marys and served them, explaining as I did so that I didn't think the meeting was really necessary.

"Maybe not," Tom said, "but we ought to agree on a course of action anyway. Just in case."

I shrugged and gave them a résumé of the two telephone calls, keeping it as low-keyed as possible and watching them closely for their reactions. Mark's expression as he listened was slightly bored, which didn't necessarily mean that he was bored, and Tom chose to mask his anxiety by savoring his Bloody Mary as if it were a rare cognac.

"Twenty-three million," Mark said when I finished. "That'd be quite a ripoff."

"If somebody actually stole the stuff," I said.

"Do you think it's possible?" he asked.

"That's not the point," Tom said. "The point is, suppose somebody did steal it—what business is it of ours? Our obligation is to our customers, not to the stockholders of Interlake General." He glanced at Mark. "Right?"

"If I remember correctly," Mark said, "some of our customers

15

are stockholders of Interlake General." And he glanced at me. I nodded. I'd recommended the stock.

Tom lost some of his cool. He put his glass down sharply on the table beside him. "What the hell. How big is Interlake General? I'd like to know exactly. Look it up, Brock."

I took *Best's* off the bookshelf and, almost staggering under the weight of the enormous volume, put it on the desk. I flipped the pages until I came to Interlake General. "Total assets $375,391,-020," I said.

"So a loss of twenty-three million wouldn't put them out of business."

I looked at him. So did Mark. Tom flushed. "I'm concerned about our customers too," he said. "After all, I'm the one who sold them the stock and I'm the one who has to deal with them day after day. All I'm saying is, Interlake isn't in danger of going under even if twenty-three million was stolen. And," he added darkly, "next time we *will* draw a suspension."

"Come off it," I said. "First of all, we don't know that the man will call me again. I may have discouraged him. Second of all, we don't know that he isn't a nut. And thirdly, I can't imagine any stocks or bonds being stolen from an insurance company. They're audited like you wouldn't believe. By their own outside auditing firms as well as by the state insurance commissions. A theft like that would have to be an inside job, and anyone on the inside would know that he'd be caught. You're being too pessimistic, Tom."

"Maybe," he said. "But you never know."

"Balls," Mark said with scorn, and held his glass out to me. "I'll have another drink, if you don't mind."

"Damn it, don't act so superior!" Tom told him furiously.

I was about to take Mark's glass, but I was so surprised that I dropped my hand. Tom rarely lost his temper. "But why take such a dim view?" I asked.

He got himself under control. "I don't like Anton Lipp."

"Neither do I," Mark said, "but that doesn't prove anything."

I glanced from one to the other. It was one of those moments. Anton Lipp was chairman of the board of Computech, the conglomerate that controlled Interlake General. We'd never exchanged opinions of him, but I didn't like him either. "That makes three of us," I said. "But I agree with Mark. That doesn't prove anything. And God knows, he's built a hell of a business."

Mark waved his glass. "A drink, please."

I gave him another Bloody Mary.

"So I'm not altogether out of line, am I?" Tom asked.

Mark said nothing. I was certain, though, that he appreciated Tom's intelligence as much as I did. For regardless of his inner stresses, Tom was no fool. He could size up a man or a situation with considerable accuracy. Intuitively.

"Not altogether," I said. "But I think you're letting your feelings get in the way of your judgment."

"And you're jumpy," Mark threw in.

Tom flushed again and started to reply, but checked himself. I felt sorry for him. He'd obviously expected Mark to back him up or he wouldn't have called for a meeting. And Mark wasn't performing as anticipated.

Mark turned to me. "It *is* possible, I suppose, that someone might deliberately be trying to get us into trouble."

"Like who?" I asked.

"One of the Yankee Clipper crowd."

"They're too busy trying to stay out of jail. Besides, what would they gain?"

"Revenge."

Tom looked at him. "I may be jumpy," he said, "but you're paranoid."

And before Mark could reply, the telephone rang.

None of us moved.

It rang again.

I took a deep breath and went across to the desk.

"Mr. Potter?"

I covered the mouthpiece with my hand. "It's him."

Tom jumped up and hurried over to join me. He put his ear close to mine.

I uncovered the mouthpiece. "Yes."

"Have you thought about what I told you?" the man asked.

Tom put his hand over mine so that he too was holding the telephone.

"Yes," I said. "I still think you ought to go to the Insurance Commission. And if it's a case of theft, the police. I'm a securities analyst, not a criminal investigator."

"If I tell you who I am, will you help me?"

I hadn't expected him to give in on that point. I didn't know what to say. I could feel Tom shaking his head. I glanced at Mark. He was regarding me with the same bored expression he'd been wearing earlier. "What kind of help do you need?" I asked.

"Immunity from prosecution. And protection."

"I'm in no position to offer either one. That's up to the law."

"But if I gave you the evidence and you explained things to them I'd have a better chance."

My doubts vanished. "O.K.," I said. "I think I understand. Call me back in half an hour, and I'll give you a definite answer." I put the telephone down. Tom's hand went with it.

"That was quick," he said.

"I believe he's on the level." I went back to where I'd been sitting.

He followed me.

I told Mark what had been said. "He's looking for an intermediary," I added. "Someone to clear a path for him so that he can go to the police. He doesn't think the Insurance Commission would do that, so he wants me to."

"Therefore you're convinced he's done something illegal," Tom said.

"Exactly."

18

Mark raised an eyebrow. "And you're inclined to go along with him?"

"I believe I should," I said.

He crossed his legs and considered the hole in his right sneaker. "Tom's right, you know. We really could do without another rhubarb."

"On the other hand," Tom said, "if there's something wrong at Interlake, we owe it to our customers to find out what it is."

I shouldn't have been surprised. I'd learned early on that there was one thing you could count on when you had partners: they'd change sides at least once on every issue. Yet I was surprised.

"I'm not saying we don't," Mark said. "All I'm saying is, we haven't yet recovered from the last rhubarb."

"What's the point of having a research department," Tom asked, "if we don't give it any scope?"

I said nothing. I just listened. Each of them presented the other's arguments. Then they switched back again.

But finally I entered the fray. "Look. The man's called three times. He obviously has a story he wants to tell. I don't know how true it'll turn out to be, but I don't think I should ignore it and I don't think either of you really wants me to. Regardless of what happened the last time, I think each of you wants me to keep on trying to get information, as much as possible, no matter what kind it is, because in the long run that's the only thing that makes us different from any other house—the quality of our information. Am I wrong?"

Tom shook his head.

Mark sipped his drink.

"So," I said, "I'm going to take a chance. You both know damn well that whatever I find out, I'll talk to you before I go further. Any objections?"

Neither of them spoke. So it became simply a matter of waiting for the telephone to ring again. And presently it did.

Tom kept his seat this time.

I told the man I'd come to Chicago on two conditions: that when I got there he'd identify himself and that he'd back up whatever he said with concrete evidence. He agreed. I also said that I was making no promise to do anything for him in return; I'd hear his story, period. He hesitated, but in the end he accepted that condition too.

"All right," I said. "How shall we proceed?"

He instructed me to check into the Astor Tower Hotel in Chicago the following evening—there'd be a room reserved in my name. He'd come to see me at ten o'clock.

I said that I would, and the conversation ended.

And since there was nothing further for Tom and Mark and me to discuss, they left shortly after that.

I went back to *Best's* and read the rest of the page.

5

Forty-three percent of the assets of Interlake General Insurance Company of North America were in stocks and bonds. A little over $162 million. The rest were.in mortgages, treasury notes and real estate.

I closed the book and put it back on the shelf. It had served to refresh my memory but hadn't told me anything new. Founded forty-eight years before by J. J. Oliver, the company had grown from a fly-by-night outfit that peddled small life-insurance policies to factory workers, mainly employees of the steel mills around Chicago, into one of the giants of the industry, with almost two billion dollars' worth of insurance in force. It was conservatively run and immensely profitable.

I'd only met J. J. Oliver once. He'd come to address a meeting of the New York Society of Security Analysts. He was eighty-one years old at the time, and on the edge of senility. His glasses kept slipping down his nose, and he kept pushing them back. He misread his notes and had to correct himself. He forgot the punch line of the one joke he tried to tell. But in spite of all that, he was an admirable figure. An aging tiger who'd gone the whole route and who, even though he was failing, could still outwit most of the men in the room.

The following year he'd let Interlake get taken over by Computech.

Computech was the creation of Anton Lipp, who was even more of a legend than J. J. Oliver was. A Lithuanian immigrant, he'd run a tiny computer-leasing company, which he'd started on five hundred dollars, into a multibillion-dollar conglomerate that controlled everything from a hospital-equipment firm to a fleet of tuna-fishing boats. But his biggest coup was the acquisition of Interlake. Having decided that it would make a nice addition to his empire, he went after it boldly, with a tender offer for Interlake stock at five dollars above the market price. And J. J. Oliver surrendered without a fight. Not only didn't he resist the takeover, he sold his own stock to Lipp. For something like $71 million. Which was a coup for him too. His one son had died in a plane crash, and his grandchildren weren't interested in the business: there was no one to carry on. So Interlake became a virtual subsidiary of Computech, and J. J. Oliver retired with his bankbook and two nurses to Delray Beach, Florida, where he became increasingly senile and, after two years, died.

A few of his cronies retired about the time he did and were replaced by Lipp's men. But there were no important changes in the way Interlake was run. Lipp didn't interfere much with management, and in my conversations with the Oliver people who'd stayed on I found them to be a contented lot. They liked the handful of new officers Lipp had placed in their midst, and the company was doing as well as it ever had.

Interlake stock was still traded independently of Computech, and I thought well of it. I thought well of Computech too, for that matter, even though I had reservations about Lipp personally. He'd come too far too fast, it seemed to me, with too few setbacks.

I brooded for a few minutes about what I was letting myself in for, then made a conscious effort to think about something else. My father had, in a manner of speaking, brooded himself to death, and I was determined not to follow in his footsteps.

The effort succeeded. I went out to learn what I could about Monica.

We'd met at The Cyclops, a bar on Christopher Street. I'd noticed her (a) because she was a good-looking woman; (b) because she was alone; and (c) because like myself she was too old for the place. The Cyclops catered to a mixed crowd. All kinds of people went there. But most of them were under thirty. Anyone over thirty-five was conspicuous. I was thirty-nine. Since the breakup with Carol, however, I'd had a lot of free evenings and I'd taken to dropping into The Cyclops a couple of times a week. I liked the atmosphere and in spite of the generation gap I'd managed to make friends.

"Haven't we met somewhere before?" I asked. Not original, but true. I really did feel that we had.

She looked me over and smiled. "Anything's possible," she said.

She was as willing to get acquainted as I was, and conversation was no problem. Neither of us could remember where we'd met or even whether we had, but we discovered that we had certain things in common. Both of us had been born in the Midwest, preferred cold weather to hot, had an inexplicable yen to see Australia and had once broken an arm.

About her present life she was evasive. All I was able to find out was that she sculpted, that she lived in the neighborhood and that she'd never before been to The Cyclops. Nor did she ask me questions about my present life. Which was all right with me. Except that I began to get certain vibrations. The strongest of them was that if I propositioned her she'd accept. The next strongest was that if I didn't proposition her she'd wait around until someone else did.

So I suggested that she come home with me. And she said yes. Proving to me once again that I should never doubt my vibes.

But sometimes they didn't tell me enough. In this case they didn't tell me that she'd be a very imaginative lover. Or that I'd end up pursuing her.

23

The bartender on duty was Dennis McMahon. Dennis was by training a singer. He'd come to New York to find a show to sing in, but hadn't found one. Though he made good money at The Cyclops, he was dissatisfied.

"What's happening?" he asked as he put a beer in front of me.

"Not much," I said. "You?"

"Not much. Friend of mine called up yesterday. Has a place in Boston. Needs a bartender."

"Are you interested?"

Dennis shrugged.

I tried to remember whether he'd been behind the bar when Monica came in. "You know the girl I was talking to night before last?"

"Friday night?" He frowned.

"Long black hair, black eyes. She was wearing a blue sweater. Said her name was Monica."

"I remember you were talking to the guy who's always talking about dogs."

"Cal Ringer. It was after that."

"Doberman pinschers are gentle, he was trying to tell you."

"It must have been around nine-thirty."

Dennis shook his head. "I went off duty at nine. In a pig's eye, they're gentle. Killers is what they are. There'd be less competition in Boston."

"We were sitting over there."

"The thing is, my agent's in New York. But for all the good he does me, I might as well be in Boston."

I gave up. There was no one else in the bar at the moment. The Cyclops did most of its business at night. I sipped my beer.

Larry With The Rings came in. At least that was what I called him, for his first name was Larry and he always wore a lot of jewelry. He made the stuff in his spare time. I was quite certain he'd been there when I was talking to Monica.

He recalled seeing her. "The broad with the blue sweater and the big tits?"

"That's the one. She said her name was Monica."

"Never saw her before." He held out his arm. "How do you like the bracelet? I just finished it."

"Very nice. She said she lives in the neighborhood."

"Could be. Chris wants it, but I think I'm going to keep it myself."

Larry With The Rings was followed by a man I'd never seen before. He, in turn, was followed by an airline steward. I couldn't think of the steward's name but I knew he worked for Pan Am and was on the transatlantic run. I wasn't sure whether he'd been in The Cyclops on Friday night or not. I asked him. He said he hadn't, he'd been in London. London had had nothing but rain recently.

At three-thirty I left. I walked down Christopher Street toward the river, looking at faces. Then I went over to Seventh Avenue and looked at more faces. I saw several women who resembled Monica until I got close. I wondered whether she really had gone to Long Island. And whether she really did live in the neighborhood.

After an hour of idle walking I decided to go over to Eighth Street. The stores there were open on Sunday, and I needed a pair of shoes.

At the corner of Eighth Street and Avenue of the Americas I heard a familiar voice say, "Brock."

I turned.

It was Carol.

She always seemed to cross my path when I was daydreaming about someone else.

"Going my way?" she asked.

"Sort of," I replied. "I had in mind to buy a pair of shoes."

She took my arm. There was an intimacy about the way she did it that made me uncomfortable. She wanted to remain friends even though we were no longer lovers, and that was the sort of relationship I'd never been able to handle.

The light changed. We crossed the street.

"So what have you been up to?" she asked, still holding my arm.

"Same old thing."

"How are Tom and Mark?"

"O.K. How's Perry?" Perry was her boss. He operated a firm that bought women's wear for small clothing stores around the country that couldn't afford to send buyers to New York every few weeks.

"He was home with the flu all week. He always seems to get sick when we're the busiest. I've been running my legs off."

The sidewalk was too crowded in places for us to walk side by side. She let go of my arm. I felt relief. It wasn't that I didn't like her. It was that I could no longer muster the emotion which had once come naturally, and felt guilty. Our drifting apart hadn't been entirely my fault. Both of us had the same flaw, Carol said: we couldn't sustain love. But I wasn't in analysis, as she was, and I couldn't accept my flaws as readily as she could accept hers.

"Tough," I said, then noticed that I was alone. Carol had stopped to look in the window of a bookstore. I waited for her to catch up with me.

We reached the shoe store. Everything on display seemed too gaudy. We walked on. Carol took my arm again. "Incidentally," she said, "I've got a tip for you."

She was always giving me tips. The stock market interested her.

"Really?"

"Vagabond is in trouble."

"Apparently," I said. Vagabond Sportswear had come up from nowhere and got itself listed on the American Exchange. The stock had had a steep rise and was now having a steep decline. I'd never liked garment industry stocks: they were too volatile. This was a case in point.

"I feel sorry for Victor," Carol said. "I haven't seen him lately, but they tell me he looks terrible."

26

"Victor?"

"Victor Lane. You remember him. I introduced you to him at the party the Grosses gave last Christmas. He owns Vagabond."

"It escapes me."

"The tall man with the mustache. He was getting a divorce at the time."

I had no recollection of him.

"Anyway," Carol went on, "he got the divorce right after that and married the woman he was running around with. The artist. She paints or sculpts or something. But now everything's going to pot. The line is terrible, and he's not paying his bills. I've heard there might be a creditors' meeting. If you ask me, he just wasn't paying enough attention to business."

Something registered. "The woman he married, the artist—was she at the Grosses' too?"

"Yes."

"Black hair, black eyes, tall?"

"That's the one. Her name's Monica or something like that. She's supposed to be a pretty good artist but the world's worst tramp. They say she'll sleep with anybody."

6

Every Monday morning at nine o'clock the research staff went into a huddle. That was the only time during the week when we worked together formally as a group. On Monday mornings we pooled our information and opinions for the weekly market letter that went out to our customers on Tuesday.

The staff consisted of five guys plus myself. I include Harriet Jensen as one of the guys, because that was what she considered herself. She was an attractive young woman, but she chose to overlook that and insisted on being treated the same as the men —which suited me fine. I hadn't hired her for sexist reasons, any more than I'd hired Jaime Ortega because he was a Latin. Every member of my team had been picked for only one reason: because he had a talent for ferreting out information and interpreting it.

Irving Silvers was my number one boy. He'd been with me the longest and he was the one who was in charge when I was away. He was no more than five feet five inches tall even in shoes with platform soles and he weighed all of a hundred and twenty pounds. But he had a tough and inquisitive mind, and it was hard to fool him on any subject, and when it came to the workings of the automotive and steel companies he was a real authority.

Irving, Harriet, Jaime, George Cole and Joe Rothland—that was my staff. Five highly individualistic people. But while there was often friction between us, there was also a certain team spirit that I was proud of. An us-against-the-rest-of-the-world attitude that made for cooperation even in the midst of disagreement.

On that particular Monday morning there was a minimum of disagreement, however. We discussed the performance of the market during the preceding week, which didn't take long. The market hadn't done much. Then we got into the study of banks which Harriet was working on. She'd been occupied with it for two weeks and estimated that she'd need another week. She was mildly optimistic about bank profits but pessimistic about certain banks that had large foreign investments. She intended to go to Boston the following day, she said, and from there she was going to the West Coast for three days. Being Harriet, she didn't ask whether she could; she simply said that she was. And being me, I raised no objections.

Irving reported on a meeting he'd had with some American Motors people on Thursday, in the course of which he'd picked up some interesting scuttlebutt on impending personnel changes at Ford.

Jaime brought up some conflicting stories he'd heard about Clark Laboratories. Jaime was the newest member of my staff. I'd run across him at, and hired him away from, the Mercantile Trust Company, where he'd been tucked away in an obscure corner of the trust department and stymied. He was coming along beautifully, especially in pharmaceuticals. He hadn't started out with any special knowledge of the drug houses, but was developing into something of an expert on them. Clark was giving him a bit of trouble, though. He'd heard a rumor that the company was testing a new blood anticoagulant—one which would be less apt to cause hemorrhaging than any product previously used. But everything was so secret that he couldn't get a definite confirmation.

"I've got a friend who used to work there," George Cole said.

"He's with Billings-Smithson now. Maybe you ought to get in touch with him."

"Speaking of Billings-Smithson," Harriet said, "I heard something interesting the other day. They're supposed to be close to a cure for herpes simplex Type 2."

"What the hell is that?" Joe Rothland asked.

I wondered too. The name was familiar. I'd read something about the ailment, but I couldn't remember what or where.

"A form of VD," Harriet said.

The article I'd read came back to me. Herpes simplex Type 2 was a recently identified venereal disease which was more widespread than anybody thought and for which there was no known cure. "Where did you pick up that rumor?" I asked.

Harriet told me.

"I'd check it out if I were you," I said to Jaime. If the rumor was true, Billings-Smithson stock might be in for a rise.

Jaime nodded.

We traded a few more bits and pieces of information. Most of them wouldn't amount to anything, but every now and then a stray fact that someone came in with turned out to be important.

I asked Irving to remain for a few minutes after the meeting broke up. He'd mentioned that he wanted to go to Detroit for a couple of days. I asked him when he was planning to leave.

"This afternoon," he said.

"I'd like you to reschedule the trip," I said. "I'm going away this afternoon myself." It was my policy that when one of us was out of town the other shouldn't be. Especially on Tuesday, when the letter went out.

"For Christ's sake, Brock, I've got three appointments scheduled out there tomorrow!"

"Can't be helped."

He groaned, then asked, "Where're you going?"

"Chicago."

He groaned again but didn't argue. He got up to leave.

"By the way," I said, "have you heard anything about Computech recently?"

He paused. "Like what?"

"I don't know. Anything."

"Nothing special. You want me to ask around?"

"You might, Irving. In a general way."

"What, particularly, are you interested in?"

"Damned if I know. Just see if there've been any changes that haven't been made public."

"Will do. How long will you be gone?"

"I'll be back tomorrow afternoon probably."

Irving went out. Helen Doyle came in. Helen was my secretary. She gave me the telephone messages that had accumulated during the meeting. The one on top was from Jim Berry. I called him back. We talked for a few minutes about Dr. Chang's prospects and about some bonds that I thought were a good buy. Then I began to jot down the points I wanted to make in Tuesday's letter. Irving could do the actual writing; we always waited until Tuesday afternoon for that, in order to allow for any last-minute developments.

I was still making notes when Mark stalked into my office. He looked angry.

"Harriet's drawing more expense money," he said. "She claims she's going to Boston tomorrow."

"That's right," I said.

"She was just there two weeks ago. What's the matter with that girl?"

"Nothing. She believes in being thorough."

"You ought to speak to her. We're not the Bank of England, you know."

I didn't reply.

His tone changed. "What time are you leaving?"

"I don't know. I haven't made a reservation yet."

He waited around for a moment, then left. I called the airline.

The five-o'clock flight was sold out, but there was space on the six. I booked a seat.

I went back to my notes, but couldn't remember what I'd been about to write. Mark had annoyed me.

I looked up to find Jaime standing in the doorway. "What do you want?" I asked irritably.

He looked stricken. Of everyone on my staff, he was the most easily offended.

"Sorry," I said. "Come on in. What's on your mind?"

He crossed the room. "I wanted to ask you to have dinner with Elizabeth and me Friday night," he said hesitantly. "I'd like her to meet you." Elizabeth was his fiancée.

"I'm afraid I can't on Friday. I'm invited to a party." It was true. The Nordikes, friends from my earliest days in New York, were celebrating their wedding anniversary.

"Oh." There was disappointment in Jaime's eyes.

"What about Thursday?" I suggested. "You and she can come to my house for drinks, and we'll go on from there."

The disappointment vanished. "Thanks, Brock. That would be very nice."

"You'll come home from the office with me, and Elizabeth can join us about six."

He nodded and thanked me again.

As I watched him depart, it struck me that in some ways he was like Irving. Both were small men with great determination and courage. Jaime's inner toughness wasn't as apparent as Irving's, for he was sensitive and soft-spoken. But it was there. Transported by his mother when he was five years old from Ponce, Puerto Rico, to New York's Spanish Harlem, he'd survived every adversity that could be thrown at a kid and emerged as the one in a thousand from his neighborhood to get himself a college education and a job with a substantial five-figure income.

Yet the dinner invitation bothered me a bit. I suspected that there was more to it than the simple desire on Jaime's part for

Elizabeth and me to meet. The two of them had been having problems. Elizabeth's father objected to Jaime because he was Catholic, and Jaime's mother objected to Elizabeth because she wasn't. No wedding date had been set. What Jaime probably wanted from me, consciously or subconsciously, was the approval he couldn't get elsewhere and the assurance that religious differences and family opposition weren't important.

I pondered the matter briefly, then picked up my pen and went back to work.

The afternoon passed quickly.

At four o'clock Tom popped into my office. "What time's your flight?"

"Six."

"I'll give you a ride to the airport."

That wasn't necessary, I said. It was no trouble, he assured me. O.K., I said. I figured he had something on his mind.

And I was right. He did have something on his mind. Two things, in fact. Both were matters of conscience.

First, he wanted me to know that he was sorry he'd kicked up a fuss about my looking into Interlake. He'd thought it over. I was doing the right thing.

I glanced at him. He was gazing straight ahead, his back stiff, his jaw muscles pulsing. For an instant I saw a very young man apologizing to a stern parent for an act of dishonor. There were some things that people never outgrew, I guessed. In his case it was a fear of fear. "What you said wasn't entirely wrong," I replied.

He took a deep breath and went on to the next point. He'd had three long telephone conversations during the day with Hardin Webster. Hardin was with Amalgamated Investors Services, one of our largest customers. Amalgamated was going to put up for sale 230,000 shares of Philadelphia Steel. Tom had talked it over with Irving. Irving felt strongly that Philadelphia Steel should be held and not sold.

"I'd go by what Irving says," I told him.

"It's really not my decision, Brock. It's Amalgamated's. And I'd like to get the business." He paused. "That's not the whole story, though. They want to put the proceeds into Computech."

"You think they know something that we don't?"

"Possibly. On the other hand, if there should be something wrong at Interlake, that would affect Computech, so Amalgamated could be making a double mistake. I thought I ought to mention it to you."

I nodded. I didn't know what to say. "I'll do the best I can," I said finally.

We drove the rest of the way to the airport in silence.

7

There was an air traffic problem over Chicago. And a shortage of taxis at the airport. And a tie-up on the expressway. I didn't reach the hotel until nine-thirty.

A reservation had been made for me.

I followed the bellboy up to the suite, which had been done by a decorator who was deeply committed to red and white, and settled down to wait. I tried to clear my head of all thoughts about the man who was coming to see me and what he might say. To become an empty vessel. It was a fairly difficult process, and I didn't altogether succeed. Was the man young or old? Tall or short? Upper echelon or lower? His voice had told me nothing about him.

The image of Harry Wickoff kept presenting itself. Wickoff was the one who'd tipped me off to the criminal activity at Yankee Clipper. A tall, slender, bespectacled twenty-eight-year-old clerk in the actuarial department who'd been disappointed because he hadn't been given the promotion he was expecting. A complicated man and not a very pleasant one. The last I'd heard, he was still looking for a job. No company would touch him.

But this man could be entirely different. There was no way of knowing in advance, and it was foolish to guess. Nevertheless, I found myself doing just that. The figure that I kept coming up with was that of a man slightly older than Wickoff, less pale, more frightened, and on a higher rung of the corporate ladder.

There was no particular reason for me to expect that sort of man, but somehow I did. Except for the frightened aspect. He'd made no attempt to conceal the fact that he was afraid.

And, of course, he was a drinker.

So at ten o'clock I ordered up a bottle of Scotch. To make the ordeal easier for him.

The Scotch arrived at ten-fifteen. I still hadn't heard from my caller.

At ten-thirty I checked with the switchboard operator. Yes, my name and the number of my suite had been posted on her board. No, there were no messages for me.

A cunning man. One who hoped to use me to get himself off the hook. Who had no qualms about damaging the company he worked for. Who'd done something dishonest.

If he'd done something dishonest. If he really worked for Interlake. If the whole thing wasn't some sort of joke.

Eleven o'clock. No knock at the door, no telephone call. I opened the bottle of Scotch and poured myself some.

Had he lost his nerve? *Was* the whole thing some sort of joke? What motive could anyone have for a stunt like that? Simply to get me away from New York for a night? It didn't make sense.

I drank the Scotch and reproached myself for giving in too readily. I should have insisted on a name or at least a telephone number before agreeing to make the trip. This way I had nothing. Tom was right: I did go off half cocked at times.

Eleven-thirty. No word. More Scotch. Had I misunderstood the man? Had he said ten o'clock in the morning instead of ten o'clock in the evening? I'd been in too much of a hurry. The presence of Tom and Mark had created a pressure to get the matter settled, and I'd decided too quickly.

A quarter of twelve. Nothing. In a way it was good. At least I'd made an effort. Now I was in the clear.

I didn't like it, though. I didn't like being made a fool of.

At midnight I drank my third Scotch and not long after that I fell asleep.

I awoke at three o'clock, got up from the chair and went into the bedroom.

I awoke again at five and drank a glass of water.

Then at seven I awoke once more, and this time I stayed up. I shaved and took a shower. I was hungry. I started to go out to breakfast but changed my mind. There was still a chance, however slim, that I'd hear from the man. I decided to wait until ten o'clock, in case I really had misunderstood him.

I ordered breakfast from room service and tried to watch television. But I couldn't concentrate on what was happening on the screen. I kept wondering why someone would want to send me off on a wild-goose chase to Chicago.

No answer came to me.

At ten minutes past ten I checked out of the hotel and went to the airport. I got there in time for the eleven-o'clock flight. I bought my ticket and a newspaper and went to the gate. The boarding announcement was coming over the loudspeaker. I joined the line that was forming at the jetway.

I found my seat and stowed the small carry-on case I'd brought with me under it. I fastened the seat belt and opened my newspaper, turning the pages idly.

The news was varied. The chief of police was expected to announce sweeping personnel changes. Two aldermen were accused of making windfall profits on land which they'd sold to the city. A teen-ager had shot his girlfriend's new boyfriend. A survey showed that venereal disease had risen ten percent in the past year.

I thought of Jaime. I hoped he was investigating the lead Harriet had given him. He probably was.

A story on page nine caught my eye. I sat up straighter. "NO CLUES YET," the headline said, "IN SLAYING OF INSURANCE EXEC."

37

"Police are still seeking clues," the article began, "in the gang-land-style murder of Wesley Harrington, who was found shot to death Sunday night in the garage of his house at 1120 Foster Dr., in Chicago Heights. Harrington, 37, Asst. Treasurer of Interlake General Insurance Co. . . . ."

I stopped reading.

I unfastened the seat belt, pulled out my suitcase and got off the plane.

I rented a car and drove back to the Astor Tower.

8

The woman who opened the door was, I judged, in her early sixties. You couldn't tell it by her hair, which was frosted blond, but you could tell it by the lines of her face, the loose, brown-spotted skin of her hands and the disillusionment in her eyes.

"Is Mrs. Harrington home?" I asked.

"Not yet."

"Will she be home soon?"

"I don't know. She's with the police."

"My name's Potter. I'm from New York. I had a date with her husband and just found out about his death."

She nodded.

"I'm very sorry."

She nodded again.

"I'd like to talk to Mrs. Harrington."

She sighed. "I don't know when she'll be back. She's been with them for hours. It's terrible."

"Are you a relative?"

"I'm her mother. Mrs. Ackroyd."

I was hoping that she'd invite me in. She didn't appear to be about to, however.

"Perhaps you'll come back later," she said, "when Vera's—" She stopped, peering over my shoulder.

Hearing a car engine, I turned around. A car was pulling up, a man and a woman in the front seat. The car stopped behind my rented Buick. The woman got out.

Mrs. Ackroyd heaved a sigh of relief. "It's Vera."

The car drove away. Vera Harrington came slowly up the walk. She appeared to be utterly exhausted. When she reached the door I stepped aside. She took no notice of me. Her face was milk white.

"Are you all right?" her mother asked anxiously.

"I'd like to lie down," Vera said in a small voice.

"Mrs. Harrington," I said.

She gave me a blank look. And suddenly she swayed.

I caught her. She didn't quite lose consciousness, but she went limp in my arms. I scooped her up and carried her to the couch. "Get some brandy," I said to Mrs. Ackroyd.

Mrs. Ackroyd hurried from the room. I began to rub Vera's hands. They were like ice.

Mrs. Ackroyd returned with a bottle of bourbon. I made do with it. Color began to return to Vera's face. She tried to sit up.

"Don't," I said.

"Um," she said, and closed her eyes. But presently she opened them. "Thank you," she said in a voice that was stronger.

"I'll call the doctor," Mrs. Ackroyd said.

"No," said Vera. "I'm all right. It's just that those awful men . . ." She didn't finish. She looked at me. "Who are you?"

I gave her my name.

It didn't seem to mean anything to her.

"Some nice hot tea," Mrs. Ackroyd suggested.

Vera nodded.

Mrs. Ackroyd went back to the kitchen. I offered Vera more bourbon, but she said no. She made an effort to sit up and found that she could. The terrible pallor was gone. She resembled her mother, I thought, except that her hair wasn't frosted and the disillusionment, although it was there, wasn't as pronounced.

A pretty woman, really.

"I'm sorry," she said. "I don't know what came over me. I haven't been able to sleep, and those awful policemen. The way they talked, you'd think Wes was a criminal or something."

I made a sympathetic sound. And meant it. The shock of the murder, the funeral arrangements, the interrogation—she'd been through a lot in the past day and a half. "You'll feel better after you've had some tea," I said. "Can you stand?"

"I think so." She tried it. "Yes."

We went into the kitchen. The kettle started to whistle. We sat down at a Formica-topped table. Mrs. Ackroyd brought tea for all of us, then sat down herself. I looked around the room. It was like what I'd seen of the rest of the house: neat, pastelish, nothing special. The place had cost maybe forty, forty-five thousand. It appeared to have been built at the same time as all the other houses on the street by a developer who had one basic design which he varied slightly here and there.

Vera sipped her tea. She eyed me over the rim of the cup. "Are you a friend of Wes's?"

"No," I said. "We had a business appointment. I couldn't understand why he didn't keep it. Then I read in the newspaper . . ."

Her hand began to tremble. Some tea spilled. She put the cup down. "It was ghastly."

Her mother patted Vera's arm. "Try not to think about it."

"I can't help it," Vera said. "It keeps going through my mind."

I'd read all the available news stories before coming to the house. Wesley Harrington had gone out on Sunday evening. He'd come home shortly after eleven. His wife had gone to bed. She'd been awakened by the sound of the garage door being opened. Then she'd heard a car being driven away at high speed. She'd waited for her husband to come into the house. He hadn't come. She'd got out of bed to investigate. The garage was attached to the house. She'd opened the door that led to the garage from the kitchen. Harrington was on the garage floor. He'd been shot four times and was dead.

I glanced toward the door which I guessed was the one Vera had opened. It was now closed.

"Simply ghastly," she said.

"You *must* try not to think about it," Mrs. Ackroyd told her. Then she said to me, "Vera's a college graduate."

I gave her a startled look. So did Vera.

"Well, she is," Mrs. Ackroyd insisted. "She won a four-year scholarship to Syracuse." She sounded aggrieved. As if Vera's education had somehow been betrayed.

"Mother!" Vera protested.

Mrs. Ackroyd fell silent. But her expression indicated that she still thought it very unfair for the husband of a college graduate to be murdered.

"According to the papers," I said, "your husband had been to see a friend. Someone named Malcolm Davis, who also worked for Interlake."

Vera nodded. "You know him?"

I shook my head.

"You're not missing anything."

I drank some tea.

Vera made another attempt to drink some herself. Her hand was none too steady, but she managed to get the cup to her lips. "This is good," she said. She put the cup down. "He was a bad influence on Wes."

"Davis?"

"He's a lush."

"You know I don't like that term, dear," Mrs. Ackroyd said.

"A lush," Vera repeated. "Wes never had a drinking problem until he began going around with Malcolm. I mean, he drank, but he never used to stay out until all hours, and if he wasn't going to be home on time he'd call me, and he never used to say he was going to work late when he wasn't. I blame it all on Malcolm."

"Is that why you didn't go with your husband Sunday night?"

Vera thought for a moment. "Have you ever wished you could unsay things?"

"Very often."

"Well, that's the way I feel about Sunday night. I wish with all my heart I could unsay the things I said to Wes before he went out. I was angry. We'd been having a nice day, and then right in the middle of dinner Malcolm calls. He wants Wes to come over. I mean, it's not enough that they go out together during the week, and Wes doesn't come home until all hours, and he's had so much to drink that it's all I can do to get him up the next morning—now it's supposed to be weekends too. Well, I put my foot down. I told Wes he couldn't go. We're together little enough, I said. Well, he said he had to go, and one word led to another, and we ended up having a fight, and I said some pretty awful things, and now I feel just dreadful, because those are the last things I ever said to Wes. I didn't really mean them but I said them, and he died before I had a chance to say I didn't mean them. Now it's too late." Her chin began to quiver.

"I don't think you ought to be telling this gentleman all that," Mrs. Ackroyd said.

Vera bit her lip. Her chin stopped quivering. "Have you got a cigarette?" she asked.

I gave her one and lit it for her.

"And it wasn't all Malcolm's fault either," she went on. "I mean, his wife's left him and taken the children with her, and he's all by himself and he needs a friend. I can see that. I don't like him and I think he was a bad influence on Wes, but I can understand." She inhaled smoke deeply, the way someone in great pain might inhale an anesthetic.

"You must try not to think about it," Mrs. Ackroyd said, "or you'll make yourself sick."

Vera transferred the cigarette to her other hand and drank some tea. "Do I sound like a shrew?" she asked me.

"No," I said.

"Well, I feel like one. I really do." She paused. "Mother's right, I suppose. I shouldn't be telling you all this. I don't even know who you are."

"I'm a securities analyst. Your husband never mentioned me?"

"Not that I recall."

"He didn't telephone me? Friday night or Saturday morning?"

"He was out Friday night. With Malcolm. And Saturday morning he went to the nursery."

"The nursery?"

"Tree nursery. Our little crab apple got blown over, the last storm we had. Wes bought another."

"Say between ten o'clock and noon?"

"He was at the nursery."

"He was going to show me a list of some securities. Would you know anything about that?"

Vera shook her head.

"What about Sunday?" I asked. "Sunday morning, that is. Did he make any telephone calls then?"

"I couldn't say. I was at church. Wes never went, but I do. What kind of securities?"

"Some securities that belong to Interlake."

"Wes never brought problems home from the office. That's one thing I'll say for him."

"We're Episcopalians," Mrs. Ackroyd said. "Vera was always very good about going to church."

I looked at her. I got the impression that she hadn't had an easy life. And that she was meddlesome. "Do you live here?"

"Goodness, no. I'm from Utica. I just came yesterday. Vera called me in the middle of the night, to tell me. I took the first plane. I had to change in Buffalo."

I turned back to Vera. "Your husband liked his work?"

A note of annoyance came into her voice. "You sound like one of those awful policemen. Was Wes having trouble at the office? Are we in debt? Did he gamble? Who are his enemies? Like—like —Wes didn't *have* enemies. He wasn't that kind of a man. He was happy in his work. As happy as anyone is, maybe more so. He didn't gamble. We aren't in debt. He did drink, yes, but he wasn't what you'd call an alcoholic."

"I'm sorry," I said. "I didn't mean it the way it sounded. But I can understand how the police might think the way they do. The shooting was done so fast, so efficiently, and there were no clues. They evidently figure it was a professional job. And, according to what I read, there was no sign of robbery."

Vera sighed. "I know. I can understand too, I guess. But that doesn't make it any easier. Anyway, Wes was doing all right at work. Mr. Rasher liked him."

The name Rasher was familiar to me, from *Best's.* Richard Rasher. Treasurer of Interlake. "He was your husband's boss?"

"Yes."

"And he's been just wonderful," Mrs. Ackroyd put in. "He came to the house last night and he's helping with the funeral arrangements and—"

"If you had a date with Wes," Vera interrupted, "Mr. Rasher's the one you'll probably have to see. He won't be at the office tomorrow morning—he's coming to the funeral—but I imagine he'll be there tomorrow afternoon."

"I'll call him," I said. "I'd also like to meet this Malcolm Davis, I think. Do you happen to have his address?"

Vera regarded me thoughtfully. "More than likely he'll be at the office tomorrow afternoon also." She paused. "A securities analyst, did you say?"

"Price, Potter and Petacque," I told her. "Our office is in New York. I'd like to catch as early a plane as possible. If I could see Davis this evening, it would save time."

The thoughtful gaze continued.

"We're rather a well-known brokerage house," I said. "Interlake has done business with us." In a sense it was true. I'd interviewed Interlake executives and mentioned the company in my reports.

"Well," Vera said slowly. Then she stubbed out her cigarette, got up from the table and left the room. She still didn't appear to have regained all her strength.

She returned presently with the city telephone directory. She

45

read me Davis's address and telephone number. I wrote it down. After a moment she said, "The list Wes was going to show you—what would it look like?"

"I don't know," I said. "Stocks and bonds. Maybe treasury notes. Mostly bonds, though." Good quality bonds, too, no doubt.

"I'm almost positive it's not here. Wes hardly ever brought work home from the office. I'll look around, though. Where are you staying?"

"At the Astor Tower."

"Finish your tea," Mrs. Ackroyd told her daughter. "It's getting cold. Then I think you ought to lie down."

Vera obediently picked up her cup. Her hand was all right now. So was her color. But there were dark shadows under her eyes. I was suddenly reminded of my mother. She'd looked like that once. The same shadows, the same haunted expression.

I got up abruptly. "I won't take up any more of your time. Thank you for talking to me. If there's anything I can do . . ."

Vera put her cup down. "Thank *you,*" she said. "I'm sorry I was such a nuisance."

Both women walked me to the door. We said good-bye. Vera and I shook hands. She let her hand linger in mine for a moment. I left. She closed the door. I started down the walk to the street. When I reached my car I paused and looked back at the house. It didn't appear to be any different from the other houses on the block. Yet it was different. A man had been shot to death in it.

My eyes traveled to the garage door. It was shut. I imagined it open. I imagined a car standing in the driveway with its headlights on. I imagined a body on the concrete floor, illuminated by the beam of the headlights.

I shuddered.

9

Sheridan Road. The far north end of the city. A few old mansions, gone to pot, diminished by the string of new high-rise apartment buildings on the other side of the street.

The Lakeside. Thirty-odd stories of concrete and glass behind a semicircular driveway, an angular arrangement of steel pipes spouting water into a small basin and a sign saying: "THE LAKESIDE. LUXURY LIVING. ONE, TWO AND THREE BEDROOM CONDOMINIUMS, FROM $39,500. MODELS OPEN DAILY."

I found the garage, which was down a ramp on the side of the building, and turned my car over to an attendant who didn't really want to take it. I opened a door that said: "TO LOBBY" and climbed some steps. The doorman, who was maybe eighteen years old, was engaged in conversation with a young lady who was maybe sixteen years old. I studied a panel of buttons with names and numbers next to them. Davis, M., was in 23F. I picked up the telephone next to the panel and stood there, trying to decide what to say. A woman with a shopping bag in one hand and a set of keys in the other made it unnecessary for me to say anything. She unlocked the door that led to the inner lobby and held it open for me. I thanked her, and we rode up in the elevator together. She asked me whether I knew when the laundry room would be completed. I said I wasn't sure.

The corridor smelled of paint. F was opposite the elevators and a little to the left. I hesitated before pushing the buzzer. It was possible that he wouldn't be home. It was possible that he would be home but wouldn't let me in. It was possible that he'd let me in but wouldn't tell me anything.

I pushed the buzzer.

I could hear it ring on the other side of the door. I listened for footsteps. There were none. But suddenly the door was flung open and I found myself facing a big man with a red face and a scowl. He was barefoot and naked from the waist up.

"Mr. Davis?" I said.

"Where's the pizza?" he demanded.

"I'm Brockton Potter," I said.

His scowl deepened. Then he slammed the door in my face.

The suddenness of the action left me astonished. As did the sound of his voice. For the anonymous telephone calls hadn't come from Wesley Harrington; they'd come from Malcolm Davis.

10

It was eight-thirty when I got back to the hotel. I called Irving. He was at home. I told him that I was staying in Chicago an extra day and asked him what was new at the office.

He'd got the letter out, he reported. He'd also heard from Harriet; she was already in San Francisco. And Jaime had talked to George Cole's friend at Billings-Smithson. Jaime wanted to go to Cleveland to get more information. Irving had told him to go ahead. Jaime was planning to leave the following morning and would be back on Thursday.

"Have you found out anything about Computech?" I asked.

"I haven't had much time," he replied. "Tom talked to me this afternoon. Amalgamated is definitely going to buy some. And I spent a few minutes on Computech's last financial statement. They've made some changes in their accounting procedures. Is that what you wanted to know?"

"Not exactly." I'd read the statement myself at the time it was published. I didn't remember the details, however. "But what changes did they make?"

"Accelerated write-offs. And the money from the sale of the Martin Pump division went into profits. Nothing illegal, but you have to read the fine print to catch it."

"Well, keep checking. See what else you can come up with."

"Will do. But what's this all about, Brock? If it's any of my business."

"I heard a strange story about Interlake. I'm trying to get to the bottom of it. Anything that affects Interlake could affect Computech and vice versa."

"I see."

"Maybe you'd better postpone your Detroit trip to next week."

"I did that yesterday."

"Good boy." I hung up.

Notices with a Toulouse-Lautrec look were planted here and there, stating that Maxim's was in the hotel. I decided to find it. I found it in the basement, at the foot of a curved, red-carpeted stairway.

"Do you have a reservation?" the maître d' asked. The room was half empty.

"No," I said.

He thought about it for a while, then grudgingly seated me.

I ordered chicken with a fancy name and an endive salad and settled back to contemplate the rose in the silver vase in front of me. Presently a small orchestra began to play. One elderly couple got up to dance. They were joined by another elderly couple. One of the elderly men was wearing a green velvet jacket over a white turtleneck.

Not Wesley Harrington, I thought; Malcolm Davis. Not Wesley Harrington; Malcolm Davis. Not Wesley Harrington; Malcolm Davis.

The door had been open for ten seconds at the most. Yet there were things to recall. About the man himself and even about the room he was standing in. A large room, carpeted from wall to wall but with scarcely any furniture in it. Davis had evidently just moved in or was just getting ready to move out. Maybe both. A powerful-looking guy. At least six feet two, with shoulders like railroad ties. Red-faced from alcohol or from anger. A tendency —judging by the way he'd thrown the door open—toward violence. Broad cheeks, heavy black eyebrows, the beginning of a double chin. All in all, a man who'd once been tough and attractive, was still reasonably so, but wouldn't be so for much longer if he kept on the way he was going.

Not at all like Harry Wickoff. Except perhaps for the anger. And even that was different. Wickoff's was cold and internal. Davis's was out in the open. But then, Davis had recently been deserted by his wife.

The waiter brought the salad. And applied pepper to it from a grinder the size of a bowling pin.

I turned on the television set. A movie was beginning. The credits were being shown. Between the credits were shots of various people getting on an airplane. All of them appeared tense and nervous. You got the feeling that something was going to go wrong as soon as the plane was in the air.

The director's name appeared on the screen, and the plane took off.

My telephone rang.

It was Vera Harrington. She was in the lobby. She wanted to come up.

"Sure," I said.

I was taken aback when I saw her. She looked different. She'd done something with her hair and she was all in black.

"I'm sorry to disturb you so late," she said. "I tried to call you earlier, but you were out." She seemed more composed than she'd been during the afternoon.

"You're not disturbing me."

She came into the suite. She'd been at the funeral home, she explained. Visitation. And when the visitation was over she'd driven her mother back to Chicago Heights.

I'd salvaged the bottle of Scotch from the night before. I offered her some.

"Just a little," she said.

I poured drinks for both of us.

"Thank you," she said as I handed her one of the glasses. "I really didn't want any visitation, but Mother insisted, and I'm glad she did. It helps to have people around. And things don't seem so . . . abnormal." She paused. "Did you see Malcolm?"

"Very briefly."

She didn't pursue the subject. "What I wanted to tell you is I found a list. It may be the one you asked about."

My heart skipped a beat. "You did?"

She opened her pocketbook and took out an envelope, which she gave me.

The envelope contained a single sheet of memo paper. "From the desk of Wesley Harrington" was printed across the top. Beneath that were two columns of neat handwriting. The first line of the first column said: "Nev NG 8½ 89 19472–610."

I understood immediately. Nevada Natural Gas bonds which yielded 8½ percent interest and were due to mature in 1989, with serial numbers 19472 through 19610. Each bond was worth in the neighborhood of a thousand dollars. A hundred and thirty-nine thousand dollars in all.

The second entry was for a hundred and ninety-six thousand dollars' worth of Northeast Telephone bonds with a maturity date of 1991.

"Is this your husband's handwriting?" I asked.

Vera nodded.

"Where did you find it?"

"In the humidor."

"The humidor?"

"A cigar humidor. Someone gave it to Wes one Christmas. Wes didn't smoke cigars, but the humidor was so pretty he kept it. He used it for papers, like until he could get around to putting them in our safe-deposit box, or sometimes receipts that he wanted to save. Things of that sort."

I scanned the columns. About half of the entries referred to the bonds of public utility companies, the rest to municipals. I didn't make an exact count of the sum involved, but twenty-three million seemed quite possible.

"Is that the list you were talking about?" Vera asked.

"I believe so."

"What does it mean?"

"It's a list of bonds. May I borrow it?"

"I don't know," she said dubiously. "I don't know what Wes would want me to do."

"He'd want you to let me have it."

"I don't know. Maybe I ought to show it to Mr. Rasher."

"That's up to you. It's possible that Mr. Rasher's already seen it. All I need it for is a few hours. I'll mail it back to you tomorrow."

She still looked undecided.

"If I'm going to talk to Mr. Rasher, I have to know what I'm talking about."

She hesitated a moment longer, then said, "All right. But you will mail it back to me, won't you?"

"I promise." I put the list in my pocket before she could change her mind.

She sipped her drink and frowned. "Was Wes in any sort of trouble?"

"I don't know, Vera. I don't know anything about him."

Her frown lingered. "I was married to him for thirteen years but I'm beginning to think I didn't know anything about him either." She put her glass on the table. "I used to think I knew him better than anybody in the world, but what it was, I think, is I was taking him for granted. Taking people for granted isn't the same as really knowing them. Has that ever happened to you —you took someone for granted, thinking that you knew them, and all the time you didn't? It's kind of sad, actually. It happens mostly between husbands and wives, I think. Are you married?"

"No."

"It starts out nice but sometimes it changes. In fact, I guess it always changes. Maybe it would have been different if we'd had children."

I said nothing.

"I don't know, though. These past few months, with the drinking and everything . . ." She picked up her glass, studied it, then drank some Scotch. "I'm not sure I was being fair when I blamed everything on Malcolm. Maybe some of it was something else."

"In other words, the past few months weren't so good."

"Wes was changing. It wasn't just his drinking. He was more irritable. He wouldn't tell me what it was. Every time I tried to find out he told me everything was fine. But something was bothering him. I'm sure of it. That's why I'm asking if he was in trouble." She paused. "Do you think he knew someone wanted to kill him?"

"Did he ever say anything like that?"

"No. But something was on his mind. And someone did kill him." She finished the drink and put the glass down. She glanced at my pocket as if she still wasn't sure that giving me the list had been the right thing to do. She didn't ask me to give it back, however. "Do you know Mr. Jars?"

"Jars?"

"Jars or Yars. I'm not sure which. His first name is Clifford."

"No. Should I?"

"I don't know. I thought you might."

"Who is he?"

"That's what I'd like to find out. Wes mentioned the name a couple of times when he was drunk."

I searched my memory. The name meant nothing to me. "In what connection?" I asked.

" 'That Jars!' he said one time. He sounded upset. 'What Jars?' I asked. 'Clifford Jars,' he said. 'Who's he?' I asked. 'Nobody,' he said. 'Leave me alone.' Then the next time he said, 'If it weren't for Jars!' and we went through the same thing. It could be Yars, though. I'm really not sure. When I tried to question Wes he got angry."

"Never heard of anybody with that name," I said.

"Well," she said, "I don't suppose it matters. I'd better be going.

It's a long ride, and Mother'll be worried." She got up.

I got up too. But then she didn't move toward the door. She just stood there, looking indecisive and unhappy.

"I hate to go home," she said. "I'm going to miss him. In spite of everything, I'm going to miss him."

I wanted to say something apt, something comforting. I took her hand. "Time has a way," I said. It was the best I could do.

"I suppose." She let me hold her hand for a moment, then withdrew it and hurried from the suite.

I thought about her for a while. I poured myself another drink. I took the list from my pocket.

It contained some of the safest securities in the entire world. No insurance company would limit its portfolio to the bonds of public utility companies or the most solvent municipal governments. But if someone wanted to steal from the portfolio of an insurance company, those were the items he'd take. For they were negotiable everywhere.

11

● ● ● ● ● ● ● ● ●

"Mr. Rasher is in conference," the secretary said.

"Will you ask him to call me, please, as soon as he can?"

"Your name?"

"Brockton Potter. I'm at the Astor Tower, 12A."

"And what was it you wished to talk to him about?"

"Interlake General."

"Could you be more specific?"

"I'm afraid not. Just tell him Brockton Potter, of Price, Potter and Petacque."

"I'll tell him. But—"

"Thank you." I hung up.

The conference ended in a hurry. Five minutes later my telephone rang. "Mr. Potter?" the same secretary said. "Mr. Rasher would like to speak with you."

Rasher came on the line. Although we'd never met, he made it sound as if we had. "Brockton Potter! I didn't know you were in town! What can I do for you?"

"I'm updating my last survey and I'd like to get together with you to chat about Interlake."

"Of course. I'd be delighted. But actually, I'm sure, Mr. Sayre would like to speak with you himself." Sayre was the president of Interlake. He'd never had much time for me before the Yankee Clipper publicity.

"Fine. But what I'm most interested in falls into your department, I believe."

There was a slight pause. Ever so slight. "I see. Well, unfortunately this is a crowded day for me. I have to attend a funeral later this morning, and after that I have a luncheon appointment, and this afternoon there's a directors' meeting."

"I understand. I don't think I'll need much time, however. And I imagine Mr. Sayre would want you to be present anyway."

"Oh?"

"There's a rumor I've heard which on the surface sounds rather preposterous, but nevertheless I feel I should ask you about it."

He laughed. With all the sincerity of a department store Santa Claus. "Then perhaps you should speak to the rumor division. Mr. Lipp heads that. Rumors follow him wherever he goes." He reconsidered. "I could break away from the luncheon early, I suppose. Can you be here at one-thirty?"

"Certainly."

"Good. One-thirty, then. I'm on the twenty-first floor."

"I'm looking forward to meeting you."

"Righto," Rasher said, and hung up.

I put on my shoes and went out for breakfast.

The photocopy shop was located in the John Hancock Center. It took the man only a few seconds to make a Xerox copy of the list.

I returned to the hotel and mailed the Xerox to myself at the office. Then I used the original to make another copy in my own handwriting on plain white paper. This copy I put in my pocket. The original I mailed back to Vera.

The Interlake Building was on North Michigan Avenue. It had been completed shortly before Lipp bought control of the company. It was a nice structure of glass and steel, but there was nothing extravagant about it. J. J. Oliver had personally supervised the design and J. J. Oliver had never been one to waste a buck.

The one concession to art which he'd permitted was a small bronze statue in the lobby. It was literal enough not to need a title, but it had one anyway—"The Helping Hand." It showed a stalwart man who looked like Abraham Lincoln without the beard, lightly touching the shoulder of a woman whose head was bowed and who had a small child in her arms. Any of the art dealers I knew would have frowned at the statue as a creative work. Yet on the few occasions I'd seen it I'd found myself liking it. Not for its artistic merit but for what it said about J. J. Oliver. He was the one who'd commissioned it, and I was positive that he saw himself as the Lincolnesque figure. As a businessman he'd been plenty tough, and in its early years Interlake had undoubtedly dodged as many claims as any other insurance company, but there was another side of his personality: for most of his career J. J. Oliver had considered himself a protector of widows and orphans—and had taken the responsibility seriously.

The statue was still there.

Other changes had taken place, however. The twenty-first floor, where the executive offices were located, had been completely redone. In lavish style. The reception area now looked like the library of an English manor, and the stunning Japanese girl who sat facing the elevators was so dwarfed by the enormous desk in front of her that she seemed like a mere ornament.

I gave her my name. She pushed a button and spoke into a brass and porcelain telephone.

"Mr. Rasher will be with you shortly," she said. "Would you care for some coffee while you're waiting?"

I said I would. She got up and went into an adjoining room. I sat down on one of the tufted leather couches. The Japanese girl returned with a silver tray of coffee things. The coffee things were of Royal Crown Derby. I wondered what J. J. Oliver would have said.

I sipped coffee and admired the calf-bound sets of books which lined the wall on both sides of a portrait of Anton Lipp. The atmosphere was hushed.

Presently a door opened. A man appeared. He started toward the elevators, saw me, hesitated, then detoured in my direction. He was a small man with a large head and lots of black hair. I recognized him immediately. He was Anton Lipp, looking much livelier in person than he did in the portrait.

"Haven't we met?" he asked.

"I'm Brockton Potter," I said, getting up to shake hands.

He pumped my hand vigorously. "Of course." And to my surprise he mentioned the exact dates and occasions of our two previous meetings—a fund-raising dinner for Senator McDermott and a breakfast that Lipp himself had given for a group of security analysts to tout Computech.

"You have an excellent memory," I said.

He smiled. He had the kind of mobile face that good actors have, and when he smiled it wasn't only his mouth that moved —his other features went into action too. "I know. It's often a handicap—it disconcerts people. To what do we owe the honor of this visit?"

"I'm being nosy. In a professional capacity, that is."

"Splendid. The company's doing beautifully, as you probably know. Are you an astrology freak?"

The question startled me. So did his use of the word "freak." He hadn't come to the United States until he was in his middle teens, and he still had a slight eastern European accent. The colloquialism, coming from him, seemed strange. "Not exactly," I said.

"Neither am I. But sometimes, I think, the stars do favor certain people. And the day I decided to buy Interlake they were definitely favoring me."

I nodded.

"An extremely profitable company. Extremely. Who are you waiting to see?"

"Richard Rasher."

"Rasher? Not Sayre?" He frowned. His frown was like his smile —everything went into it.

"For present purposes—Rasher."

"Well, finish your coffee and let me take you in. A man like you shouldn't be kept waiting."

I put the cup down. "The coffee doesn't matter. I was admiring the décor, though."

"It's a big improvement. Oliver was brilliant, but like so many men of his generation he pinched pennies. I've never believed in that. It's bad for morale." He placed his arm on my shoulder. "Come along."

He guided me through the doorway from which he'd emerged and down an L-shaped corridor. The corridor was thickly carpeted and hung with good pictures. Walking behind him, I noticed that he wore the same kind of shoes with platform soles that Irving sometimes wore. The two men were of about the same height.

Rasher's office was beyond the turn of the L. The door was open. Rasher was lighting a cigar.

"You have a visitor," Lipp said. "An important visitor."

Rasher dropped the match. It fell into an ashtray and went out. "Mr. Potter?" he said. He struggled to his feet. He was shaped like a cello.

"How do you do," I said. We shook hands across the desk. His hand was as soft and smooth as a satin pillow.

"A pleasure," he said. "I've heard so much about you."

Lipp pointed to a chair. "Sit down, Mr. Potter."

I sat down. So did Rasher. "A pleasure," he said again. For a man who was having all that pleasure, he looked kind of unhappy.

He offered me a cigar. I declined. He made another attempt to light his own. His fingers were trembling slightly. I wondered who was making him nervous—Lipp or I.

Lipp seated himself in one of the other chairs. He slid all the way down until his weight was on the lower vertebrae, extended his legs, folded his arms and crossed his ankles. He assumed a grave expression. "Now then," he said to me, "fire away."

I took my time. I hadn't figured on his being there. I'd intended to start slowly with general questions, then spring the list as a surprise. With Rasher alone it would have been possible. With Lipp present it wasn't going to be. Nevertheless, I directed myself to Rasher. "What I'm mainly interested in," I said, "is your investment portfolio."

Lipp spoke up immediately. "Are you here as a securities salesman or a securities analyst?" he asked.

"A securities analyst," I replied. I turned back to Rasher.

"Then I'm surprised," Lipp said. "What could you possibly want to know about our investment portfolio? It's a matter of public record."

"It is and it isn't," I said. "I know the general breakdown of your investments but not the specific stocks and bonds and treasury instruments that are included."

"It's an enormous number of items, and they're constantly changing. I'm not an insurance man and I don't participate very actively in the day-to-day operations of the company, so I myself don't know what all of them are, but if you're interested I suppose we could get you a reasonably current rundown." He paused. "*Are* you interested? Or are you merely leading up to something else?"

"I'm not being devious, if that's what you mean," I said. "I really am interested in your investment portfolio."

"Very well. What particular aspect of it are you interested in?"

"The bonds, primarily."

"What do you want to know about them? We own some of the best."

I glanced at Rasher. He was intent on his cigar.

"I'm not questioning your motives," Lipp said, "but I can hardly believe that you came all the way out here just to ask what bonds we own."

"You're right," I said. "I'm concerned not so much with what bonds you own but with whether you actually own them."

He sat up straighter. His eyes narrowed. "I beg your pardon?"

"When I spoke to Mr. Rasher this morning I said that I'd heard a rather preposterous rumor. I'm trying to check it out."

The room was very still. Lipp's eyes were mere slits. "What did you hear?" he asked.

"I heard that a large number of the bonds that are supposed to be in your portfolio aren't there—that they're missing."

His eyes widened. His lips parted. He grinned. "Be serious," he said.

"I am serious. I heard that there's been a theft of securities from this company."

"A theft?"

"That's the way it was put to me."

"Well, you certainly used the right term, my friend: preposterous."

"Twenty-three million dollars' worth, to be exact."

Still grinning, Lipp turned to Rasher. "Can you even conceive of such a thing, Dick?"

Rasher made an effort to look amused also. "No, sir."

"You're putting us on," Lipp said to me.

That line too struck me as incongruous. There was nothing really wrong with it, just as there was nothing really wrong with his hair, which he wore over his ears, or his clothes, which seemed more appropriate for a thirtyish movie director than for a sixtyish businessman. But there was something studied about it all. Lipp seemed to enjoy projecting the image of a man younger and looser than he actually was, which was all right with me. But why did he have to project it? "No," I said. "I didn't believe the story myself at first—and I'm not sure that I do yet—but I have come into possession of a list of the securities which are supposed to have been stolen, and that makes the whole thing seem a bit more real."

I took the list from my pocket and put it on Rasher's desk.

Lipp got to it before Rasher did. He pulled out a pair of half-moon glasses and without opening them held them to his eyes. "Nevada Natural Gas 1989's," he read aloud. "Oklahoma Gas Transmission 1996's." He tossed the list to Rasher. "Do we own these?"

Rasher took the cigar out of his mouth, but didn't look at the paper. "Yes, sir."

"Where did you get that list?" Lipp asked me. There was a lot of suppressed emotion in his voice, and the emotion was rage.

"I'm afraid I can't tell you," I said. I wondered whether his hair was naturally black or whether he dyed it. "But do you think that there's a remote chance that the story could be true?"

He let the emotion explode. "There'd damn well better not be!" He hurled his glasses across the room. "Goddamn it to hell, there'd better not be!"

The glasses landed on the carpet, a few inches from the leg of a table. The carpet was so thick that they didn't break.

"I demand that you tell me where you got that list and who told you that story!" Lipp shouted.

I looked at Rasher. He'd gone very pale. "That's hardly important, is it?" I said to Lipp. "The important thing is whether the bonds have been stolen or not. It would be awfully serious if they have been."

"Serious! It would be a goddamn disaster! We're due to be examined soon by the Insurance Commission."

There was no reason for me to have been surprised, but I was. "In that case—"

Lipp didn't give me a chance to finish. "You're right," he said, struggling to master his anger. "It doesn't matter who told you the story; what matters is whether it's true." He leaned across the desk. "What the hell's been going on around here, Rasher? What have you people been up to?"

Rasher had jowls. They quivered. His voice was steady, however. "There's been no theft, Mr. Lipp. I'm positive."

"How can you be sure?" I asked.

"I'm positive," he repeated.

Lipp straightened up. He looked at me and smiled. "Forgive my bad temper," he said. "My friends say I'm mercurial." His smile broadened. "My wife uses a less flattering term."

I smiled back at him.

"I hope you'll accept Rasher's word," he said.

"I'd like to," I said, "and actually I do. But if there were some way of verifying it . . ."

"You don't, then. Well, I don't suppose I blame you." His eyes went back to Rasher. "Why don't we have a look in the vault?"

Rasher's jowls started to quiver again. "Mr. Lipp!" he protested.

"You're acquainted with Mr. Potter's reputation," Lipp told him. "He isn't going to take anybody's word. And if I were in his position I don't think I would either. Perhaps he and I should both have a look."

"It's against all the rules!" Rasher exclaimed, his voice rising. He was beginning to get angry himself.

"Can't we bend the rules a bit?" Lipp asked. "Come to think of it, I've never been to the vault myself."

"It's not one vault; it's several. And there's the board of directors meeting in a few minutes."

"To hell with that. Sayre can preside until we get back."

Rasher appeared to want to throw something too. He didn't do it, though. "We'll have to have someone else with us," he said stonily. "It takes at least two signatures to get into any of the vaults. One isn't enough. Not even mine."

"That's sensible," Lipp said. "Please make the necessary arrangements."

Rasher hesitated a moment, then yielded. He opened one of the drawers of his desk and took out a huge leather-bound notebook. "It would take us days to check every single stock and bond certificate," he said to me. "Would you be satisfied with a spot check?"

"Of course," I replied.

"It would be easier," he said, "if we only had to go to one of the vaults. But you can select which of the issues you'd like to inspect."

I studied my list. I picked several entries at random. Rasher checked them against the master list in the notebook, which evidently had been prepared by a computer. After some dickering, we agreed on three series of bonds, all of which were housed at the Monroe National Bank. My feeling was that if even one of the series was intact, all of them would be, but I insisted on three.

Rasher put the notebook back into the drawer and picked up the telephone. "Tell Malcolm Davis to meet me in the lobby in five minutes," he instructed someone.

My stomach muscles tightened. I said nothing, however.

Rasher went to a wall safe, fiddled with the combination lock and got the door open. He removed a large assortment of keys and selected one. "Shall I have one of the company cars sent around?" he asked Lipp as he closed the safe.

"Don't bother," Lipp said. "We can cab it."

We filed past Lipp's glasses on the way out. He didn't stop to pick them up.

Davis was waiting by the statue. He blinked when he saw me, and his ruddy complexion went a shade ruddier, but he didn't say anything. No one introduced us. We simply left the building, a silent group of four.

Lipp flagged a taxi, and we got in. Rasher took up more than one man's share of the back seat, but Lipp took up less, so we came out even. And Davis rode in front with the driver.

Rasher and Davis signed the card. The attendants wheeled out the box. It was so large that they had to transport it on a cart, which one attendant pushed and the other pulled. They escorted us into a private room and left us.

"The wealth of America," Lipp observed to me as Rasher opened the box. "Fancy pieces of paper that are worth maybe fifty cents apiece."

"Until they're sold," I said.

He nodded.

I watched Davis as he went through the thick manila envelopes in which the bonds were kept. The envelopes were well identified by issue, maturity date, coupon date and serial numbers. He found the first series we'd agreed upon and took the envelope out. Davis withdrew to an inconspicuous corner of the room.

I could see immediately that all of the bonds were there. Nevertheless, I took out my list and checked each certificate by serial number.

All of them were exactly where they belonged, in their proper numerical order, with the correct number of coupons attached.

The same with the second series.

And with the third.

"Are you satisfied?" Lipp asked finally.

"Yes," I said.

"Well, I'm not," he said. He asked for my list and searched it for another series of bonds which might be in the same box. He found one. He checked that series of bonds himself.

It too was in perfect shape.

Handing the envelope back to Rasher, he said, "False alarm."

"That's what I tried to tell you," Rasher said grimly.

Davis went to summon the attendants.

"Now," Lipp said to me, "Perhaps you'll tell us how you came by that list."

"I received an anonymous phone call the other night," I replied.

He gave me an enigmatic smile.

"You've gone out of your way to be helpful," I said. "I'm grateful."

The smile became less enigmatic. "I've enjoyed it."

"And I'm sorry I put you to so much trouble."

"Keeps us on our toes. We need that."

Davis returned with the attendants.

"You'd be amazed," Lipp said as we followed them down the corridor, "how much I own that I've never even seen. Sometimes it frightens me. You have to rely on other people, I know, but I keep having nightmares about having bought something that doesn't exist."

The cart went up the ramp and into the vault. Rasher went with it. We waited for him to return. I couldn't think of anything to say.

Rasher appeared.

"Can we give you a ride back to the office?" Lipp asked me.

I could have used the ride, for my car was parked in a lot near the Interlake Building, but I was suddenly anxious to get away from the group. "No, thanks," I said. "I'm going to make some other stops." I had the feeling I'd forgotten something. I thought for a moment and remembered what it was. "By the way," I asked Lipp, "have you ever heard of a Clifford Jars?"

Half a dozen furrows appeared on his brow. "Is that a man or a company?"

"A man."

The furrows deepened. He rubbed his chin. "Afraid not."

I turned to Rasher. And was shocked by the look he was giving me. It was one of pure hatred. "How about you?" I said.

"The name means nothing to me," he said stiffly.

Lipp led the way to the escalator, and we went up to the ground floor. Lipp and I shook hands. "If you should ever find out who made the anonymous phone call," he said, "I'd appreciate your cluing me in."

I avoided Davis's eyes. Also Rasher's. "The man wouldn't give his name," I said. "That's the truth. But he did say that he worked for Interlake."

"Thank you," Lipp said. "Thank you very much." He turned to Rasher. "Apparently you have a troublemaker in your midst."

"Um," said Rasher.

"You ought to investigate," Lipp advised him.

"Um," he said again.

Davis said nothing.

I told them all good-bye and entered the revolving door. With a moderately clear conscience and a deep feeling of relief.

12

Thursday got off to a good start. For one thing, Louise, my housekeeper, came to work on time, which she hardly ever did, and for another, the weather changed. It had been uncomfortably hot and smoggy for weeks, but on Wednesday night the wind shifted, causing the temperature to drop and the air to clear.

I'd slept well and felt rested. Before going to bed I'd spoken to Tom and Mark and given them a report on my trip. Both had been as relieved as I was. Tom told me he'd lined up buyers for Amalgamated Investors' Philadelphia Steel shares and made a couple of other deals besides.

Over a second cup of coffee I chatted with Louise about one of her grandsons, who'd come up from Arkansas to spend the summer with her and now didn't want to go home. I also asked her to put out some cheese and things before she left, as I was expecting guests. She said we were out of cheese. I gave her money to buy some.

Sometimes I drove to work, sometimes I didn't. This morning I decided not to. The weather was too nice. I'd walk part of the way, then take a cab.

Strolling eastward on Eleventh Street, I paused a couple of times just to look around. I'd lived in the neighborhood for a year and a half but still hadn't got over the novelty of it. The strange blending of past and present, of ordinary and offbeat, of mainstream and backwater. It wasn't typical of New York. It wasn't typical of anyplace I'd ever been, although in some ways it reminded me of Beacon Street in Boston and of the area around the Astor Tower in Chicago.

The Astor Tower.

Much of what had happened during the past few days still didn't make sense to me. I'd done as much as I could for the time being, however. Evidently someone had wanted to make trouble for Interlake: Davis. And had probably had help: Harrington. Beyond that I couldn't go. Future developments might provide additional answers. But then again, there might be no future developments.

Strange man, Rasher. Lipp too, for that matter; part financial genius, part ham actor.

Vera Harrington? I felt a pang of sympathy. Life was tough at times.

Davis? A downhill racer, not of the skiing variety. Any further conclusions would be pure guesswork.

At the corner of Eleventh Street and Fifth Avenue I paused again, to admire the First Presbyterian Church and the quiet churchyard. A half acre or so, straight from a European village; an oasis of peace where you wouldn't expect to find it.

I walked another six blocks, then hailed a cab, and when I got to the office I found that it was Irving's birthday.

One of the girls in the bookkeeping department had baked him a cake, and during the morning coffee break we had a party. Which made the day even nicer.

Shortly before noon Jaime popped into my office, suitcase in hand, eyes glowing. He'd come straight to the office from the airport and couldn't wait to tell me what he'd learned. Billings-Smithson was indeed close to developing a drug which would cure herpes simplex Type 2, and the disease was certainly one which needed a cure—the effects could be terrible. Furthermore, if the drug would cure herpes simplex Type 2, there was a good chance that it would also cure other viral infections which at present were uncurable. I complimented him on having dug into the matter so quickly and so thoroughly. He asked whether our dinner date was still on. I said that it was. He left to call Elizabeth.

Right after that I received a telephone call from Dr. Chang. He wanted to say that he was about to return to Boston; he'd enjoyed talking to me and hoped I'd look him up when I was in the area. No sooner had that call ended than another came in. From Rodney Alpert. Alpert was one of the art dealers I bought from. He told me that he'd received some new canvases from Claude Goulet and thought I'd like to see them. I said that I would. Goulet was a French-Canadian artist. I'd met him at his first one-man show in New York and liked him. We'd gone to dinner together, and I'd purchased one of his paintings.

At one o'clock Mark asked me whether I wanted to have lunch with him. We didn't often eat together, but he seemed reasonably mellow, and I had no other invitation, so I said sure.

Over martinis we talked about his favorite subject, the telephone bill. But when the steak sandwiches came he began to question me about my trip. I gave him all the details I hadn't given him the night before.

I'd found I had to watch Mark rather closely at times in order to know how he really felt about things. His usual posture was one of not being interested, of considering the matter at hand as being unworthy of his concern. Showing emotion was, according to his code, bad form. He was as capable of emotion as anyone else was, I'd come to realize, but you had to pay a lot of attention in order to detect what the emotion of the moment was. It therefore surprised me when he made a face and said, "I just can't stand that man Lipp."

"I don't know," I said. "I'm a little suspicious of him myself. But when you're with him he kind of gets to you. He *is* dynamic. And I must say he went out of his way—way out of his way—to cooperate with me."

"He comes on like the host of a talk show."

I smiled. "That was my reaction too. He'd have done well on the stage. But you can't sell him short as a businessman. Look what he's built."

Mark's face continued to register disapproval.

"Where do you know him from?" I asked.

"He's a friend of my father's."

That helped me to understand. Mark didn't care much for his father. He also didn't care much for people who spoke with foreign accents or for people who were flamboyant. A flamboyant man who spoke with a foreign accent and was a friend of Mark's father had, as far as Mark was concerned, three strikes against him before he even came up to bat.

Mark changed the subject. "That list," he said. "How do you know it wasn't a fake?"

"I don't. I didn't check out the handwriting. And even if the handwriting was Harrington's, there's no way of knowing whether the list was accurate or not. Someone could have deliberately made up a list of the wrong bonds, simply to mislead me."

"That's what I mean."

"On the other hand, whoever made up the list knew exactly which securities are in the inventory. Even the serial numbers. There aren't that many people who'd have access to such information. That doesn't prove anything, I know, but somehow or other I have the feeling that the list wasn't a fake—at least in the sense that someone was trying to make *me* look bad."

"You think, though, that Harrington and Davis were working together to stir up some kind of mischief?"

"It would appear so. Not for me but for Interlake."

"And that's why Harrington was killed?"

"Who knows, Mark? That's a matter for the police. They seem to have it in their heads that he was mixed up with some kind of criminal outfit. His wife insists that he wasn't, but you never can tell. The way he was killed indicates that a pro did the job, but you can't be sure about that either. Who knows what elements there were in the guy's life? He'd begun drinking heavily, he and his wife weren't getting along so well, he was worried about something—for all I know, he may have been a gambler, up to his ears in debt to the loan sharks. In spite of what his wife said."

Mark nodded.

"The one I didn't like," I said, "is Rasher."

"Is he one of Lipp's men?"

"Probably. He wasn't there the last time I was in the office. A man named Jordan was treasurer then. But Jordan was due to retire soon, and I guess he did. I don't know where Rasher comes from. From one of Lipp's other companies, possibly, or from some other insurance company. Or else he was at Interlake all along, somewhere down the ladder. I can't keep up with all the personnel changes. Wherever he comes from, though, he isn't my cup of tea."

"I wonder if Lipp attends all of the board of directors meetings or whether he just happened to be in Chicago for this one."

"I don't know. Come to think of it, it might not have been pure coincidence that he happened to pass through the reception room while I was there. More than four hours had elapsed between the time I spoke to Rasher on the phone and the time I showed up at the office."

The waiter approached. He asked whether we wanted more coffee. We said we didn't. Mark asked for the check. The waiter went off to get it.

"The bonds you saw," Mark said, "were made out to bearer rather than to Interlake, I take it."

"Yes," I said. "They could be cashed by anyone."

The waiter returned with the check.

Mark outfumbled me.

I was annoyed.

We walked back to the office. But when we got to the entrance to the building I decided to stay out for a while. The weather was so nice. And I was anxious to see Goulet's new paintings.

"See you later," I said to Mark.

He went into the building. I kept walking. I headed up Broadway. It seemed to me that there were just as many people on the street now as there had been in the days when stockbrokers were doing better and there were fewer computers. That everyone was in just as much of a hurry, just as unsmiling. That no matter which way the market was going, the folks who worked in the area called Wall Street seldom looked happy.

After a few blocks I flagged a taxi and got in. "Seventy-fifth and Madison," I said. The driver grunted and began to tell me his troubles. He'd had to wait in line at La Guardia for an hour before picking up a fare. He'd had to go to Harlem. The passenger before me had only tipped him a lousy thirty-five cents after a trip from the Sherry-Netherland to 14 Wall Street.

"The richer they are, the cheaper they are," he observed bitterly.

I thought of Mark. And fragments of our conversation at lunch came back to me. My own words, in particular.

I wondered where Rasher really had come from. Perhaps I should find out, just to satisfy my curiosity. It was hardly worth the effort, though. For I was quite certain that, wherever he came from, he was one of Lipp's men. Indebted to Lipp, afraid of Lipp.

13

• • • • • • • • •

The canvases were in Alpert's office. He hadn't yet got around to framing or hanging them.

There were three. And all were magnificent.

"It's a new direction for Goulet," Alpert said.

"It certainly is," I agreed.

Goulet's previous subjects had been people. The people of his native province, Quebec. Inhabitants of the small towns along the St. Lawrence River, north of Montreal. Poor, tough, wise, enduring people, weathered by hardship and the extremity of the seasons. His choice of such people as subjects was logical, for he was one of them. He understood them and loved them. He viewed the world as they did—but with broader knowledge than they had. He'd traveled for six years before coming home to settle down in Trois-Rivières, where he'd grown up.

Although I liked him enormously as a person, I didn't really understand him. A huge, burly, bearded creature who was only thirty-five but looked fifty, he spoke three languages and was inarticulate in all of them. And when he did express himself he usually did so in the form of questions, even when he was quite sure of what he was saying. He was fond of aphorisms, to which he always amended a "no?" or an "isn't it?" But despite his great size he managed to convey gentleness, and his difficulty with words had nothing to do with a lack of intelligence. He was plenty bright. He just didn't trust himself when it came to speech. Painting was his way of saying things, and he preferred not to have to use any other.

He'd evidently undergone some sort of change, however. The new pictures didn't deal with people at all. They were landscapes. Stark seacoast scenes, painted during the late winter or early spring. A beached rowboat, half covered with a tarpaulin. Rocks. Melting snow. A lone gull. What they indicated was a concern with time and with solitude.

"Where did he do them?" I asked.

"Nova Scotia," Alpert replied. "He's been up there since late February."

I studied first one and then another. Avidly. My appetite was whetted. I'd begun buying art as a hedge against inflation, but was now buying it because I enjoyed having it around. Initially, not knowing anything about it, I'd let the dealers guide me. They'd guided me into the blue chips of the art world—to the extent that I could afford them—much as a stockbroker would guide a novice investor into blue-chip stocks. After a while, though, I'd found that there was nothing wrong with picking up a picture for no other reason than that it pleased me. Goulet's work was a case in point. He was gaining recognition, and the painting of his that I owned was now worth more than I'd paid for it. But I'd bought it simply because I liked it.

"They're just great," I said.

"I'm glad you like them. Claude will be too. He asked about you in his last letter. Why don't you drop him a line? I'm sure he'd like to hear from you."

"Maybe I will. Give me his address." I continued to study the paintings. "I know I want at least one, but I don't know which."

"Take one home. See what it does for you. If you decide you want one of the others we can switch. There's no hurry."

I nodded. We often operated on that basis. The picture belonged to Alpert until I was sure I wanted to keep it, but it hung in my house.

He wrote Goulet's address on a slip of paper and gave it to me. I put it in my wallet. "Take your time," he said.

I did. And finally decided that I wanted the picture of the gull. It said so much about survival.

"Would you like me to drop it off at your house?" Alpert asked.

"Fine. I'm going out to dinner but I'll be home between six and seven."

"I'll be there."

Riding back to the office, I felt very good.

And at four-thirty I felt even better. For Tom had come in a few minutes before with the news that we had a new client: the Maryland Fund. He'd been trying to get a portion of its business for two years and during a four-hour lunch at the Plaza with two members of M.F.'s top brass he'd not only won them over but got their first order. To buy twenty thousand shares of Consolidated Business Machines.

We had a drink, to celebrate. Mark joined us. And while we were drinking Jaime appeared, ready to go home with me. I invited him to have a drink also.

"How was the trip?" Tom asked him.

"Better than I'd hoped," he replied. "Billings-Smithson are on to something."

"Like what?"

Jaime glanced at me, as if requesting permission to speak. This wasn't unusual. People in my department often hesitated to reveal information to people in the sales department without my consent, just as people in the sales department were, on occasion, reluctant to tell me the terms of a deal without first consulting Tom. I wondered whether the employees of other companies felt the same way—more loyal to their immediate superiors than to the company itself. I guessed that they did.

"Like a cure for herpes simplex Type 2," I said.

"Never heard of it," said Tom.

I told him what it was.

"What's the big deal?" he asked.

77

Seeing that Tom had been given security clearance, Jaime proceeded to offer some of his newly acquired knowledge. "The virus wasn't really isolated until 1967. Now that it's known, it's estimated that about a quarter of a million people in the United States have it. It's contagious—and very dangerous. Babies can catch it from their mothers at birth and become brain-damaged and a lot of other things. Some of them even die."

"I didn't know that," I said.

"It's a fact," Jaime said. "But that's not all. It's been linked to cancer."

Tom sat up straighter. So did Mark and I. Anything that related to cancer was important.

"They haven't proved yet that it actually causes cancer," Jaime went on, "but there's evidence which points in that direction. Cancer of the cervix, mainly."

"Man!" Tom exclaimed. "And Billings-Smithson will have the only cure?"

"There's a German company that's supposed to have one, but the Food and Drug Administration won't clear it for use over here."

"Man!" Tom exclaimed again.

"Herpes simplex Type 2," Mark said thoughtfully. "And what, may I ask, is herpes simplex Type 1? Who's got a cure for that?"

Jaime shrugged. "A cure for that isn't so important."

"Why not?"

"Herpes simplex Type 1 is the common fever blister."

Tom laughed and said, "I give up. I'm glad I'm just a salesman." He put his glass on the desk and got up. "I'm going home. I've been drinking off and on since twelve-thirty. Enough is enough."

He left. And shortly after that Mark did too.

Jaime relaxed noticeably. As if he'd been under a strain with Tom and Mark in the room.

"We're all part of the same company, Jaime," I said with a smile.

He got my meaning. "I know, Brock. But you're the one who hired me and you're the one I'm responsible to. And you're the one who understands the problems."

I let the matter drop.

He sighed. His expression became very serious. He hesitated a moment, then spoke. "I don't think I've ever really thanked you, Brock, for hiring me."

"Aw, come on now."

"I mean it. I love this job. I can't imagine anything else I'd like as well. I stopped being religious a long time ago, but every morning I sort of say a prayer of thanks that you got me out of that bank."

I was embarrassed but pleased. "What you ought to be thankful for is that you have the kind of head that can handle the work."

"That too. And the education. If only more kids where I came from could get the breaks I got."

"You didn't get them, Jaime. You made them."

"Well, whatever." He fell silent. Not for long, though. "About tonight," he said. "I want you to be my guest."

"That wasn't what I had in mind."

"Please. I want it that way. So does Elizabeth."

"O.K. If you insist."

"Thanks. And thanks for giving us the evening. I appreciate it." Another silence. "Maybe, Brock, when we're all together you could talk to Elizabeth . . . you could say something . . . you could . . . well . . ." He didn't finish.

"Still the same problem?" I asked.

He nodded.

"You're two grown people, Jaime. You know how you feel about each other."

"We love each other."

"O.K., then."

"It's just not that simple, Brock. We can't live just the two of us in a world with nobody else in it. There're other people to think about. My mother's taking it very hard that I want to marry out

79

of the faith. I know, I'm twenty-nine years old and my own man and all that, and I'm not a believer, in the old-fashioned sense, but, hell, I'm all she has and she worked like a dog so that I could have an education, and to go against her . . ." He shook his head sadly and began again. "It's the same with Elizabeth's dad. Not only am I Catholic, but I'm Puerto Rican, and as far as he's concerned there isn't a Puerto Rican in the world that's good enough for his daughter."

"I don't know what I could say, Jaime. To you or to Elizabeth."

"It would be different, maybe, if we didn't both come from broken homes. But we do, see, and neither of us wants to have kids and put them through that. I mean, suppose it didn't work out. Suppose something happened. I mean, I promised myself one thing, Brock—I promised myself when I was no more than a little kid: if I ever had children, I'd never leave them or let my wife take them away from me. I know what it's like. So does Elizabeth. That's what's hanging us up more than anything else, I guess."

"Sometimes, Jaime, you have to be willing to take a chance."

He looked at me. The troubled expression went away. He smiled. "I know. But would you mind telling that to Elizabeth?"

"I'll be glad to." I glanced at my watch. It was almost five. "What arrangements did you make with her about tonight?"

"She's going to meet us at your place at six-thirty. I thought I could clean up there. I have an extra shirt in my bag."

"Fine."

We finished our drinks, Jaime picked up his suitcase, and we went out to tangle with the rush-hour traffic.

The traffic was worse than usual. As the taxi inched its way up Broadway I began to have visions of Alpert bringing the picture to my house, finding no one there and leaving again. Louise never stayed later than four o'clock, even on the days when she didn't come to work on time.

I suggested an alternate route, and the driver took it, but things were no better there. When we reached Eleventh Street and University Place my patience finally ran out. "We can make better time walking," I said.

Jaime paid the driver, and we got out. We walked briskly to Fifth Avenue. The light was against us. We waited for it to change. I gazed beyond the stream of cars to the First Presbyterian Church. The day had passed very quickly; it seemed no more than a couple of hours since I'd stood at the same intersection, admiring the same building from a different angle.

Jaime's gaze followed mine. His reaction was different, though. "Churches always look so peaceful," he said. "How come they make so much trouble for everybody?"

"Because they're run by people," I said.

The light changed. We crossed Fifth Avenue. I could see a car parked in front of my house, where parking wasn't allowed. I wondered whether it was Alpert's. "Let's hurry," I said, and we quickened our pace.

My house was in the middle of the block. As we drew closer I peered at the car. It was a black sedan. I couldn't identify the make, but I could see two people in the front seat.

"Hi, Mr. Potter."

I paused for an instant. The speaker was Eddie Marshak. He was six years old and lived in the building three doors east of my house. He was on roller skates and was clinging to one of the frail trees that bordered the curb. "Hi, Eddie," I said.

"I got skates," he said. "For my birthday."

I smiled and nodded and took a long stride to catch up with Jaime. We reached my house. I looked at the men in the car. Neither of them was Alpert. The one on the curb side blinked as our eyes met and moved to get out. I turned and started up the steps to my front door, taking my keys from my pocket as I did so. A woman came out of the building next door. I recognized her. My neighbor Mrs. Negronsky. She stopped suddenly and, staring at something behind me, froze.

"Look out!" Jaime yelled, and gave me a hard shove.

I staggered against the railing, slid off the step, went down on one knee, dropped my keys and spun around.

The man who'd blinked was on the sidewalk. He was wearing gloves, and in his left hand he had a gun.

In one swift movement Jaime flung his suitcase at the man and leaped between the man and me.

There was a soft pop. Jaime stiffened. Mrs. Negronsky screamed.

Jaime came down on top of me. I tried to get out from under him. Mrs. Negronsky continued to scream. An engine roared. Tires shrieked.

Jaime rolled over. Blood was trickling from his chest and from the corner of his mouth. I looked around wildly. The car was already at the end of the block. Jaime's suitcase lay on the sidewalk. Eddie Marshak was skating unsteadily toward it.

"Call an ambulance!" I shouted at Mrs. Negronsky.

Jaime stared at me. I cradled his head in my arms.

"Call an ambulance!" I shouted again.

Jaime's eyeballs rolled upward, and while I was holding him he died.

14

● ● ● ● ● ● ● ● ●

I slid into a robotlike state in which I could function but couldn't feel.

People came and went. Police officers, newsmen, my partners, Eddie Marshak's parents, Mrs. Negronsky. Mrs. Negronsky and I took turns working with the police artist. Between us we managed to come up with a pretty good likeness of the man who'd stepped out of the car and fired the gun.

Eddie Marshak had noticed more than anyone would have expected. He supplied the information that the car's left rear fender was dented and that Jaime's suitcase had knocked the gun out of the killer's hand. Neither Mrs. Negronsky nor I had seen the gun fall or the killer pick it up, but Eddie had. I hadn't been aware that there'd been another eyewitness, but Eddie had seen that too, and so had Mrs. Negronsky. A car had pulled up to the curb behind the killer's car almost at the instant of the shooting, and the driver had honked the horn. That man was identified. He was a friend of a woman named Charlotte Gaines, who lived in the house to the east of mine, which had been converted into apartments, and he'd come to pick her up.

The police theorized that the suitcase had struck the killer a fraction of a second too late, that dropping the gun and hearing the honking of the horn had caused him to take off without firing a second shot. I was inclined to agree.

At no point during the long hours of questioning did I get confused. At no point did I not know what I was saying and doing. But at no point was I a complete human being. My emotions were out of order. They didn't start working again until Friday afternoon.

The jolt was enormous.

I was standing at the corner of Ninety-sixth Street and Second Avenue. I'd been to see Jaime's mother, who lived in the housing project at Ninety-ninth and Second, and I'd walked down to Ninety-sixth, trying without success to hail a taxi. And suddenly, as I stood there, I began to shake. The shaking got so bad that I had to lean against the wall of a building for support. At the same time I lost all sense of my surroundings. The mental picture of Jaime's mother sitting blank-faced on the side of her bed, fingering her rosary, was so overwhelming that it blocked out everything else.

As breakdowns go, it was very brief. The fit of trembling lasted only two or three minutes. It left me feeling weak, though, and I continued to lean against the wall, not sure of where to go or what to do.

A pregnant woman came up to me as if to speak, then changed her mind and walked on. A brown and white dog sidled over to sniff at my shoes. Finally I felt sufficiently together to make another attempt to get a taxi. This time I succeeded.

I gave the driver the address of my house but halfway there I changed my mind and decided to go to the office instead. For I was now able to face the fact which for almost twenty-four hours I'd kept hidden from myself. The fact that someone might have taken out a contract on my life.

15

· · · · · · · · ·

The atmosphere was more subdued than usual. No one was smiling. Voices were lower. People weren't milling about.

Helen Doyle gave me a startled look as I passed her desk. She brought in the mail and telephone messages and instead of leaving she hovered beside my chair. "I'm very sorry," she said. "It's a terrible thing."

I nodded.

"Are you all right?"

I nodded again.

"Is there anything I can do?"

"Not right now, Helen. Thank you."

Word that I was there got around fast. In less than five minutes both Tom and Mark were in my office, wanting to know whether there'd been any new developments. I said that I'd been to see Jaime's mother and that I'd met his fiancée at the mother's apartment and that Mass was going to be said at ten-thirty the next morning.

"Have the police come up with anything?" Tom asked.

"Not that I know of," I replied. "I haven't seen them since this morning."

"They were here around noon," Mark said. "I spoke to them."

"What did they want?" I asked.

"General information. About Jaime."

"I've been getting phone calls all day," Tom said uneasily.

"Anything special?" I asked.

He shook his head. "Just people wanting to know." He looked as if he hadn't slept any more than I had. "Would you like to stay at my place for a while?"

"Thanks, Tom, but I don't think it's necessary."

"I don't know," he said dubiously. "It might be safer."

I ignored the implication. But evidently he and Mark had discussed the matter, for Mark said, "You shouldn't stay at home, Brock. Alone, I mean."

I saw Irving standing in the doorway as if he didn't know whether or not to interrupt us. I motioned for him to come in. Tom and Mark hung around until I said to Irving, "Sit down. We have a lot of rearranging to do." Then, reluctantly, they left.

Irving eyed me with concern. As if expecting to find visible scars. "Are you O.K., boss?" He only called me "boss" when he was emotionally shaken, which wasn't often.

"More or less."

"You had a close call."

"Very."

"Harriet's back. She came in a little while ago. Everybody's pretty upset. Including me."

"How do you think *I* feel, Irving?"

"I can imagine."

I considered what he'd said. "Upset" had many meanings. And morale was important. "I'll speak to everyone," I said.

"That'd be a good idea, boss. Scotch the rumors."

"Are there rumors?"

"Naturally."

"Like what?"

"Like that Jaime found out something that someone didn't want him to know, or that you did, or that we handle money for the Syndicate."

"The Syndicate? Whose idea is that?"

"Mine."

"Irving!"

"It wouldn't be unusual, Brock. Maybe without our knowing it. Plenty of brokerage houses do."

"Well, we don't. To the best of my knowledge, at least. If the Syndicate has money in one of the funds—I suppose that's possible—otherwise no. Believe me."

"Then why, Brock? Why would someone want to assassinate one of us? Unless the TV guys are wrong, and the newspapers, that's what it was like: an assassination."

"I haven't turned on television or read the papers, but it all happened so fast, I don't know how anyone could be sure."

Irving didn't appear to be convinced. And he was the most level-headed of the bunch.

"Call everyone in," I said.

He left the office. I flipped through the mail. The second envelope from the top was addressed to me in my own handwriting. It contained the Xerox copy of Harrington's list. I put it into the top drawer of my desk. I tried to think of what I'd say to my staff.

It took Irving no time at all to round them up. I watched them as they filed in. They were a grim-faced group.

"We suffered a hell of a loss yesterday," I said when they'd pulled up chairs. "I'm not going to pretend otherwise. It's going to be tough to get along without Jaime, but one way or another we will. That I'm certain of. Eventually I'll find someone to replace him, and when I do I hope that whoever it is will turn out to be as good as Jaime was. In the meanwhile you'll all have to pitch in and cover what he was doing as well as your regular work. Irving will make the decisions as to who does what. The main thing is to carry on."

There was no response. They didn't want a pep talk.

"I don't know what's been going through your minds since you heard the news and I don't know what you heard. The fact is, I myself don't know what happened, or why. All I know is that two men were in a car in front of my house and when Jaime and I started up the steps one of them got out and fired a shot at us. That's all I know, and there were several eyewitnesses, and that's all *they* know, and the police are investigating, but as far as I can tell they themselves don't have any answers."

I looked around. Still no response. Generalities wouldn't do either.

"A number of things have gone through my mind. First of all, the whole thing could be the work of some maniac, or pair of maniacs, who had no understandable reason for doing what they did. Secondly, if they weren't crazy, if there was some plan behind what they did, it may be a case of mistaken identity; they may have intended to kill someone and fired at us, thinking that we were the men they were after. And lastly, they may have really wanted to kill Jaime or me or both of us, but if that's what it was, it's going to be awfully hard for anybody to dig up a reason, because neither Jaime nor I nor this company has been even remotely involved in any criminal activities."

This time there was a response. It came from Joe Rothland. "The last possibility you mentioned," he said. "I mean, that they knew what they were doing. It could be that one of us has run across something that's more important than we think."

I gave him a sharp glance. He didn't flinch from it. He was a thick-necked, beefy young man with some of the same bulldog qualities that Irving had. "Take yourself," I said. "Have you?"

"Not that I know of. But I may have. Or Jaime may."

"Or even you," George Cole added.

I shifted my gaze to him. He was the opposite of Joe. A tall, painfully thin, prematurely bald man of forty who looked more ascetic—and sounded more shy—than he actually was. "Possibly," I said. "I've made a lot of enemies recently, as a result of exposing Yankee Clipper. Is that what you mean?"

Harriet spoke up. "I should think it'd be something more recent," she said softly. She paused. "If that woman was right, and Jaime was trying to protect you."

Mrs. Negronsky, I thought. "If," I said. None of them appeared to be satisfied.

"I don't know what else to tell you," I said.

"Is there any way we can help?" Irving asked.

"If there is, I'll let you know. Meanwhile I'd like you to stick around for a few minutes after the others leave."

He nodded. The other three took the hint and got up.

"I don't think I accomplished much," I said when they were gone.

"Anything is better than nothing," Irving replied.

I repeated that the reassignment of work would be up to him, but I outlined how I thought he should do it. He told me not to worry. Then he asked me whether I wanted him to continue looking into Computech.

"Yes," I said.

"I don't suppose I should ask, Brock, but your trip to Chicago —could it be related to what happened yesterday?"

"I don't know, Irv." I thought it over. I definitely needed assistance. "I'll tell you about it, and you can make up your own mind."

I told him about it.

He did make up his mind.

We talked it over.

He left.

I took the envelope from the top drawer of my desk and opened it. I studied the list. Somehow Harrington seemed more real to me now than he had before.

I pictured the house in Chicago Heights. I pictured the bullet-ridden body in the garage. I pictured Jaime on my front steps. I tried not to believe that the killer, having failed, would try again.

I asked Helen to have Miss Jensen step into my office.

I put the list away.

Harriet came in briskly. She no longer looked as grim as she had before. "Is there something I can do?" she asked eagerly.

"Maybe," I said. "Sit down. That relative of yours in Washington—is he still there?"

"Uncle Bill?"

"The one who's a lobbyist."

"Uncle Bill. Yes, he's still there."

"How good are his connections?"

"He knows a lot of senators and congressmen, if that's what you mean."

"I'd like some information. Maybe you can get it for me, through him. It would be in the Justice Department, in the FBI files, and it's hard to get that sort of thing."

"I don't know whether he can or not, but I'll ask him. Does this have anything to do with Jaime?"

"It might. In any event, I'd like it kept strictly between you and me."

Harriet squared her shoulders. She could be very purposeful. "Of course. What information do you want?"

"I'm interested in someone named Clifford Jars or Yars—I'm not sure how it's spelled."

She repeated the names.

"It's only a guess on my part," I said, "but there may be a record on him in the Justice Department."

"In connection with what, Brock?"

"In connection with counterfeiting."

16

• • • • • • • • •

A light went on. I opened my eyes. Irving was standing in the doorway.

"You ought to go home," he said.

"What time is it?"

"Seven-thirty."

"I must have fallen asleep." I tried to get up, but my body felt like lead. "How come you're still here?"

"I didn't think you ought to be alone."

"Is anyone else here?"

Irving shook his head. "They've all gone. Tom said his offer still stands. You're welcome to spend the night at his house." He eyed me critically. "You look awful, boss."

"Reaction, I guess."

"When did you eat last?"

I shrugged. I couldn't remember.

"What you need is a meal and a good night's sleep—someplace."

I stretched. Even that was difficult. "I had in mind to go back to Mrs. Ortega's. I was there this afternoon, but she was in such a state of shock I couldn't talk to her."

"She probably still is."

"The only one who could get her to respond even a little bit was Jaime's fiancée." Which was true. By dying Jaime had brought the two women together as he'd never have been able to do if he'd lived.

"They may be better off left alone."

"I wanted to tell her that we'd pay the funeral expenses and, in addition to the insurance, we'd continue to pay Jaime's salary for the rest of the year."

"You can tell her that in a few days."

A telephone rang in a distant part of the office. Irving frowned.

"Maybe you'd better answer it," I said.

"Everybody knows we're closed. It must be a wrong number." Nevertheless he went.

Presently he returned. "It's for you. A Detective O'Brien. On Charlie's line."

I remembered the name but couldn't associate a face with it. O'Brien was one of the police officers who'd questioned me the night before. I forced myself to get out of the chair.

"We tried to reach you at home," O'Brien said. "We wondered, Detective Sestino and me, whether we could come over."

Not again, I thought. "Of course," I said.

"How soon?"

"Well, I was just about to leave the office and go out for something to eat."

"Nine, nine-thirty?"

I sighed. "Fine. At my house."

He hung up. I sighed again. "More questions," I reported to Irving.

"I'll eat with you," he said.

We went to Patricia Murphy's restaurant. Because it was near my house, and because, despite that, I seldom met anyone there whom I knew.

Irving wasn't a drinker. An occasional glass of Rhine wine was about as far as he went. But now, before we even unfolded our napkins, he ordered a Scotch on the rocks, and when it came he seized the glass like an alcoholic.

"Suppose it isn't true," he said.

We hadn't spoken in the taxi. Bone-weary, I'd rested my head against the back of the seat and dozed off again. But his mind had evidently been racing, and he was merely voicing the last of a long chain of thoughts.

"You lost me," I said. "Suppose what isn't true?"

"Suppose there really isn't anything wrong at Interlake."

"I didn't say there was."

"Suppose Lipp doesn't know anything about it."

"I didn't say he did."

"Well, then, *you* lost *me*. What were you talking about?"

"I was telling you why I went to Chicago and what happened when I got there. I said there may be a connection between that and the shooting." I sipped my own drink. It tasted better than any I'd had in years. Two more gulps and it was gone. "What I said at the office I meant, Irving. It could have been a maniac, or mistaken identity. Or someone could have been trying to kill me. I don't believe anyone was trying to kill Jaime. I believe Jaime saw the gun pointing at me and, being the kind of guy he was, he instinctively tried to protect me."

"Is that what you told the police?"

"No. It didn't even seem possible to me until this afternoon."

"Are you going to tell them now?"

The waiter, seeing that my glass was empty, came over. "Something else from the bar?" he asked.

"Another Scotch," I said.

"Me too," Irving said, and quickly emptied his glass.

The waiter left.

I pondered Irving's question. "No," I said at last.

"But suppose—" Irving began. He lapsed into silence.

"What could the police do?" I said. "Question Lipp? Question Rasher? Neither of them shot Harrington, you can be damn certain, any more than they shot Jaime. And the two killings may not even be related. And the bonds, if they ever were missing, have possibly been put back. All I'd be doing is slandering a couple of men who are smart enough to make anything I said appear ridiculous."

"But suppose the police catch the guy who shot Jaime. They seem to have got a pretty good description. It's possible."

"I hope they do. But if he's a professional killer they may not. And if they do, and he is a professional killer, I very much doubt that he'd tell who paid him. Guys like that just don't."

The waiter brought the second round.

"So what are you going to do?" Irving asked.

"Help the police as much as I can to catch the man who shot Jaime. And continue to look into Interlake. But really *look*. Then, if I find anything, any proof—well, we'll take it from there."

Irving sampled his new drink. He was beginning to perspire.

"But meanwhile, Brock, you have to protect yourself."

I wished that I knew how. I nodded, though.

Irving dabbed at his upper lip with his napkin. "It seems warm in here."

Both of us fell silent. I thought about protecting myself. And about how destructive fear could be. I saw myself in hiding. The picture wasn't attractive.

I opened the menu. "Let's order."

We did.

I stared at the tablecloth.

"Well, if it isn't the researcher!"

I looked up—and blinked. "Monica!"

She was smiling broadly. There was a man beside her. A tall man with a mustache. He seemed familiar. I recalled Carol's words. The Grosses' party. Victor Lane.

I tried to think of something to say. "How was Long Island?" was what I came up with.

"An orgy," Monica replied. "An absolute orgy." She sat down beside me on the banquette and said to her husband, "Sit down, Victor. Brock is a very close friend of mine." She emphasized "close."

Victor sat down beside Irving. There was agony in his eyes. Monica didn't introduce her husband or show any interest in Irving. "Brock owns the loveliest Picasso," she said, addressing all of us. "A nude from the early fifties, after he broke up with Françoise, I think. The sort of thing I'd love to own. And some other choice items."

Her hand touched the inside of my leg and began to stroke it. I never blush. But at that moment I began to.

Irving looked at her with admiration. "Do you collect art?"

"In a small way," she replied, continuing to stroke my leg, her hand moving upward toward my crotch. "Mostly my own, I'm afraid."

I glanced uneasily at Victor Lane and tried to remove Monica's hand. She took it away but brought it back, this time placing it on my penis. "Brock seems to like it too."

I felt myself going from pink to crimson. I wanted to say something, but all I could do was swallow.

Monica fingered my penis. "He has a definite feel for it," she said to her husband.

He made an attempt to smile.

In spite of myself I began to respond. I was certain that Victor couldn't see what was going on, yet I felt guilty as hell. I swallowed again. "I'm still learning," I said in a tight voice.

Monica laughed delightedly. "You know more than you think you do." She addressed herself to her husband. "He really does."

"Jesus," I said.

"Look at him," Irving said. "He's blushing."

The waiter arrived with the shrimp cocktails.

Monica gave me one last stroke, then removed her hand and slid out of the booth. "We don't want to disturb your meal," she said, "so we'll run. Come along, Victor."

Victor was already on his feet.

Monica stood there a moment longer. "Didn't I read something about you in the paper this morning? Something about a shooting?"

"You may have," I said.

"A jealous husband, no doubt." She gave me a parting smile. "It's been lovely. We must get together again soon." She took Victor's arm, and the two of them headed toward the front of the restaurant.

"Good-looking woman," Irving observed. "Maybe you shouldn't be drinking. You're flushed."

"It's warm in here. You said so yourself."

He nodded and speared a shrimp.

I picked up the lemon from the plate and gave it a vicious squeeze. Juice squirted into my eye. "Damn," I said.

But I really felt better than I had before. Less tired. More alert.

17

● ● ● ● ● ● ● ●

I recognized both of them as soon as I saw them. They'd been at my house the night before but had come late, after the patrolmen had taken my first statement. They were from Homicide.

O'Brien was the older of the two. He was in his late forties, I judged. A stocky, blue-eyed man with hair that was in the process of going from red to gray. Sestino was at least ten years younger, and very Italian-looking, with black hair, olive complexion and big brown eyes that kept darting here and there as if he didn't quite trust the furniture.

"I hope you managed to get some sleep," O'Brien began in a friendly enough manner.

"Not very much," I said.

He nodded sympathetically. "Sometimes it's worse the day after."

"It didn't really get to me until this afternoon," I admitted. "Then all of a sudden I was walking down the street, coming from Mrs. Ortega's, and right there on the street I damn near cracked up."

He nodded again. "It can happen that way." His eyes narrowed. "Mrs. Ortega—the man's mother?"

"Yes."

"You were pretty close to him? You knew his family?"

"Close to him, yes. His family, no. In fact, he didn't have much family. Just his mother—and his fiancée, whom you met last night." Elizabeth had arrived at six-thirty, in the midst of everything. It had been a terrible scene. "I'd never met his mother before."

"But you were close to him, you say."

"He'd been with me less than a year, but yes, I guess you could say we were close. We worked together, and I liked him, and there was something about him—yes, we were."

Sestino's eyes returned from another of their surveys. "What kind of man was he, would you say, sir?"

"A good man."

"Good? Good in what way, sir?"

"Good in all ways. His work, his feelings about people. Just good, that's all."

"What Sestino means," O'Brien said, "is, what we're trying to get is a sort of picture of the man. Like look at it this way. A man just doesn't get himself shot for no reason at all. Not usually. Usually there's something about him, about the way he lives, who his friends are, that sort of explains things. Like if a man drinks or gambles or is involved with women or is hooked on something—you know what I mean?"

"I know what you mean, but there was nothing like that with Jaime."

"How sure are you about that, sir?" Sestino asked.

"Very sure. As sure as you can be about anyone you've worked with the way I worked with Jaime. And before I hired him I did some checking. Believe me, he was a fine human being."

"He was a Puerto Rican, though," Sestino said.

I looked at him.

"I've got nothing against Puerto Ricans," he added quickly. "We've got some on the force and we get along fine. But sometimes—well, dope, for instance."

"Not in Jaime's case," I assured him.

"And yet," O'Brien said, "somebody had it in for him enough to hire someone like Arco to hit him."

"Arco?" I asked.

"Timmy Arco. He has quite a record."

"You *know* who killed Jaime?"

"Could be. We're not sure, of course. But that picture you and the lady came up with, and the style of the killing, and the fact that the man was left-handed—we think it might be Arco."

"Who is he?"

"A hood," said Sestino. "A bad number." He gazed around again—at the lamp, the table, the fern next to the window. His eyes came back to me. "Last anybody heard, he was in California."

"But before that," O'Brien said, "he was a member of Sal Serafina's outfit in Chicago. North Side loan sharking. An enforcer. Then after Serafina's murder he put in with Tony Muratto, when Muratto took over Serafina's operation. There was a rumor at the time that Arco's the one who shot Serafina, on Muratto's orders. It's never been established, though. Anyhow, after Muratto got sent up, Arco dropped out of sight for a while. Recently he's been seen around Los Angeles." He paused. "He's not the kind of guy you'd want to get on the wrong side of. He's been credited with six murders, not counting Serafina's."

I tried to comprehend that there was a man walking around who'd committed six murders. "And he's never been caught?"

"He's been arrested plenty of times. What he's never been is convicted."

"But that's incredible."

"No, sir," Sestino said. "It happens all the time. Lack of evidence. Whatever witnesses there've been have either refused at the last minute to testify or have disappeared."

The temperature in the room seemed suddenly to drop.

"The only crime Arco's ever been convicted of was stealing a car when he was seventeen," O'Brien said. "He drew a suspended sentence. So you can kind of see how anxious we are to find out all we can about this Ortega murder."

I nodded.

99

O'Brien took a folded-up piece of paper from his pocket and handed it to me. "You might want to take a look at this."

I unfolded the paper. It was a Wanted poster. The photograph on it was unmistakably that of the man who'd shot Jaime. Younger, thinner, with more hair—but the same man. Wanted for murder: Timothy Arco, also known as Thomas Arch, also known as John Burns, 5'11", 155 lbs., brown hair, brown eyes, scar on right cheek, dangerous, and various other morsels of information. "That's him," I said with certainty.

"That's what the lady—Mrs. Negronsky—says too. And the Marshak kid seems to agree."

I continued to study the photograph. The man looked angry, but not particularly dangerous. An ordinary male with a small mouth and narrow shoulders, caught by the camera at a moment when he was in a bad mood.

Six times a murderer. Maybe seven. Or eight or nine.

O'Brien handed me another Wanted poster. "Recognize him?"

Paul Arco. Accessory to murder.

"His brother?" I asked. There was a resemblance.

"Yes. He may have been the driver of the car. They often work together."

"I didn't get a good look at the driver," I said. Paul Arco appeared to be the younger of the two. His hair was lighter, and his expression was less grim; he gave the impression of being startled to find himself in front of a camera.

O'Brien sighed. "He's never been convicted either."

"A good driver," Sestino said.

I thought of the car pulling away from the curb in front of my house. And of a car pulling away from the Harringtons'.

No one spoke for a few moments.

"In this case," O'Brien said finally, "it'd be hard to get a conviction if we couldn't prove a motive."

"And," Sestino added, "there's nothing about Ortega that gives us one. Everybody we talk to says the same thing: he was a great guy."

"The thing that doesn't exactly make sense," O'Brien said, "is that the car was parked in front of *your* house." He paused to note my reaction.

I made an effort not to have one.

"I mean," he went on, "someone like Arco, the way he operates, it'd be more likely if he was going to hit Ortega, he'd be waiting someplace around Ortega's house."

"I see what you mean," I said.

"And the way Mrs. Negronsky saw it, Ortega was sort of trying to protect you."

"It happened so fast," I said, "I just don't know."

"So the thing is, it's possible that Arco wasn't trying to kill Ortega, if you know what I mean—he was trying to kill you."

They were fishing. But they were fishing in the right stream. And they seemed to be capable men. I was tempted to tell them about Interlake. The connection was too tenuous, though. Arco had probably never heard of Lipp or even of Rasher; they'd have made damn certain he'd never heard of them.

"I'd give that some thought if I were you," O'Brien said. "There's always the chance that if someone tried once he'll try again. If you know what I mean."

"Are you trying to tell me to be careful?" I asked.

"That wouldn't be a bad idea," Sestino said.

"But what we're also saying," O'Brien said, "is that you ought to think about why Arco was waiting outside your house."

My nervous system asserted itself. I shuddered.

And for the moment that seemed to be enough for the two detectives. O'Brien got up, and Sestino followed suit. "We'll be in touch," O'Brien said.

Sestino gave the room a final inspection. "That's a nice fern," he said. "I like plants."

I sat in the den for a while after they left, looking at the Wanted posters.

The house seemed very quiet. And not particularly safe.

18

● ● ● ● ● ● ● ● ●

I had a nightmare.

Two men were chasing me. One of them had a hand grenade. He kept trying to get close enough to throw it. I ran around the corner from Eleventh Street onto Fifth Avenue, thinking I could escape into the churchyard, but the gate was closed and pad-locked. The two men narrowed the distance between us. I made a desperate attempt to climb the fence. It was very high and had iron spikes on top. I grabbed one of the spikes and flipped myself over, landing on the grass. The two men followed. I raced across the yard toward the church house on Twelfth Street. The men had almost caught up to me now. The door of the church house wouldn't open. I banged on it with both fists. The man with the grenade pulled out the pin and drew back his arm.

I awoke.

My heart was pounding and my neck was damp with sweat. The inside of my mouth felt as if it were stuffed with dry oats.

I turned over. The streetlight outside my window was still on, but the sky was beginning to go from black to gray. I looked at the clock. Five-twenty. My heart continued to pound.

Jesus, I thought.

I went into the bathroom and drank some water. Then I went to the window and looked out. The two men I'd dreamed about still seemed quite real.

I'd left my cigarettes downstairs. I wanted one but was reluctant to leave the bedroom; a killer might be lurking in the hall.

I forced myself to open the bedroom door and went down the steps, turning on lights at the top and at the bottom. I found the cigarettes and lit one. Then, turning on more lights, I walked into the kitchen. I put a fire under the teakettle and spooned instant coffee into a mug. Waiting for the water to boil, I tried to explain away the noises I heard. The refrigerator switching itself on, the grandfather clock in the hall ticking at its usual pace, a car passing. But when the teakettle suddenly began to whistle I jumped, and my hand was so unsteady that I spilled some of the steaming water.

The Arco brothers are back in California, I told myself. And no one would dare to make a second attempt.

Gradually I talked myself out of the more irrational fears. But some of the rational ones lingered. If someone wanted me dead, Jaime's death wouldn't satisfy him.

I began to wonder whether I'd be safer at a hotel. But that would be running, and I didn't like the idea. Besides, I could stay away from the house but I couldn't stay away from the office; I had a job to do, now more than ever.

I took the coffee into the den and stood there, gazing at Goulet's picture of the gull. Alpert had arrived shortly after the shooting but had seen the police cars and the crowd outside my house and, realizing that something was wrong, had driven away without coming inside. But the next morning he'd phoned, and, being in that unnaturally calm state, I'd told him to bring the picture over. It was now on the table next to the door, resting against the wall.

Each of us is alone, it said. Each of us must survive.

I thought of my father. And began to get angry. I damn well had to see things through. One quitter in the family was enough.

At eight o'clock I was in the kitchen again, having a second mug of coffee and munching on one of the doughnuts Louise had made, when the telephone rang.

The call was from Tom. He wanted to know how I was and

whether I wanted a ride to the church for the Mass.

I said that I was all right, and that I did.

He picked me up at a quarter to ten. He wasn't as ebullient as usual, and there was a nick on his chin where he'd cut himself shaving.

We drove in silence until we reached Fifty-eighth Street. Then as we turned to go over to the East Side Tom said, "I don't suppose you feel like a few games of squash this afternoon."

I looked at him. Bravado, I thought. But I admired him for it and decided to show a little of the same. "Sure," I said, "but I'll have to buy a new racket first."

He gave me a startled glance and shut up.

Was it only a week since the last time we'd played squash? It seemed more like a month.

The crowd in the church was large. At least two hundred people. Most of them, aside from our office group, were Puerto Rican. Scores of older women with scarves over their heads, but a surprising number of teen-age boys too. The boys sat in clusters, tieless, solemn-faced, impassive. Jaime, I guessed, had been their benefactor. He'd occasionally mentioned little things he'd done, like hiring a lawyer for some kid who was in trouble or getting a specialist for one who had a rheumatic heart.

I paid my respects to Jaime's mother, but she still seemed dazed and gave no sign of recognizing me. Elizabeth sat beside her, pale but composed. She thanked me for coming.

I found a seat in a pew next to Tom and two members of the sales force. Irving was in front of me, between George Cole and Harriet. I was surprised by how many of our employees had showed up. Even Clair Gould, our receptionist and switchboard operator, was there. I caught a glimpse of her on the other side of the aisle, a few seats down from Mark. Jaime had made friends, all right. His quiet personality had reached a lot of people.

During the service I made an attempt to follow what the priest was saying, but my mind kept wandering. I recalled the first time I'd met Jaime. I couldn't remember what had prompted me to speak to him or what we'd said, but I remembered how noticeable he'd been, the one Puerto Rican in a room with a couple of dozen Anglo-Saxons. He'd been hired, I later learned, less for his ability than because the management of the bank wanted to prove that it wasn't prejudiced against minorities, which it had a reputation for being. Jaime had known this, just as he'd known that he'd never make it to the top in that company, but it wasn't until he'd come to work for me that he'd begun to realize how cramped he'd been, how much he was capable of doing.

He'd just started to grow.

And now it was ended.

I was dreadfully sorry.

The pallbearers carried the coffin out through a side door. The crowd rose. Tom and I walked up the aisle without speaking. When we got outside we stood on the steps for a moment while our eyes adjusted to the sunlight. Ward Carlton and Milt Radison, the two salesmen, joined us. Irving came over, along with George and Harriet. No one said anything, but presently Harriet motioned for me to step aside with her. I did.

"I talked to Uncle Bill," she said in a low voice. "I'd like to go to Washington tomorrow."

"Go ahead," I told her.

We went back to the others. Mark approached with his wife. There was a round of greetings. Mark's wife seldom came to the office, and most of the group hadn't seen her in months.

Mark eyed me. "Everything all right?" he asked.

I shrugged.

"Did you bring your car?"

I shook my head.

"Joyce and I'll give you a ride. We're on our way up to Greenwich."

"Thanks," I said, "but Tom's taking me."

His wife looked around at all the Puerto Ricans. "I wish I had a camera," she said.

Mark took her arm. "Come along," he said. "It's an hour's drive."

They started down the steps.

"We might as well shove off too," Tom said to me.

I nodded. We parted from the others and headed for Tom's car. I caught sight of the hearse and of the limousine behind it. I thought of buying a squash racket, of going to the club, of returning to my silent house. And suddenly I knew that I just couldn't hack it.

"Never mind," I told Tom. "I'll go with Mark."

He opened his mouth, but before he could say anything I took off, pushing my way through the crowd on the sidewalk. I saw Mark and his wife down the block and ran to catch up with them.

They were getting into the car when I reached them.

"I've changed my mind," I said. "I'll go with you."

Joyce slid over to make room for me on the front seat. Mark got behind the wheel. He started the engine.

"What's the best way?" he asked. "The East Side highway or the West Side?"

"Neither," I said. "I want to go to Connecticut with you."

Both of them looked at me.

"Just for a day or two. Until I can get my bearings."

"Sure," Mark said.

"The house isn't really open," said Joyce. "We're simply camping there."

"I don't want to be alone," I said.

That ended the discussion. Mark pushed the gear lever into drive and guided the car away from the curb.

It wasn't until we were on the Hutchinson River Parkway, skimming past Pelham, that I began to have second thoughts.

Mark and his wife hadn't invited me to be their houseguest; I'd thrust myself upon them. All I had with me were the clothes on my back. And I was doing what I'd never done in my life before —I was running away from something.

It's only for a couple of days, I told myself. I'll come back on Monday morning. I'm not afraid. I simply don't want to be alone.

But I had a hard time convincing myself.

19

The day got better as it went along, however. In fact, it turned into one of the most enjoyable days I'd had in years.

The improvement was due partly to the locale. Mark's house was situated near the Round Hill Country Club, midway between the Boston Post Road and the Merritt Parkway. I'd been in the neighborhood before—once to see Mark and twice with Carol to visit business acquaintances of hers, people by the name of Ross, whose house was a couple of miles north of Mark's. I'd also spent a weekend with some friends of my own, the Dedmans, who had a place in New Canaan, which is also in Fairfield County, a few stops down the pike. Oscar Dedman was a banker who'd befriended me when I was just getting started.

On those occasions I'd found the area annoyingly perfect. Unreal. Too rich for my blood. I'd been told that the people who live in that corner of Connecticut have the highest per capita income in the United States, and I guess they do. You can drive for miles and not see a house that cost under a hundred thousand dollars, and most of them cost a damn sight more than that. Tough zoning ordinances make it impossible for anyone to build on less than a couple of acres, and there aren't many houses which occupy plots that small.

Like all sites chosen by people who can afford the very best, Fairfield County is beautiful. Rolling hills, meadows, brooks, ponds and a great variety of magnificent trees. But beauty is easier to appreciate when you have something to contrast it with, and where Mark's house was you didn't. Or where the Rosses' house was. Or the Dedmans'. North of the Boston Post Road, everything is nice to look at, and on past visits I'd had the feeling that I was in a world which, being ideal, didn't really exist or, if it did exist, was too fragile to last. I'd been uncomfortable.

But this time I didn't have that feeling. I was glad to take the landscape at face value and simply enjoy it. The air was clear, the sun was bright, there was a nice breeze from Long Island Sound, and the birds chattered agreeably about where they were going to spend the winter or whatever well-fed birds do chatter about as summer draws to a close. Mark's house was a twenty-two-room white frame place that was built on a slight rise. The land in the back of the house sloped down to a pond, beside which stood the most superb willow tree I'd ever seen. There were a couple of nice pines on the property also, and half a dozen oaks which, to judge by their appearance, had been growing there when Connecticut belonged to the British.

Sitting on the terrace, sipping a Campari and soda, gazing at the trees and the pond, I forgot about the events of the morning. Forgot about most other things too. I began to think about matters such as what the country must have looked like before it got all cluttered up with people, how long it might have taken to go from New York to Greenwich in the days of horses and buggies, and why trees in the South didn't grow to be as tall as trees in the North.

I was alone at that point. Mark and his wife were playing tennis. They had their own clay court at the side of the house, and apparently they used it whenever they came up. I could hear the ping of the ball in the distance and the occasional sound of a voice. It was a delightful hour.

There was something else that made the day good, though: I got to know Mark and Joyce as I'd never known them before. And I got to like them better.

It was strange. I'd been seeing Mark five days a week for years.

I'd been with Joyce on any number of social occasions. And I hadn't really cared for either of them. I could appreciate Mark's good qualities—his intelligence, his eagerness to work even though he didn't have to, his honesty—but there were too many things about him that put me off. His stinginess, his lack of warmth, his inability to trust people. And Joyce had struck me as being not only as stingy as Mark but also totally oblivious of everything beyond her own little world of Southampton, Palm Beach, Fifth Avenue and Greenwich.

But I found, suddenly, that I'd been wrong about both of them.

Joyce was stingy. And she was no great thinker. And she did live in a restricted world. But she was nevertheless a good woman, utterly devoted to Mark, deeply concerned with the up-bringing of their son, who was due back from a bicycle tour of France in another week, and practical. She was interested in sports, in animals, in nature and, for some reason which she herself couldn't explain, in the problems of unwed mothers. She felt that there should be no stigma attached to illegitimacy and that unmarried women should be allowed to raise their children as freely and openly as married women.

She was concerned primarily with the people she was closest to—her family and the small circle of friends she saw regularly. She had no desire to broaden that circle and regarded people beyond it as picturesque natives in a foreign country. But she did have a shy curiosity about how others lived. Including how I lived. She wanted to know why, when I could have a nice apartment uptown, I'd chosen to buy an old house on West Eleventh Street which had been converted into apartments and convert it back into a house. I explained to her what I liked about the house and the neighborhood and as I did I got the feeling that she was really making an attempt to understand.

And Mark revealed facets of his personality which I'd never suspected. Some were good, others were bad; but I liked him better for all of them. He was, I discovered, a man of really intense likes and dislikes. I'd known, for instance, that he didn't get along with his father. But I was surprised by the bitterness with which he now spoke of him. His father, apparently, had always favored Mark's sister and had deeply resented the closeness which existed between Mark and his mother. But what Mark held against his father more than anything else was his treatment of Mark's mother, which according to Mark was harsh enough to drive her to alcoholism. And when she'd become an alcoholic and Mark wanted his father to send her to Silverhill for treatment, the old man had refused. With the result that during a night of solitary drinking she'd fallen down a flight of steps in her own house and broken her neck. It was shortly after that that the final rupture occurred between Price senior and Price junior.

On the other hand, Mark's affection for his wife, his son, his in-laws and certain people in our company was deeper than I'd imagined. Furthermore, he was privately supporting an old chauffeur and housekeeper who'd been with the family when he was a boy and who were no longer able to work. Also three South Vietnamese orphans whose plight had come to his attention through a television newscast.

We talked about Tom, whom Mark liked but worried about. What made Tom such a good salesman, in Mark's view, was his basic insecurity. He had a constant need to prove that he was worthy and he satisfied it by accumulating friends, then turning the friends into clients. But the insecurity that made Tom a good salesman made him a risky partner. There was no telling what he might do if he ever felt acutely threatened.

We talked about me too. For the first time Mark told me what he thought about me. What he thought about me wasn't bad. He had a higher opinion of me than I'd believed. But he said something that bothered me. He said that I was by nature a moralist and a reformer and that I enjoyed finding the worms under the stones. I didn't agree with him then and I'm not sure that I do now, but the statement has stuck in my mind.

I can't fully account for the closeness that developed between the Prices and myself that day, but one of the things that contributed to it, I think, is the fact that the house really was, as Joyce had said, closed. It's hard to be stand-offish when you're eating in the kitchen and lounging around on furniture that's covered with sheets.

I'd known that they hadn't been using the house much for the past year but I hadn't known that they'd given up trying to maintain it as more than a place to sleep every now and then and were actually trying to sell it. That was the case, however. Too hard to get help. Too expensive. The couple that worked for them in the city wouldn't come to the country, and they hadn't found anyone in the country who wanted to come to the city. Even without domestic help, Mark told me, the house was costing him twenty-five thousand a year. The landscape service alone ran seven hundred a month, and if the grounds weren't kept up the house would be more difficult to get rid of—although so far there hadn't been any takers anyway, for the area was full of people who wanted to unload their big places, and the market was glutted.

My own opinion was that Mark could actually afford the house but was just tired of it. Nevertheless, it was for sale, and the Prices were living like squatters on their own property, and that made for a certain informality which wouldn't have existed otherwise. Joyce fixed lunch herself. We'd stopped on the way up at an A & P on the Boston Post Road, and she'd bought provisions —a loaf of bread, six slices of Swiss cheese and two tomatoes— which she seemed to feel were adequate. For dinner we went out to a restaurant called The Gaslight, which looked like an ordinary roadside joint but was an exceptionally good, and expensive, French restaurant. And on Sunday they planned to do most of their eating at the party they were invited to—a tea which the Hansfords were giving for their daughter Patricia, who was making her debut. They urged me to go to the party with them.

Aside from playing tennis, Mark and his wife didn't do very

much, and I did even less. I sat on the terrace, walked around the grounds and accompanied Mark and Joyce on a ride to Darien to visit Joyce's horse, a big brown filly named Martha, which she was boarding at the Ox Ridge Hunt Club. While Joyce and Martha were having their reunion I strolled through the stable, admiring some of the other horses. The Ox Ridge Hunt Club, I gathered, was the Waldorf-Astoria of the Connecticut horse world, and the animals quartered there seemed to know it; they were a contented-looking bunch.

At eleven o'clock Joyce went upstairs to bed, and Mark and I had a nightcap in the kitchen. From the moment we'd left New York neither of us had mentioned Jaime. But now the subject came up, more or less by accident.

"You will go to the Hansfords' with us tomorrow, won't you?" Mark asked.

"I don't think so," I replied. I'd never been to a debut party and had no particular desire to go to one. I was even a bit surprised that families were still giving them. "I wasn't invited."

"What the hell, you're with us; that's good enough. They'll be glad to have you."

"I didn't bring any clothes. Not even a clean shirt."

"You can wear one of my shirts. It'll fit. You'll look all right. Any suit that's O.K. for a funeral is O.K. for a debutante tea." He frowned. "Well, you know what I mean."

I said nothing.

He continued to frown. "I'm sorry about Jaime. He seemed to be taking hold quite well."

I nodded.

"Better him than you, though, Brock."

"Let's change the subject."

"Of course," Mark said quickly.

Apparently I didn't really want to change the subject, though, for I said, "It should have been me, Mark. I'm the one the guy was aiming at."

Mark gave me a somber look. "That thought has crossed my mind."

"It's crossed the minds of the police too. A couple of detectives from Homicide were over last night, questioning me. They didn't come right out and say it, but they hinted."

"What did you tell them?"

"What could I tell them? I couldn't tell them about Interlake, because I still don't know that there's anything wrong there—and I don't think the police have the means to find out. But I'm going to keep digging and if I do find anything wrong I'm going to make damn sure the police know about it—the police and the Illinois Insurance Commission and everybody under the sun. I'm going to let out such a howl that there'll be no way an investigation can be avoided."

"Do you think that's smart?"

"I don't know what else to do, Mark. The police know who shot Jaime. A professional killer named Arco. They showed me his picture. I'm positive he's the one and I said so. What they're looking for is a motive, and so am I. Because as long as anyone has a motive, it doesn't make any difference whether Arco is caught or not—I'm still in danger."

"And you think Lipp is behind the whole thing?"

"I don't know. But I can't think of anyone else who might be. What do *you* think?"

Mark was silent for a while. "I think he might be," he said finally, and added, "I'm glad you're up here."

"I'm glad I'm up here too," I said. "Because frankly, pal, I'm scared."

"Maybe you ought to stay on for a little while. Joyce and I'll drive back tomorrow night, but you're welcome to use the house. You can lay in a supply of food and just camp, the same as we do."

That idea hadn't occurred to me. I considered it. "I'm afraid not, Mark. I could hide for a little while but sooner or later I'd have to go back."

"I suppose you would. But meanwhile if the police know who the killer is they may catch him, and that might make a difference."

"It might," I said. But I didn't really believe that it would.

20

I awoke early, dressed, made my bed and went downstairs. The house was quiet. I strolled into the kitchen and found some coffee. I also found what was left of the loaf of bread Joyce had bought. No butter. But dry toast and black coffee were better than nothing.

After breakfast I went outside. The weather wasn't as nice as it had been before—fast-moving clouds were sweeping across the sky, and there was a chill in the air—but it was nice enough. I wandered down the driveway toward the road and presently heard a strange clopping noise. I couldn't identify it and went to investigate.

An elderly gentleman in a red riding jacket and black velvet jockey cap was approaching on horseback. He was accompanied by his groom, a young black man, also on horseback. I stared at them.

The elderly gentleman smiled and said, "Good morning."

I managed to say, "Good morning."

I watched them, bemused, until they'd disappeared around the bend. And as I turned to go back to the house I found that I'd been joined by a rabbit. The rabbit was gazing at me with some doubt, as if pedestrians were as puzzling to him as equestrians were to me.

"Hello, Harvey," I said, but evidently that wasn't the rabbit's name, for he simply did an about-face and loped off across the grass.

I walked down to the pond and listened for a few minutes to a frog that seemed to be upset about something.

A nice place, I thought; a really nice place. And I considered Mark's suggestion that I stay on for a few days. It wasn't such a bad idea. I could pick up some clothes in Greenwich, rent a car, eat at various roadside restaurants, keep in touch with the office by telephone.

I couldn't decide. And while I was still weighing the pros and cons Mark came out.

"You scared me," he said amiably. "I thought you'd been kidnapped."

"No," I said. "I was just asking that frog whether I ought to buy the place."

"I hope to God he said yes."

"He said I couldn't afford it."

We went up to the house. Joyce was at the kitchen table, drinking coffee. Mark had evidently told her that I might extend my visit, for she began to explain about the appliances. There was something wrong with the left front burner of the stove, so don't use it, and the cold-water faucet on the sink had to be turned all the way to the left, otherwise it dripped.

"I still haven't made up my mind," I said.

"It might be wise," she said. "Under the circumstances."

I didn't ask her how much she knew about the circumstances. I said, "We'll see," and let it go at that.

"There's plenty of booze in the cabinet behind the bar," Mark said, "but be sure you lock it when you leave. I'll give you the key."

In their own way, I realized, they were trying to protect me.

They went out to the tennis court. I found my way into the library. The room had a musty smell. I examined the books. There were some nicely bound sets of various English novelists,

117

including the collected works of Sir Walter Scott, which took up several shelves. There was also an ancient edition of The Encyclopaedia Britannica and an assortment of biographical reference books. On impulse I pulled out a five-year-old edition of *Who's Who in Commerce and Industry,* the most recent one I could find. I looked up Richard Rasher. He wasn't listed. So I settled down with Volume I of *Ivanhoe.*

Later in the morning Mark took out a backgammon set, and we played backgammon until my stomach began to growl.

"How about some lunch?" I suggested.

"Aren't you going to the party?" Mark said, surprised.

I still hadn't made up my mind about that either, but I said, "Even so."

He said he wasn't hungry, although I didn't see how he couldn't be. Instead, he gave me the keys to the car and told me how to get to the nearest McDonald's.

I went.

I had a hard time finding the place and an even harder time finding my way back. I couldn't remember the corner at which I'd turned onto the Boston Post Road and I picked the wrong one. I ended up on a street that looked like Round Hill Road but wasn't. Then, in trying to get over to where I thought Round Hill Road was, I took various lanes, drives, terraces and courts, all of which ended in immaculately landscaped dead-end circles. And when I finally did locate Round Hill Road I turned right instead of left and presently found myself crossing the Merritt Parkway.

I didn't get back to Mark's house until almost three o'clock. He looked as if he'd been genuinely worried, but he didn't say so. He merely said that Joyce had gone upstairs to dress and that he'd put a clean shirt in my bedroom.

"But I've been thinking," he added. "Maybe it'd be better if you didn't go to the party. If you don't want people to know where you are, that is."

I'd decided by then, however, that I'd had enough of the Connecticut countryside and would go back to New York in any case. "It doesn't matter," I said. "I'll go to the party."

The Hansford place was so far from the road that you couldn't even see the roof. You could tell that something was going on, though, for there were two policemen at the gateposts, directing traffic. There were cars everywhere, and attendants parking them. I counted over twenty Mercedes-Benzes alone.

The house itself, when at last you got to it, was a huge, sprawling Norman affair with a flagpole extending from the porte-cochere. There was no flag on the flagpole, but the mast was encircled by ropes of green leaves and white orchids.

Joyce introduced me to the Hansfords, who stood in a receiving line at the foot of a curving staircase that was hung with flowers like the flagpole. Papa Hansford, Mama Hansford, the three Hansford girls—Patricia, Esther and Rosemary—both sets of grandparents and a few other people whose relationship to the family was more obscure. All of them said they were glad I could come—all except Patricia, for whom the party was being given. She offered me a sort of cold over-the-shoulder how'd'ya do. But there was nothing personal in it; she offered everyone else the same greeting. She was a slender, good-looking girl with straight blond hair, but either she hadn't wanted the party or she'd done the receiving-line routine too many times in the past, for she looked terribly bored.

There was an orchestra on the terrace. There were bars indoors and outdoors, buffet tables in the dining room and on the lawn. A small platoon of waiters kept circulating with trays of champagne and hors d'oeuvres. Everything that could be wrapped with white orchids was wrapped with white orchids, and a rope of them had been placed around the swimming pool.

I headed first to the indoor bar, then to the outdoor buffet table. McDonald's hadn't done all that much for me, and I was still hungry. A salmon at least three feet long shimmered through an aspic of the same length. One waiter was carving a roast turkey, another was serving slices of beef tenderloin. There were bowls of iced shrimp, platters of salads, a couple of chafing dishes of lobster Newburg and a pastry tray that included every kind of fruit, custard and chocolate concoction I'd ever seen.

I wondered what, if this was tea, a dinner might consist of. But that didn't keep me from enjoying it. I took my plate over to a quiet spot beside a bush which had been trimmed to resemble a mushroom and surveyed the scene as I ate. There was a moderate amount of action on the terrace. Older couples were dancing to something that sounded like a fast samba, and most of them appeared to be quite good at it. Presently, however, the orchestra quit for a break and a small rock group took over. The crowd on the terrace grew at that point, some of the older people remaining and a flock of younger ones joining them. Bodies began to move rather violently as the strongly accented notes poured from the amplifiers. I noticed one couple in particular. The man was in his sixties, the girl maybe sixteen. He was a better dancer than she was. It seemed to me that I'd met him before, under somewhat different circumstances, and after a few minutes I realized that I had. He was John Patterson, the principal stockholder in the company that controlled Amalgamated Investors Services. Hardin Webster's boss. He looked a lot different now from the way he'd looked in his office in Boston.

There were a few other people I also recognized. Melvin Lamson, president of Consolidated Carbide. Dick Welch, chairman of the board of Welch and Rooney, the real estate firm that managed the building in which we had our offices. The former wife of one of the senior partners in the brokerage house where I'd met Tom.

I made no attempt to get into things, but when I finished eating I did wander around a bit. First to the swimming pool, which was being presided over by two white poodles and enjoyed by two young men who'd taken off their shoes and were soaking their feet. Then around the side of the house to inspect something that looked like a maze and turned out to be one. And finally into the house to see what Mark and Joyce were up to.

Joyce was standing by a French window, drinking champagne and talking to a friend of hers whose name I didn't catch. Mark, she said, had been at the bar the last time she'd seen him and was drinking too much—would I please try to slow him down? I said I would if I could and went off to locate him.

Crossing the foyer, I found the Hansfords still in position at the foot of the staircase, greeting new arrivals. I smiled at Mrs. Hansford, who'd forgotten that we'd already met and told me how glad she was that I could come. She called me Harry.

The bar, as I recalled, was in a room next to the living room. I started toward it. The living room was crowded with people coming and going, drinks in hand. The bar was where I thought it was, but there were so many people trying to get through the doorway that I had to go in sideways.

And as I did I brushed against a man who was trying to get out. He too was moving sideways.

"Brockton Potter," he said. "What a pleasant surprise."

It was Anton Lipp.

21

● ● ● ● ● ● ● ● ●

Once, while in college, I'd gone with a friend to visit his parents
at their summer home in northern Wisconsin. The house was by
a lake, and the second afternoon I was there I went swimming
alone and stretched out afterward on the dock to sun myself. I fell
asleep. And awoke suddenly to find a black widow spider crawl-
ing toward me. The spider was the size of a quarter and was, at
the moment I saw it, about two inches from my right armpit.

The sensation I'd had then was the sensation I had now.

But there'd been more room to maneuver on that dock, narrow
as it was, than there was in this crowded doorway.

"Well, hello," I said hoarsely.

Lipp eyed me with a pleased expression. "I've been thinking
about you."

I tried to smile. It didn't work.

Someone said, "Excuse me," and gave me a push. I went on into
the room. Mark was standing by the window, holding a tall glass.
I worked my way over to him. "I just saw Anton Lipp," I said.

Mark nodded. "So did I."

"Did he say anything?"

"He asked about you. I didn't tell him you were here."

I glanced around. We were in a sort of sun room. The only way
out was through the same doorway by which I'd come in. It
hardly mattered, though, since Lipp already knew I was there.

"Maybe you ought to talk to him," Mark said.

"And tell him what?"

Mark shrugged. He didn't seem drunk to me, but I told him what his wife had said. He shrugged again. "You could use another drink yourself, I imagine."

I felt as though I could. I went over to the bar and asked the bartender for a Scotch. "A strong one," I added.

The bartender obliged.

Perhaps Mark was right, I thought. Perhaps I should talk to Lipp.

He wasn't hard to find. He was in the living room, only a few yards from where I'd last seen him.

"Lovely party," he said.

"Lovely," I agreed.

"Have you known the Hansfords long?"

"Not very. And you?"

"For some years. Patricia and my daughter were at school together." He'd been smiling, but suddenly, in one of those quick changes of expression that were characteristic of him, his face darkened.

A waiter came by with champagne. Lipp deftly swapped the drink in his hand for one of the glasses on the tray. His face brightened again. "I must say, you gave me quite a turn the other day."

"Just doing my job."

"And an interesting job it must be. You have a mind like mine, I think."

"What kind of mind is that?"

"Inquisitive. I could use a man like you."

I looked at him. He was dressed like a number of other men I'd seen at the party, in sports jacket and slacks. But somehow his appearance was different from theirs. His jacket was of a paisley print, the slacks were tailored to show the contours of his legs, and he was again wearing shoes that added to his height. Among other things, I thought, he's vain. "Are you offering me a job?" I said.

"Anytime you want it. Name your own price."

"I'm flattered. I like what I'm doing, though, and where I'm doing it at."

"It has its exciting moments, I suppose. Didn't one of your people get shot the other day? It seems to me I heard something to that effect."

"Yes. A very nice guy."

"That's a shame. A person never knows what fate has in store for him."

"That's true. But I think the police will get to the bottom of the matter."

"Do you?"

"Definitely."

Lipp started to say something, but at that moment the man I'd seen dancing with the young girl on the terrace came up to us. "Anton!" he exclaimed, taking Lipp by the arm.

Lipp's eyes, which had become grave, immediately began to glow with delight. "John!" He turned to me. "Do you two know each other?"

Patterson's brow furrowed. "Aren't you Brockton Potter?"

I said, "I am."

The furrows vanished. "I thought so. I owe you a debt of thanks. You're the one who got us out of that Yankee Clipper stock before it went to hell."

I smiled. It was nice to meet someone who, when it came to Yankee Clipper, wasn't mad at me. "Just tell your people to keep giving us their business."

"What do you think of Computech at the moment?" he asked mischievously.

"Well," I said, "our best source of information is standing right here."

"You couldn't make a better investment," Lipp said and chuckled.

Patterson tugged at Lipp's arm. "Do you mind if I ask you a question, Anton?"

"Of course not, John."

The two of them walked over to the other side of the room. Lipp kept looking my way as they talked. I felt certain now that Amalgamated's decision to sell Philadelphia Steel and buy Computech had come as a result of information which Lipp had given to Patterson. I waited a couple of minutes to see whether Lipp would return.

He did. Without Patterson.

"What were we talking about?" he said. "Oh, yes—about the unfortunate young man who was killed."

"That's right," I said. "And speaking of unfortunate men, I read in the paper when I was out in Chicago that one of the Interlake people had been shot, more or less like my man was in New York."

Lipp sighed. "The world is full of crime, isn't it?"

"So it seems." I wondered why he wasn't using any of his mod expressions. Evidently he could turn that kind of talk on and off as readily as his smile.

"You should—" he began, but again we were interrupted. This time by none other than Patricia Hansford.

"How's Francesca?" she asked, wrapping both her arms around Lipp's free one.

He regarded the debutante fondly. Then his face clouded over. "About the same," he replied.

"Give her my best," Patricia said. She released his arm and went toward the room where the bar was.

Lipp glared at the glass in his hand as if he suddenly wanted to hurl it at someone. "I hate parties like this!" he said savagely. "I shouldn't have come!"

I was so startled that I took a step backward.

"Forgive me," Lipp said. "I get carried away. Francesca's my daughter, you see."

I said nothing.

As if he didn't trust himself to hold it any longer, he put the glass on a nearby table. "I wouldn't have come today but I was in the neighborhood. Francesca's at Silverhill."

I hadn't even known that he had a daughter. All I'd known was that he was married for the third time. "The sanitarium?"

He nodded and reached into his pocket for a cigarette. He lit it with a trembling hand.

I didn't know what to say. "I've heard they have a good staff there," I said.

"Good? They haven't been able to do anything for my daughter! No one has! I've had her everywhere!" His voice was quivering with rage. He made an effort to control it. "For sixteen years she was fine. Perfectly fine. A normal, healthy girl. Then all of a sudden she stopped talking. Just stopped. She hasn't spoken a word in three years. Not to anyone." His voice began to quiver again. "And no one's been able to do anything! No one's been able to help her!"

He dropped the lit cigarette onto the white carpet, let it lie there for a moment, then ground it out with the toe of his shoe.

I looked at the burn mark on the carpet. And at Anton Lipp. I was certain that he'd lit the cigarette simply to do damage with it. "I'm sorry to hear that," I said, and turned abruptly away.

I walked quickly out of the room and found my way to the terrace. Skirting the dancers, I went down the steps to the lawn. I felt, just then, that I knew as much about Anton Lipp as I'd ever need to know. He was a man who couldn't accept adversity. Who, when hurt, had to destroy.

A man like that, I thought, is capable of anything.

22

· · · · · · · · ·

It was nine o'clock when we got back to the city.

Mark said that I was welcome to continue staying with Joyce and him, in their apartment, but I declined. I'd be safe enough at home, I told him—and I tried to convince myself that I would. Should there be another attempt on my life, it wouldn't occur in the same spot. In fact, my house was probably the safest place for me. The killer would think it was being watched by the police. And perhaps, without my knowing it, it was.

So Mark drove me to West Eleventh Street. He insisted on coming into the house with me. We looked around. No one jumped out from behind any doors. Everything was exactly as I'd left it, including the empty coffee mug on the kitchen table.

But after Mark left I began to regret my decision. For the uneasiness I'd felt on Saturday morning returned. I tried to talk myself out of it but couldn't. Not altogether. Which made me angry. How long could this go on, damn it?

I took two Nembutal capsules and went to bed. The capsules worked. I slept for eleven hours and would have slept even longer if the telephone hadn't rung.

The call was from Louise. She couldn't come to work; her grandson was sick. I asked what was wrong with him. She didn't know, she said. She sounded evasive. I wondered whether she'd been questioned by the police and alarmed by them, and since

127

there was no point in beating around the bush I asked her. That was the problem, all right. She didn't need no police in her life, she said, and suggested I find someone to replace her. I argued with her, but to no avail.

Exit one good housekeeper.

It was the first time in years that I was late for my Monday staff meeting. I didn't get to the office until ten-thirty. Everyone seemed relieved to see me. Irving took me aside before the meeting started, to tell me that he was afraid something was wrong with Harriet. She hadn't come to work, and he'd called her apartment three times without getting an answer. I explained that she'd gone out of town. He waited for me to say where she'd gone, and when I didn't he snapped, "I wish you'd let me know when you make decisions like that." I said I was sorry.

The meeting didn't last as long as usual. For one thing, everyone was conscious of the fact that there were only four of us and seemed ill at ease. For another, the market was having a rally. The industrials had gone up eight points in the first hour of trading, and no one seemed to know why. Irving felt that it was simply a technical reaction—the short sellers were covering. George thought that the market was anticipating favorable quarterly reports from General Motors and some of the other leaders. Joe predicted that the rally wouldn't last, and I was inclined to agree with him. But at eleven-fifteen I sent him out to check, and the industrials were up another two points.

We finished our business and dispersed. I asked Irving to let me know what was happening with Interlake and Computech. He inquired and reported back that Interlake was up an eighth and relatively dormant. But Computech was up three points and was one of the most active stocks on the board.

"It figures, though," he said. "The bulk of the action is coming from our own office. We're executing the Amalgamated buy orders."

"Are we handling both sides?" I asked.

"I don't know."

"Find out."

"Will do."

He went out but returned shortly. "I asked Tom," he said. "We're handling both sides for some, not all."

"Ask him who's selling the stock that Amalgamated's buying."

"I did. He only knows about the deals we're handling. The sellers are the Bank of Northern California and the Bristol Bank, in London."

"Ask him what accounts the banks are acting for."

"I did. He doesn't know. He's going to try to find out, but he doesn't think he can." He paused. "I've started doing some checking on my own. On Lipp personally."

"Good."

He left again.

Helen Doyle brought in the mail and accumulated telephone messages. There was more mail than usual but fewer telephone messages. The slip on top, I noticed, informed me that Detective O'Brien had called and wanted me to call him back.

I did. And found that both he and Sestino were out. I left word that I'd called and dropped the slip into my wastebasket.

But the next message startled me. Mrs. Ackroyd had called and would call again. She did *not* want me to call her back. "Not" was underlined.

I stared at the slip for a while, then tucked it under the blotter.

I started for Tom's office, to see whether he was following through, but Mark corralled me in the corridor. He was back to normal. In fact, he was worse than normal. The outfit that printed all the forms we used had raised its prices ten percent without consulting us, and he was livid. Furthermore, Tom had suggested we have the office painted, and it wasn't even dirty.

I heard Mark out, then went in to talk to Tom. He was following through. He was on the telephone as I came in, talking to someone at the Bank of Northern California. I sat down and listened to his end of the conversation. He was being his most charming self, but it wasn't getting him anywhere. Finally he gave up.

"No dice," he said. "They won't tell me. Various trust accounts, that's all they'd say."

"Try London."

"I will, but it'll be the same thing there, I can assure you."

"Try."

He picked up the telephone again but after a moment put it down. "We're both nuts," he said. "It's six o'clock in London. They're closed."

"Who'd you deal with there?"

"Sir Archibald Beardsley."

"Well, call him first thing in the morning."

"I will. It won't do any good, though. What's bugging you?"

"I don't know. I'm just curious. I saw Lipp and Patterson together over the weekend. I think Amalgamated's buying Computech based on something Lipp's been telling Patterson. And it occurred to me, maybe he's trying to unload his own stock."

"Don't be ridiculous. Anton Lipp could damn near buy the Bristol Bank, lock, stock and barrel."

"Not quite. Anyway, it's worth pursuing."

"Where did you see Lipp?" Tom asked.

I told him.

"I asked you to come with *me,*" he said. He looked hurt.

"I know. But I suddenly had the feeling that I couldn't stand it any longer, I had to get away." I smiled. "What makes you think the office needs painting?"

"Because it does, damn it." Then he smiled too. "Get lost, will you? I've got work to do."

I went back to my own office and was immediately buzzed by Helen.

"There're two men to see you in the reception room," she said.

"I don't want to be disturbed. Who are they?"

"Two detectives. A Mr. O'Brien and a Mr. Sestino."

"Hell," I said. "You'd better show them in."

23

The first thing O'Brien asked was where I'd been over the weekend.

Which led me to ask how he knew I'd been anywhere.

"We had people watching your house," he said.

Not me. My house. "If I'd known that," I said, "I probably wouldn't have gone anywhere. The place was making me nervous."

"You went to the funeral and then you disappeared," Sestino said, looking around at various objects in the room. He seemed as curious about the trappings of my office as he'd been about those of my house. I guessed that his curiosity was more personal than professional; nevertheless, I found it disconcerting.

"Were you following me?" I asked.

"No," said O'Brien. "We were at the funeral, though."

Not me. The funeral. "I didn't see you."

"We were in the back."

My house. The funeral. It made sense, in a way. They wanted to know who my contacts were. They were doing exactly what I did when I had a hunch but nothing to back it up: putting out antennae.

"You haven't answered my question," O'Brien said.

"I was in Greenwich, Connecticut, with Mark Price. He has a house there. If your people saw me come home, they probably saw him come with me. I hadn't planned to go, but after the funeral I suddenly felt I didn't want to stay at my place."

"We'll talk to him. In fact, we'd like to talk to a number of people here."

"Who?"

"Anyone who can explain what Ortega was doing."

"I can do that better than anyone else."

"We'd like to talk to others, though."

"Everybody sees things different," Sestino added.

There'd be no harm in it. My staff was reluctant to discuss our activities even with other departments, let alone with outsiders; if anything sensitive came up, they'd refer the detectives right back to me. Besides, Harriet was in Washington, and the only other one who knew what I was up to, other than Tom and Mark, was Irving, who could handle himself just fine. Yet I was irritated. The pace in an office such as ours is generally brisk, especially on a day when the market itself is active. Anything that interrupts it is unwelcome. "All right," I said. "The ones who can help you the most are the members of the research department. I'll introduce you to them."

"What about other departments?" O'Brien asked. "Didn't Ortega have any special friends there?"

"No one in particular. You're welcome to ask, though." The salesmen would be annoyed as hell at having to stop what they were doing, to answer questions.

"That'll be fine," O'Brien said. He seemed pleased.

"The first one I'll introduce you to is Irving Silvers. He's my assistant and he'll introduce you to the others."

O'Brien nodded and started to get up, but at that moment my telephone rang. He sat down again.

I lifted the instrument and said, "No calls. I'm busy."

"It's that Mrs. Ackroyd," Helen said. "The one who called this morning."

I started to tell her to inform Mrs. Ackroyd that I'd call her back, but I caught sight of the slip sticking out from under the blotter. Most of it was hidden, but it reminded me that Mrs. Ackroyd didn't want to be called back. "O.K.," I said. "Put her on."

"Mr. Potter," said Mrs. Ackroyd. "Oh, I'm so glad that I managed to get you."

"I'm afraid you caught me at a bad moment," I said, glancing at the detectives. "Let me call you back in a few minutes."

"Oh, dear, no. I'm afraid you can't do that. I'm calling from the grocery store, you see. I don't want Vera to know."

"Then let me suggest that you call me again, later in the day."

"I've already gone out twice. Vera won't know what to make of it."

"I understand," I said, "and I do want to hear what's on your mind, but later. I'll be here until five at least." And before she could protest further, I hung up. I turned to the detectives. "It's always something, in this business. Well, come along and let me introduce you to Irving."

They got up.

"By the way," Sestino said, "being in this business, have you ever heard of Amalgamated Investors Services?"

I stopped in my tracks. "Yes," I said cautiously. "They're customers of ours. Why?"

"This brother-in-law of mine, he sells mutual funds and he's been telling me I should put money with them."

"They're a good outfit," I said, relieved. And shepherded the two of them into Irving's office.

Back at my desk, I made an attempt to forget that the detectives were around and pretty well succeeded. I told Helen to let my calls through, and they began to come in one after another. Several times I went out to check the ticker tape. By one o'clock fourteen million shares had changed hands, and the averages were still up. Not as much as they'd been during the morning, however. The feeling I'd had—that the rally wouldn't last—remained with me. And presently the reason for the rally emerged. Word had leaked out that the chairman of the Senate Banking

Committee was going to make some kind of statement recommending another tax cut. But before he could even make the statement, the ranking minority member of the same committee issued a statement that he'd oppose any tax cut. Which showed how nervous the market had become, since neither one of them had all that much to do with tax cuts.

I kept wishing that Mrs. Ackroyd would call now, while I was free, but she didn't. And I wondered what she had to tell me that she didn't want Vera to hear.

Interlake stock wasn't doing any more than it had been doing before, but Computech was still trading at a fast clip. It was being overshadowed, though, by Martinson Corp. Martinson's leading product was Acidall tablets, and the Food and Drug Administration had just released a report which said that Acidall didn't relieve stomach acid as much as the ads claimed. A hundred and twenty thousand shares of Martinson had already changed ownership, and the price was dropping steadily.

Tom burst into my office, looking rather wild-eyed. "I've had four calls already. Everyone wants to sell Martinson. What do you think?"

"Tell them not to panic," I said. "The excitement won't last, and it's a good company."

He pulled himself together. "Those damn detectives are here. They seem to think we're laundering money for the Syndicate or something. Can't you get them off my back?"

"They're just probing."

"Well, I wish they'd probe somewhere else. I haven't got time for them, and neither do my men." He left.

Wondering whether I'd really given him good advice, I went out to look at the tape again. I found O'Brien and Sestino also looking at it.

"What does that mean?" Sestino asked, pointing.

"That means somebody just bought three hundred shares of A.T.&T.—and that's the price."

"A.T.&T., eh? You think it's a good buy?"

I made a noncommittal sound and turned to O'Brien. "Is everyone being helpful?"

"Everyone seems to be pretty busy."

"That's the way it is sometimes," I told him.

Sestino pointed again. "What's that?"

"That's the symbol for Martinson Corporation. The company's having a rough day today. The Food and Drug Administration said a little while ago that Acidall doesn't do as much for you as they say in the ads."

"It sure as hell don't," O'Brien observed.

I returned to my office. They followed me.

"What was Ortega's connection with VD?" O'Brien asked. "Silvers mentioned it, but no one seems to know exactly."

I glanced at the telephone. Don't call now, I told Mrs. Ackroyd. "He was interviewing executives at a company that's trying to develop a cure for a certain type of it."

"Oh." He appeared to be disappointed. "Well, what else was he working on?"

"Didn't the boys tell you?"

"Not very much. They said we should ask you."

"He was looking into a new blood anticoagulant. There're some pretty good ones in use now, but there's always a danger of hemorrhaging, and this new one is supposed to reduce that."

"I see. Medical stuff."

"Mostly."

"And you?"

"Well, I follow what everyone else is doing, and of course I sort of specialize in insurance companies."

"I guess we've got about as much as we can here, huh?" he said to Sestino.

"Looks that way," Sestino agreed.

"By the way," I said, "do you intend to keep watching my house?"

"I don't know," O'Brien said. "You think we should or you think we shouldn't?"

"I like the idea. After you left the other night, I felt kind of jumpy and I still haven't got over it."

He regarded me thoughtfully. "Well, now," he said presently, "I wouldn't want to say anything that would make you any jumpier. But I think you ought to know, see, that we have some pretty good sources of information—all over. And what we heard is that this Arco—him and his brother—left their apartment in L.A."— he took a notebook from his pocket and consulted it—"a week ago last Wednesday night."

I nodded.

"They have an apartment, the two of them, in this building there, and they left it a week ago last Wednesday night and they haven't been back since."

"In other words," I said, "you're telling me that you don't know where they are."

"That's right," O'Brien said. "That's what I'm telling you. But what I'm also telling you is there's as good a chance as not that since they haven't showed up in California, that they might still be here in New York." He paused. "So I think you're kind of right to feel jumpy. I would too if I was you."

24

I didn't exactly fall apart after they left, but I did find it harder to concentrate.

O'Brien hadn't said that the Arco brothers were still in New York, I reminded myself; he'd said that they might be. And the fact that he'd said it didn't make it true. He might simply have wanted to see how I'd react.

I'd reacted satisfactorily, I thought. I'd merely said, "Well, if they're in New York, and your sources of information are as good as you say they are, you shouldn't have any trouble catching them," and let it go at that. But now I couldn't get the two hoods off my mind.

Fortunately, however, matters came up which kept me from brooding. Irving had questions about the Tuesday letter, which for some reason he assumed he was going to write. Ward Carlton had matched buy and sell orders for 30,000 shares of International Container between two of our customers and wanted my opinion about Hopkins Tool, which one of them wanted to buy. Rose Nordike called to tell me what a nice party I'd missed on Friday night and to sympathize with me over the terrible shooting.

But the main distraction was a fight between Tom and Mark.

The three of us disagreed constantly. We rarely fought, though. It didn't pay. We had too much at stake. And since we were, for better or worse, stuck with one another, it was wise to get along —and each of us knew it. Yet at four o'clock on that particular Monday Helen rang me to say that Mr. Petacque wanted to see me in his office immediately, and when I got there I found Tom and Mark red-faced and glaring at each other.

The argument had arisen over a block of forty thousand shares of Martinson Corp. which Tom had sold a short time before. Mark felt that the commission was too low—it was a quarter of a percent under that which we'd agreed between us was rock bottom. Tom felt that he was justified in shaving the commission, because the customer was the Maryland Fund, the newest pearl in our necklace; now that we finally had them, he wanted to keep them. Mark insisted that in view of the general eagerness to dump Martinson, it shouldn't have been necessary to shave the commission. Tom insisted that there were plenty of houses that would have shaved it even more.

Both of them were right. Both of them were wrong. Both of them had had a tough day.

I tried to make peace and to a degree I succeeded. But not until after Mark had called Tom a chicken-shit salesman and Tom had accused Mark of being so stingy he wouldn't even piss. It took me a half hour to get them calmed down to the point where they could recognize the central issue, which was that what was done was done and we couldn't renege.

Shortly after that, both of them went home, leaving me to cope with an office force which had heard the shouting through the closed door and grown inquisitive. I managed to keep a reassuring smile plastered on my face, and presently the interest died.

Then I began to deal with a problem of my own: what I was going to do with myself that evening. Since breaking up with Carol, the problem had been presenting itself too often.

God got wind of my thoughts. At five minutes to five Carol called.

It was a strange conversation. She spent several minutes talking about virtually nothing. A dress she'd seen in one of the showrooms, which was made out of copper mesh but nevertheless didn't weigh much. A buyer from Omaha who'd had a gall bladder attack. A cousin of hers who was getting married.

After that she brought up the subject of the shooting. She'd read about it in the newspapers. She was worried about me. The least I could have done was call to let her know that I was all right.

"Frankly," I told her, "I was kind of busy with the police and things like that."

"I suppose. But you managed to get away for a weekend, apparently. I called Saturday and Sunday, and there was no answer."

"I went up to Mark's place in Greenwich."

But even that wasn't the number one thing on her mind. "I heard a rumor about you today," she said.

"What kind of a rumor?"

"A not very nice rumor."

"What kind of not very nice rumor?"

"Something about you and Monica Lane."

Damn, I thought. "It's not true," I said.

"My source was pretty good," said Carol.

"It's not true, I tell you."

"Well, I hope not. Poor Victor has enough troubles without that. And she wouldn't be good for you, Brock. After all, I know you. She's really not your type."

"Thanks for telling me."

"Don't be angry. I really mean it, Brock. She wouldn't."

"O.K., O.K.—she wouldn't. So what else is new?"

"I'm sorry I made you angry. But it's you I'm thinking of." She paused. "Why can't we be friends, Brock? One thing has nothing to do with the other. We ought to be able to be friends at least."

"We are friends, Carol."

"Not good friends." Another pause. "I'm going to swallow my pride for the dozenth time and invite you to take me to *Summer*

Song Friday night. Someone gave me two tickets today."

I hemmed and hawed and tried to say no. But in the end I said yes. Simply because it was easier.

Well, I thought afterward, why not?

I took the telephone message out from under the blotter. I glanced at my watch. It was ten minutes past five. I'd said five o'clock. Apparently Mrs. Ackroyd hadn't been able to get away from Vera.

Irving appeared in the doorway.

"Are you still here?" I asked.

"I'm waiting for an overseas call. I thought that was it, but it's for you."

"There's a call for me?"

"On Joe Rothland's phone."

I hurried through the now-empty offices to Joe Rothland's desk, wondering why the hell the switchboard operator couldn't plug in the phones, when she left, in such a way that they wouldn't ring all over the place.

"Mr. Potter?" said Mrs. Ackroyd. "Are you free now?"

"Yes, Mrs. Ackroyd. What was it you wanted to tell me?"

"I'm worried, Mr. Potter. I hate to bother you, but I'm really worried. I don't know what Vera's going to do about all the money."

"What money, Mrs. Ackroyd?"

"The money that they found in the box Friday."

"They found money in a box?"

"A safe-deposit box. Vera didn't even know they had the box. She'd be furious if she knew I was telling anyone, but you're a businessman, and maybe you'll be able to help us. And I don't see what difference it makes, because that man from the state treasurer's office was there when she opened the box, so he knows about it. That's why I'm so worried. I don't want them to think Vera did anything wrong, Mr. Potter. She's had a good education, and I know she didn't do anything wrong and I don't want them to think that she did."

"How much money did they find, Mrs. Ackroyd?"

"Fifty thousand dollars. Hundred-dollar bills. Five hundred of them. All in neat little packages."

"I think we'd better get together, you and I. How can you arrange to see me?"

"Oh, dear, you're not going to make a big fuss now, are you?"

"No, I'm not going to make a fuss. But I think you may be right —Vera may be in trouble."

"Oh, dear!"

"I'll come to Chicago. Where can you meet me?"

"It's rather hard, really. And I don't want to make Vera angry."

"She might have reason to thank you, in the end."

"Well, I don't know. The grocery store, I suppose. That's about the only place I can get away to."

"Then I'll meet you there. Tomorrow afternoon. Where is it?"

Mrs. Ackroyd told me.

And I promised to be by the jams and jellies at two o'clock.

25

• • • • • • • • •

The store was called Valueland. It was located at one end of a small shopping center on Route 30, about a mile from the Harrington house.

I arrived at ten minutes to two, having driven directly there from the airport. The drive, from the far north end of the city to the far south end, had taken as long as the flight from New York to Chicago.

Jams and jellies were next to canned fruits, at the rear of the store. Mrs. Ackroyd wasn't around. I began to inspect the labels on the various jars, to see which brands had been given the most space. Grocery stores had never been my thing, but grocery stocks had been, and as I looked at the labels I got the feeling that I really ought to spend more time studying products at the consumer level. For that was where the ups and downs of stocks had their origins. You could learn as much about the auto industry in a used-car lot as you could in the executive offices in Detroit. I knew this and yet I kept forgetting.

I watched the shoppers as they pushed their carts down the aisle, making their decisions. They looked worried. Buying a can of peaches had become a bigger problem than anything of that sort had ever been before, and the expressions on the faces of the women selecting food wasn't much different, it seemed to me, from those of mutual-fund managers as they tried to make up their minds about the commitment of millions of dollars. But it was the women in Valueland and their husbands and their children, and the countless families like them, who would determine whether the mutual-fund managers were right or wrong.

Mrs. Ackroyd came around the corner, wheeling her cart. On the way to meet me, I noticed, she'd stopped to pick up a quart of milk and a dozen eggs. She chose a jar of orange marmalade and glanced nervously in both directions before speaking.

"I almost changed my mind," she said in a low voice.

"I'm glad you didn't," I said.

"Not so loud," she cautioned. "The woman over there lives two houses down from Vera."

"Let's go out to my car," I suggested.

She nodded.

I waited while she went through the check-out line and led her to where the car was parked. But when we got there she was still afraid of being seen, so I pulled the car out of the lot and onto the highway, cruising toward the interstate which I'd taken from the airport.

"Now tell me exactly what happened," I said.

She'd been clutching her bag of groceries to her bosom but presently she relaxed enough to put it on the seat between us. "I just don't know what to do," she said. "And neither does Vera."

"How did she discover the money?"

"It was on account of you, I think. You asked her to look for something, some sort of paper, and there was this cigar humidor on the shelf in the closet where Wesley kept things. Vera never paid any attention to it, because there was never anything of hers in it, but the day before the funeral, when you asked her about that paper, she came across the key. She showed it to me, and it looked like the key to a safe-deposit box, but it wasn't the key to their regular box, and when Mr. Dakin came over Tuesday night with his wife to pay their respects at the chapel I told him about it."

"Who's Mr. Dakin?"

"Their lawyer. He lives around the corner. I don't suppose I should have stuck my nose into it, but I think sooner or later somebody would have found out about it anyway. Well, Thursday morning Mr. Dakin remembered and he came by on his way to work and asked for the key. Vera was still asleep, but I took it upon myself to give it to him. When she got up I told her what I'd done and that I didn't know whether I'd done the right thing. She was kind of peeved, but she said it was all right. Well, Mr. Dakin took it to his bank, and it didn't take them any time to trace it. By noon he was on the phone saying it was the key to a safe-deposit box in a bank Vera had never even heard of. It's a little bank out in Oak Park, and how Wesley found it I'm sure I don't know. Vera said there must be some mistake, but Mr. Dakin said that there wasn't any mistake—the box was in that bank, and Wesley was the one who rented it. Vera was kind of upset. So was Mr. Dakin, I think. It didn't seem right to him, somehow, that Wesley should have a box like that, that he'd never mentioned to anybody, in a little out-of-the-way bank like that, and he said that the box should be opened as soon as possible. It's kind of hard to arrange something like that, but they let you do it if you have a man from the state treasurer's office with you, because the will might be in the box, or burial instructions, or something like that."

"I know."

"Well, Mr. Dakin made an appointment with a man from the state treasurer's office, and on Friday we all went out to the bank. I thought I should go along, because after all I *am* her mother, and I felt kind of responsible, seeing as how I was the one who told Mr. Dakin in the first place. Well, after we got there I didn't feel so bad. The bank already knew that Wesley was dead and they'd put something they call a plug in the box. We had to go through all this rigmarole, but they finally gave us the box, and we took it into this room, with the man from the state treasurer's office, and opened it. And there was all this money. Well, if I'd

144

been struck by lightning I couldn't have been more surprised. And Vera too. And Mr. Dakin. Everybody was surprised." Mrs. Ackroyd paused for breath.

"How long had Wesley had the box?" I asked.

"That's the first thing Mr. Dakin wanted to know: when Wesley rented the box and how many times he'd used it. And that's what Vera can't explain. I mean, Wesley'd rented the box only four and a half weeks ago and he'd never used it since. I mean, the day he rented it he must have put the money in, and he never went back after that. Vera doesn't know where the money came from, or even whether it's Wesley's money. But there was no other name on the box, and now Mr. Dakin says that Vera's going to have to pay all kinds of taxes, and it's going to be even worse if she can't explain how the money got to be there. Is that true?"

"I'm afraid so."

"Oh, dear!" Mrs. Ackroyd put her arm around the bag of groceries and hugged it, as if for consolation. "Is it really serious?"

"That depends on what you mean by serious, Mrs. Ackroyd. She certainly won't be able to touch the money for a good long while. And if nobody else claims it—which I guess they won't, considering the circumstances—she will have to pay taxes on it. Federal and state. Inheritance and income taxes. And the government is certainly going to ask a lot of questions in order to decide how much she owes."

"But she doens't *know*, Mr. Potter. She can't tell them what she doesn't *know*."

"That may be. On the other hand, some of the money may be legitimate savings."

Mrs. Ackroyd shook her head. "Vera says no. They used to be able to save some money, but everything's gotten so expensive, they haven't been able to save anything in the past couple of years. It's the same with me, so I know. And what little they were able to save is in the bank—I mean, in their regular bank. Vera has the passbook."

"How much was your son-in-law earning?"

"I don't know exactly. I think around eighteen thousand, but maybe it was more. When Mr. Rasher made him assistant treasurer, he got a raise. But that wasn't so long ago. No, according to Vera they just weren't able to save much."

"When, exactly, did he get promoted?"

"Last Christmas."

"What happened to the man who was assistant treasurer before?"

"I don't know. Why do you ask?"

"I just wondered."

"The thing is, Mr. Potter, what should we do? You're a businessman, and it was on account of you that Vera found the key."

"Is that why you called me?"

Mrs. Ackroyd gave me a shrewd sideways glance. "Well, I thought that since the paper you wanted and the key were in the same place, maybe there was a connection between them."

"Maybe there is," I said. "Have you talked to anybody else about it?"

"No. And neither has Vera. But she's been thinking of talking to Mr. Rasher. Do you think she should?"

"No," I said emphatically. "That would be a mistake."

She gave me another sideways glance, but said nothing.

I wondered whether I'd made the point strongly enough. "A very serious mistake," I said. "She should let Mr. Dakin handle it, and not tell anyone else. You either. Do you understand?"

She nodded.

I drove the car into a gas station, turned it around and we headed back to the shopping center.

"I never did like Wesley Harrington," Mrs. Ackroyd said after a moment. "I didn't want Vera to marry him. She wouldn't listen."

I looked at her.

"But I never thought he was dishonest," she added.

"And now you do?" I asked.

"He must have been." She paused to consider what she'd said. And decided that she was right. "Yes, he definitely must have been."

I offered no opinion. But it seemed to me that she was seeing things pretty clearly.

26

● ● ● ● ● ● ● ● ●

I dropped Mrs. Ackroyd off at Valueland and went back to the interstate. It was two-thirty.

On the remainder of the ride she'd told me only one other fact that seemed important: before going to work for Interlake, Wesley Harrington had been employed by the Federal Reserve Bank in Boston. As an assistant bank examiner.

I checked into the Drake Hotel, where I'd stayed once before. Then I walked one block down Michigan Avenue to Delaware Place and checked into the Whitehall. At the Drake I used my right name, at the Whitehall I didn't. Which created a problem. I couldn't show the room clerk at the Whitehall a credit card, and he didn't want to let me in without one. He finally agreed to accept a cash deposit—two hundred dollars for two nights; anything left over would be returned to me. But that was all the cash I had.

From my room in the Drake I called Philip Quick. I'd chosen his name from the various listings in the Yellow Pages. I'd never hired a private detective before and was surprised to find five pages of the telephone directory devoted to them. Apparently the detective business was good in Chicago. Some of the agencies had large ads, explaining the things they did. I passed those up and selected Quick, because all that was given were his name, address and telephone number, which seemed properly discreet.

Besides, I liked his name; it expressed my state of mind—I was in a hurry.

The woman who answered the telephone said that Mr. Quick was out but would call me back shortly.

I waited, and after ten minutes he did. I told him who I was, where I was and that I had some work I wanted him to do. He asked what kind of work it was. I said I'd prefer to discuss that in person. He agreed to come to the hotel.

"How soon can we get together?" I asked.

"I can probably be there in half an hour," he said. He had a gravelly voice.

"Fine," I said. "Half an hour." And hung up.

He couldn't have been far away, however, for he was at my door in less than twenty minutes.

I almost changed my mind when I met him. He looked less like a detective than anyone I'd ever seen. About thirty-five years old, stocky, going bald, he fitted my image of a gambler on a winning streak. Red and black plaid jacket, black slacks, black and white sports shirt, Gucci loafers, thousand-dollar gold wrist watch, diamond-and-ruby ring. Moreover, I'd thought that a private detective would be a quiet, taciturn man, and Quick was just the opposite. He was a compulsive talker.

I told him what I wanted him to do, and he said it would be no problem. Then he launched into a fifteen-minute explanation of himself and his career. He'd been on the police force for fourteen years, moonlighting with private cases. His position in the police department made it possible for him to accomplish more for outside clients than he would have been able to do otherwise, and for that reason he'd resigned from the force with great reluctance; besides, he'd hated to give up his pension. But his private cases had been taking up too much of his time, and of course they were more profitable. Now that he had a reputation, he could make five times as much money working on his own as he could in the police department. He rarely took cases that came in off the street, preferring clients who were sent to him by lawyers, but he would take my case, because it was such a simple one and because he happened to be in the neighborhood.

He talked on and on, in that irritating voice, telling me how good he was and how in his entire career he'd never failed to accomplish what the client wanted, indicating at every opportunity that he liked expensive things and could afford them.

I was completely turned off by him, but it was getting late. "The office closes at five o'clock," I said, glancing at my watch, "and it's twenty minutes to five now. Don't you think you should get going?"

He shrugged. "Don't worry. Leave everything to me." He looked at his own watch, holding his wrist in such a way that I couldn't fail to notice the watch's quality. "But I suppose you're right. Now let me get this straight. The man's name is Malcolm Davis, and he's in the auditing department, and you want to meet him in a way that looks accidental."

"Right. I'm not positive that he's in the auditing department, but I believe he is, and that he's fairly high up in it. But I'm sure you'll be able to find him, once you get over there. If not, he'll probably be at home sometime this evening. I gave you his address—that's as much as I can give you. He's a big man, with—"

"I know, I know," Quick said impatiently. "It doesn't matter. I'll find him. Leave everything to me."

"He's a heavy drinker, so there's a pretty good chance that he'll lead you to a bar someplace, which would be fine."

"Sure, sure. Leave everything to me."

"The thing is, I'd like to meet him as soon as possible."

"Don't worry. Now where shall I send my bill?"

"First get me together with Davis, then let's talk about the bill."

"I'll get you together with Davis. I've never failed a client yet. But I have to know where to send the bill. Five hundred dollars is my minimum fee. Plus expenses, of course. Now give me your address."

I gave him a business card, and he left. I was thoroughly annoyed. The Interlake Building wasn't far from the hotel, but I doubted that Quick could get there before closing time. Yet if he hadn't talked so much, he could have done it. Furthermore, five hundred dollars was a hell of a lot of money for what I wanted him to do.

I went down to the lobby and cashed a check, since the Whitehall had left me with only five dollars. Then I returned to my room, took off my shoes, loosened my tie and ordered a double martini. Quick had promised to call me as soon as he was on the trail, and I guessed that I was going to have a long wait.

27

• • • • • • • • •

I'd told Irving where I was going. It would be all right to share the information with Tom and Mark, I'd said, but no one else. But even he didn't know what hotel I was staying at, and I thought I'd better let him know.

He was at home, having dinner. The weekly letter had gone out, he assured me, although he'd had to make some last-minute changes, because the market had gone down more today than it had gone up yesterday and there was a rumor that interest rates were again going to be increased.

"Anything else?" I asked.

"Tom and Mark seem kind of mad at each other."

"They'll get over it. What else?"

"Harriet called. She wanted to talk to you."

"Any message?"

"None that she'd give me. Just said she's at the Statler in Washington."

"O.K., I'll call her. And for your ears only I'm at the Drake in Chicago. Room 809."

"Right. How long will you be there?"

"I don't know, Irv. Another day or so, maybe."

"I've still got those dates in Detroit. I said I'd be there this Thursday. I don't think I ought to change them again—it'd look funny."

"I forgot about that. Well, we may have to bend the rules. I'll try to be back by then, but if I'm not, go anyway. Can you get everything done there in a day?"

"I think so."

"Good."

"Oh, and, Brock—that cop called. O'Brien. He wanted to know where you were. I said I didn't know but I don't think he believed me."

That was a problem. I thought about it for a moment. Honesty was the best policy. "Well, if he calls again, tell him that you heard from me, and where I am. Tell him that I came out here for a couple of days on business."

"What about Tom and Mark? Shall I tell them?"

"Only if they ask. They may not."

"Tom did. He wanted to talk to you."

"Well, all right. I'll call him. Anything else I should know?"

"Yes. We were having dinner, and mine is getting cold."

"O.K., so eat." I hung up and went back to what was left of my martini. Then I picked up the telephone again. Possibly Harriet was in her room.

She was. Having a martini, she said.

"That makes two of us," I told her. "Only mine's a double."

"Mr. Price doesn't question your expense account the way he does mine. Where are you? Irving said you were out of town."

"I'm in Chicago again."

"Oh. Something new happen?"

"Yes. But what about you?"

"Well, I talked to Uncle Bill. It's awfully hard to get anything out of the FBI, he says. But he sent me to Senator Watkins. He said if anybody can do it Watkins can—he's on the Appropriations Committee. The senator didn't seem very enthused, but while I was with him he got a call from Uncle Bill, and that helped. He was going to talk to someone at the Justice Department and let me know. Do you want me to stay here and wait?"

"How long do you think it'll take?"

"A day or two, he said."

"Then I think you'd better stay there, Harriet. In case he can't, you may have to see someone else."

"I wouldn't know who, Brock."

"I wouldn't either, but in any event I'd stay on the spot if I were you."

"All right. Where can I reach you if I find out anything?"

"I'm unreachable at the moment. Leave word with Irving."

"Tell him everything?"

"Use your own judgment."

On that note, and with an exchange of good wishes, we ended the call.

I tried to get Tom. I didn't succeed. His son answered the telephone. Tom and his wife had gone out for the evening. All I learned was that Tom's son was unhappy at the prospect of having to go back to school.

I ordered dinner from room service. I'd had an early lunch on the plane, and nothing since.

It took a long while for the meal to arrive. I passed the interval watching television. Three young policemen were trying to catch a mad killer. None of the policemen resembled O'Brien or Sestino or any other policeman I'd ever seen. They looked like nice kids, though, and their concern for one another was enormous. What's more, all of them were exceptionally good at climbing, running and leaping from ledges. The mad killer turned out to be a former policeman. In the end he got shot and fell off a fire escape.

At eight o'clock the waiters finally wheeled the table into my room, and I began to eat. I wondered whether I'd have to spend the night at the Drake. I was safe enough there, I supposed. Yet I'd feel better staying where I was registered under the fictitious name. I should have arranged with Quick for him to report back to me at fixed intervals. I'd been in too much of a hurry. And too

154

irritated. The man was so damned egocentric. Other private detectives weren't like that. Or were they? In the past I'd always been my own detective. It was better that way. But on the spur of the moment hiring a stranger had seemed like a good idea. As a matter of fact, it still did. A different kind of man, though.

A new program was under way. A very rich woman had disappeared from her house on the French Riviera. Her nephew was attempting to trace her.

I never got to find out whether he did or not. Or to finish my meal either. For at eight-fifteen the telephone rang.

Malcolm Davis was at a bar called the Pillbox, on North Sheridan Road, Quick informed me; I should come right over.

28

From the outside it didn't appear to be much of a place. It was one of three stores on the ground floor of an old high-rise apartment building. The others were a real estate office and a beauty shop. A small, crackling pink-neon sign said "PILLBOX." The show window had been painted black, but there was a small clear square in the middle, with a Hamm's beer sign.

I took a deep breath and opened the door. The room was quite dark. A long bar occupied the left side, a row of semicircular booths the right. There were a few tables in the front and a jukebox in the back. An illuminated sign near the jukebox said "REST ROOMS."

One of the tables was occupied, and there were half a dozen customers scattered along the bar. With the exception of two men, all the bar customers were sitting by themselves. The two men were Malcolm Davis and Philip Quick. They were engaged in a heated discussion.

I stood there a moment, adjusting. I hadn't expected Quick to be present. Davis had his head turned away from the door and didn't see me, but Quick was looking straight at me. He gave no sign of recognition, however. I walked over to them and sat down on the stool next to Davis's.

"It's the goddamn line," he was saying. "They're not strong enough to protect the backfield. That's the whole trouble."

"That's the fault of management," Quick told him.

"They're like a bunch of goddamn high-school players," Davis said. He didn't sound drunk.

The bartender came over to me. He had the build of a football player and the face of a man who'd never in his entire life liked anyone.

"Beer," I said.

He filled a mug from the tap.

"Ten years ago they weren't like that," Davis said.

"Ten years ago they didn't have all the competition," the bartender butted in. "That's the trouble. It's not that they've gotten so worse, it's that everyone else's gotten better." He gave me my beer.

"That's management," Quick said. "Too greedy. They won't pay enough."

The bartender nodded.

I looked at the hand-lettered sign over the cash register. "NO CHECKS CASHED," it said.

My eyes were getting used to the dim light. Davis was drinking something clear that had a slice of lime in it. He'd almost finished it. Quick was working his way through a beer.

"You're right," Davis said to the bartender. "Too many teams." He picked up his glass and finished the drink, then handed his glass to the bartender. "And give my friend another beer," he instructed him.

Quick shook his head. "Thanks, but I've got to be going. Promised the wife I'd be home."

"One more," Davis urged.

"Another time," Quick said. He finished the beer, put the glass down noisily and got off the stool. He patted Davis on the shoulder. "Nice talking to you."

"Sure I can't buy you another?" Davis asked. He sounded disappointed.

Quick glanced at me, again without recognition, wished Davis good luck and left.

"Nice guy," Davis observed to the bartender.

"Nice ring he was wearing," the bartender replied.

Davis turned and saw me. He frowned, as if he knew he'd seen me someplace before but couldn't remember where. I smiled. He continued to frown. And when the bartender gave him the new drink he ignored it.

"Hi," I said.

It came to him. There was a flicker of shock on his face, then nothing.

"I'm Brock Potter," I said.

He nodded slowly.

"It's a small world."

He did nothing. Just sat there, looking me in the eye.

"Jerry!" someone down the bar called.

The bartender went over to him.

Davis suddenly put one foot on the floor, as if he intended to leave.

"Don't go," I said, taking his arm. "I have some interesting news for you."

He hesitated. He seemed afraid to leave and afraid to stay.

"Look," I said, "let's level with each other. I know you're the one who called me in New York. I have a recorder on my telephone, and a voice-print device would identify your voice in a minute." It sounded good anyway.

He decided to stay. "What do you want?"

"To start with, I want to know why you called."

"I was doing a favor for a friend."

"Wesley Harrington?"

He wouldn't commit himself.

"There's no point in not telling me," I said. "I've got the list. You know that. And Harrington is dead."

He remained silent.

"You're not doing yourself any good by clamming up. I could take the record of those telephone calls to the Insurance Commission and to the police, and you'd have to answer their questions whether you want to or not."

"Go ahead." He was scared, though. I could see it.

"All right, I will." I started to get up.

"Wait a minute," he said quickly. He picked up his drink. "Come over here."

He led me to a booth at the back of the room.

"Harrington thought he could pull something smart," he said when we were seated. "I don't know what it was. That's the truth."

"You know what you said. Or what he told you to say. That's enough."

"I don't know what he was trying to pull. Believe me."

"Believe you? How can I? You're not that dumb. You've got a responsible job in a big company. You didn't get there because you were stupid."

"Wes was my friend. I wanted to help him."

"You're not *that* stupid either. You knew damn well you could lose your job, at the very least."

"What the fuck difference does it make? I've lost everything else."

"Who was supposed to meet me at the Astor Tower—Harrington or you?"

"Harrington."

"And what were you going to get out of it?"

"Nothing. I was doing Wes a favor, I tell you. Who the hell cares about the job? Everything's gone anyway. I wish I *would* get fired."

"I don't believe that you weren't going to get anything out of it. Money changed hands. Harrington's widow has found a bundle of cash she can't explain."

"No!"

"Yes. It's no secret. The state treasurer's office knows about the money. The state and federal revenue services will be told automatically. Questions are going to be asked."

"That has nothing to do with me. It was Harrington's money, not mine."

"But you helped him get it."

"I did not! Leave me alone, damn it!" His voice rose. Two of the men at the bar turned around.

The bartender came out from behind the bar and walked over to us. "Everything all right?" he asked Davis.

"Everything's all right, Jerry," Davis assured him. "Everything's all right."

After a moment the bartender went back to his post.

"I could get you thrown out of here," Davis told me.

"I could get you thrown into jail," I replied.

"I didn't do anything wrong. I didn't break any laws. It was Harrington."

"What laws did Harrington break?"

"I don't know. But I know that I didn't break any."

"How much does Rasher know?"

There was a silence. "Rasher?" Davis asked finally.

"Rasher. How much does he know? He's the one who put Harrington where he was, wasn't he?"

"Rasher liked him. Rasher hired him. Yes, Rasher made him his assistant. But how should I know how much Rasher knows? Ask Rasher."

"And tell him about you?"

"Oh, God!"

"And Lipp—shall I tell him about you too?"

"Oh, God! Leave me alone! Leave me alone!" You could hear him all over the room.

The bartender returned. "What's going on here?"

"This guy won't get off my back," Davis said. "Get him out of here, Jerry."

The bartender took me by the arm and pulled me from the booth. "The beer is on the house, buddy. Come on."

He hustled me to the front of the room, opened the front door and gave me a push.

I staggered across the sidewalk and bumped into a lamppost.

For the first time in my life I'd been thrown out of a bar.

29

Eight-thirty was too early, Quick said. How about nine-thirty?

Nine-thirty would be O.K., I said, adding, "I'm not at the Drake. I'm at the Whitehall. Room 2005."

"Oh?"

I didn't explain.

He arrived at a quarter to ten. With bloodshot eyes. He'd been up most of the night, he said, following someone's straying wife. She was having an affair with a clarinet player, and the clarinet player didn't finish work until three in the morning. Then he paused. "How come you changed hotels?"

"Business reasons," I replied.

"And registered under another name?"

"You know about that?"

"I asked for you at the desk."

"Business reasons," I said again. But since he didn't look satisfied, I went a step further. "The card I gave you yesterday is authentic. I'm a stockbroker. I'm in the analysis end of the business, though. I'm here investigating Interlake. It's better if they don't know where to find me. You can call my office if you don't believe me."

He still seemed skeptical.

I showed him credit cards, driver's license and a sample of my signature.

"All right," he said finally. "What can I do for you now?"

"You did a good job last night," I said. "You got me to Davis a lot faster than I expected."

"I always do a good job. That's how I got my reputation. Never disappoint a client."

"How'd you do it?"

"That's another thing I never do: explain my methods."

"Did you get onto him at the office or when he left his apartment?"

"I didn't even go to the office. I went right to his apartment." He smiled. "Let's just say I knew he was going to have some pizza and go to the Pillbox."

I thought about it. The only way Quick could have learned such things so quickly was by bugging Davis's apartment and eavesdropping on a conversation. Which was illegal. I didn't pursue the matter. "I didn't expect to find you talking to him," I said.

"Why not? It was a way of keeping him there. And I like to talk to people. You never know what they're going to say. People are interesting. That's why I enjoy this kind of work. You meet a lot of people." He launched into another long explanation of himself.

This time I paid attention, however. My opinion of him had gone up. "What do you think of Davis?" I asked when he finished.

He shrugged. "Frustrated. One of those ex-jock types who finds things falling apart. Football player. College, not pro. Wanted to turn pro but either wasn't good enough or changed his mind when he got married. That's why he goes to a joint like the Pillbox. The bartender used to be a pro football player, until he wrecked his knee. The two of them like to talk football. And I'd say Davis has more time on his hands right now than he knows what to do with. His wife left him not so long ago. Went off with somebody else. He's bitter as hell about that. She took the kids, the furniture, tied up the bank account—he got kind of a rough deal. They hadn't been getting along, I'd say, and he bought this new condominium, thinking that that might help, and no sooner did he buy it than she up and left. Now nothing seems any good to him. That's my impression, at any rate. He's a man doesn't care what happens to him."

I nodded. That seemed a pretty good summary. Especially since he couldn't have talked to Davis for more than half an hour. My estimate of him went up another couple of notches. "Would you say he was dishonest?"

"Could be," Quick replied thoughtfully. "A man like that, you don't know. I'd say he wasn't originally, but when a man doesn't care anymore—well, he can go either way. That's been my experience."

"Mine too," I said. "Now about today—I've got another job for you. Same kind. I want to bump into a man named Richard Rasher. He's the treasurer of Interlake. I don't think he'll lead you to a bar, but he'll probably lead you to a restaurant. I'd like to meet him where he's having lunch."

"I don't know," Quick said. "I've got a tough day ahead. I've got a lot of jobs going. I've got to get this ring back for a client—she knows who's got it and she can't report him to the police. Then there's this guy who's screwing around with his wife's sister. And I have a fitting on some jackets I bought. You like cashmere? Anyway, I'm going to be tied up. But maybe I can squeeze in an hour or so. What time does this Rasher eat?"

"I don't know. You mean you have all these jobs going at one time and you handle them all yourself?"

"Sure. How else could I make my kind of money? You put on extra people, you got to pay them. Cuts the profit. And most of the guys around in this business are such a bunch of clowns I wouldn't even want to hire them. Me, I put in an hour here, a couple hours there. Most jobs aren't that hard, and with the kind of equipment we got nowadays you don't have to spend a lot of time. All that stuff about detectives working on one case day and night—it hardly ever happens like that."

He reached for the telephone, dialed Information and asked

for the number of Interlake General Insurance Company. Then he hung up and dialed again.

"I'd like to speak to Richard Rasher," he said. Then he said it again, apparently to Rasher's secretary. "No, personal," he added. "I'm with the Insurance Commission in California and I'm in town and I thought maybe we could have lunch together. I'm not doing anything around one o'clock, and if he's free . . . I see. Anything serious? . . . I see. Well, I won't bother him. Thanks anyway." He hung up. "It won't work," he said to me. "He's home, sick."

We looked in the telephone directory. Rasher was listed. He lived on Lincoln Park West.

We discussed it. There was no way, we decided, that I could meet Rasher accidentally. I'd have to go to his home and hope that he'd let me in. But if he really was sick, he probably wouldn't.

"And if that's the case," Quick said, "let me know. I'll find out for you what's going on inside."

"How?"

He smiled. "Leave that to me. I've never disappointed a client yet."

"Any messages for 809?" I asked.

"Yes, there are," said the message clerk.

Tom had called. So had O'Brien. Both of them wanted me to call them back.

I put down the telephone and picked it up again.

Tom was out.

I tried O'Brien.

He was in. And annoyed. I should have told him I was leaving town, he said.

I explained that I had to carry on with my work and that I had some appointments in Chicago.

He didn't care what I had to do, he said; he wanted me to tell him when I went out of town; he wanted to know where I was so that he could get in touch with me on short notice if he had to.

I apologized.

He asked when I'd be back in New York, and I said I'd probably be there the next day. He asked whether he could reach me at the Drake in the meanwhile, and I said that he could. He instructed me to let him know as soon as I landed in New York. I promised to do so.

I hung up and went to the window. From my room in the Whitehall I could see my room in the Drake. I felt like twins.

The doorman brought my car. He explained how to get to Lincoln Park West.

It wasn't far.

The building was a nice one. A stately three-story walk-up with bay windows and fancy cornices, facing the park. The sort of building which would probably be torn down within the next few years and replaced by a high-rise that would accommodate two hundred families instead of three.

I sat in the car for a few minutes, planning what I was going to say. All I could do was what I'd done with Davis: apply pressure. Rasher, it seemed to me, was the type who didn't stand up well under pressure.

I climbed out of the car and went into the lobby. It was a spacious area with a red tile floor and a glass door that separated the outer lobby from an inner one. The stairway leading up to the apartments from the inner lobby was carpeted, and in addition there was a small automatic elevator. I tried the glass door. It was locked. I studied the mailboxes. Rasher's was the middle one. I started to push the button above it, then hesitated. Was I really making the right move? Suddenly I wasn't sure. I might accomplish more by letting Quick use his methods. But I'd lose a day.

A woman came into the lobby. A stout woman, middle-aged. Over her arm she was carrying a man's suit in a plastic cleaning bag. Mrs. Rasher? Quite possibly.

I smiled at her and left.

I walked to the end of the building and followed the driveway that ran along the side of it to the garages in the back. Toward the rear of the building was a door. It wasn't locked. I went inside and found myself in a small vestibule with a stairway. I climbed half a flight, changed my mind and came down. This is ridiculous, I thought. Either go in the front way or leave.

I returned to the lobby but still couldn't make up my mind. And while I was standing there I heard a whirring noise.

I looked through the glass door into the inner lobby. A red light was glowing from the instrument panel beside the elevator. Someone was coming down.

I went outside again and got into my car.

A man and a woman emerged from the building. I looked at them, then quickly turned my head.

They were Malcolm Davis and Vera Harrington.

I slid down in the seat and stayed like that for several minutes. When I came up they were gone.

I went into the lobby and pushed the button.

30

A garbled voice came through the speaking tube. It asked who I was.

I answered.

The glass door buzzed. I opened it, crossed the inner lobby and went up the steps.

The door on the second floor was open. Rasher was standing with his hand on the knob.

"I've been expecting you," he said, and stood aside to let me in.

"They said at the office that you were sick."

"I am. Are you the insurance commissioner from California who wanted to have lunch with me?"

"No." He looked healthy enough. But green slacks and a green and white sports shirt emphasized the width of his hips. I was reminded of a distorted hourglass. "It's nothing serious, I hope."

"You're not?" A frown creased his brow, then vanished. "Well, no matter. Serious? Not if I take care of myself. I have to take care of myself. High blood pressure. Every now and then it shoots up, you know." He led me into the living room, which was large and had a high ceiling. The view of the park from the bay window was very nice. Rasher fitted himself into a lounge chair and motioned for me to sit on the sofa. "I've heard you're a persistent man, and you certainly are, aren't you? I must say, I'm rather impressed."

"Thank you."

"How you managed to encounter Davis in that dreary little bar he goes to, I'm sure I don't know. He thinks you were having him followed. Were you?"

"I never discuss my methods," I said, borrowing a phrase from Quick.

"Well, no matter. What do you want this time, Mr. Potter? Another look in the vault?"

"No. One look in the vault was enough. Information is what I want, Rasher. Just information."

"Rasher? Come now. Either make it Mr. Rasher or Dick. We're not enemies, you know." He smiled. "Or are we?"

"O.K., Dick." He was more likable when Lipp wasn't around, I decided.

"That's better. I also understand that my assistant left a bit of an estate."

"Fifty thousand dollars. In hundred-dollar bills."

"Incredible. We're all surprised. Including his widow. He wasn't earning that kind of money, of course."

"I didn't think so."

"Vera can't explain it. And she can't explain how you happened to find out. She thinks you must have found out either from her lawyer or from her mother."

"You know how it is, Dick. News travels."

"Apparently. At any rate, Vera's admitted giving you the list of bonds which were allegedly stolen."

I nodded.

"But of course that doesn't explain the fifty thousand dollars, does it?"

I shook my head.

"Well, the fact of the matter is, I can't explain the fifty thousand dollars any more than you can."

"What about Harrington's murder?" I asked.

Rasher took a cigar from a box on the table beside his chair.

He bit off one end and put a match to the other.

"Should you be smoking?" I asked.

He sighed heavily. "No. But a man has to do something. I can't eat. I'm on this absurd diet. Life is no fun at all." He sighed again. "Harrington's murder. Well, that's an interesting point, isn't it? Fifty thousand dollars, then a gunman hiding in the garage. It's possible that the gunman was after the fifty thousand dollars, wouldn't you say?"

I shook my head.

"You wouldn't?"

"No. Harrington was killed because of something he knew."

"You insist on that?"

"Dick, I don't want to fence with you. Harrington had a list of bonds which were supposedly stolen from Interlake. He wanted me to make it public. He was killed to keep him from getting together with me. It's as simple as that. And someone tried to kill me last week, too."

Rasher chuckled, and his chins quivered. "It's easy to understand, the way you operate, that someone would want to kill you. You're very annoying." His expression became serious. "Forgive me. That wasn't funny, was it?"

A woman came into the room. She was the woman I'd seen with the cleaning bag. "I *thought* I smelled smoke," she said severely. "Richard, put that cigar out. At once."

Rasher jumped. He put the cigar out.

I felt sorry for him. Caught between Lipp and a woman with a voice like that—no wonder he had high blood pressure.

"My wife," Rasher said. "Brockton Potter, my dear."

Mrs. Rasher gave me a brief nod. "I saw Mr. Potter downstairs." She turned and left the room.

Rasher gazed fondly at the cigar, but didn't relight it. "I'm afraid I was wrong about Harrington," he said presently. "I trusted him."

I said nothing.

"I brought him into the company, you know. Promoted him. Made him my assistant. I don't know how I could have been so wrong."

"Where did you find him?"

"In New England. He was working for the Federal Reserve."

"And you?"

"Me? I was comptroller for a company that made bedsheets, in a little town in southern Maine. It was like being buried alive up there."

"How did you get to Interlake?"

"Anton Lipp bought the company I was working for. We met. He liked me."

"So he brought you to Chicago."

"Thank God. I was miserable up there. Small towns aren't for me."

"He brought you, and you brought Harrington."

"In effect. I'd known Harrington for a number of years. He used to travel in Maine, auditing banks. I was impressed by him. He had a good head on his shoulders. But evidently Chicago didn't agree with him morally. Or else I promoted him too fast. At any rate, something must have gone wrong."

"What about Davis?"

"Malcolm? Malcolm was with Interlake before. Didn't you ever meet him?"

"No." I wondered whether Davis had admitted making the telephone calls.

"Well, I don't suppose you would have. He's a good man too. Or at least he was. He's having personal problems now, and I think that's affecting him. He's drinking more than he should. I don't quite know what to do about him. I keep hoping he'll straighten out."

"He and Harrington were friends, I understand."

"Yes. And Harrington was probably a bad influence on him."

"Or vice versa."

Rasher shook his head. "No. If anyone did anything wrong, it was Harrington. I realize that now. I should have realized it before. I think he was exposed to too much."

"I don't understand."

"He was a bank examiner. You'd be surprised at some of the things bank examiners run across. Harrington was exposed to all sorts of fraud and embezzlement. He may have picked up a few ideas of his own. Maybe even blackmail."

"Are you suggesting . . . ?"

"I'm not suggesting anything. But he evidently got fifty thousand dollars recently, and I very much doubt that he did it legitimately. I'm as anxious as you are to find out what he was up to, because it's a reflection on me. Therefore I'm saying you ought to look into his past. His boss at the Federal Reserve was a man named Jack Williams. If I were you, I'd have a talk with him. He may be able to tell you some of the irregularities Harrington uncovered, and that could be useful to you. I have a hunch that he may have been doing himself what he'd found others guilty of doing. Or else he was blackmailing someone."

"That could be."

"I'm glad you think so. I've never met Williams myself, but Harrington used to speak of him, and I know he's still there. He's one of the examiners. I don't think he'll tell you anything over the telephone, but if you talk to him in person and show him your credentials he probably will."

"Thanks for the tip. I may do just that." I smiled. "You're being more helpful than I expected."

"I have no reason not to be. Contrary to what you may think, I too want the truth. I brought Harrington into the company. I promoted him. I feel responsible for his actions. The only thing I ask is that you don't tell Mr. Lipp about this meeting. He's a peculiar man. He can be one of the nicest people you ever want to meet, when things are going well. But when they're not, he doesn't like people to know. Which is understandable, of course.

And I'm sure he'd prefer everyone to forget about this little episode. The fact that I'm talking to you as I am—well, as he said himself, he's mercurial."

"Mercurial? That's one way of putting it. Me, I'd say he has a vicious temper."

"Call it what you will, but I'm not anxious to make him angry."

"I don't blame you."

"I hope not. For just as Harrington was indebted to me, I'm indebted to Anton Lipp. Everything I have I owe to that man. If it weren't for him I'd still be holed up in an ugly little dump of a mill town where the temperature goes down to twenty below zero in the winter and the snow drifts up to the eaves of the house and there's no place to go and nothing to do and no one to talk to, and where I was working for peanuts, and where my wife and I were driving each other crazy. I try to be a realist, Mr. Potter. I try not to kid myself. I know I'm not a particularly attractive man, and I'm not the smartest man in the world either. I'm pretty good with figures, but so are a lot of other people. There's no end to the number of men Mr. Lipp might have given a break to, but he chose me. He took me out of that rut I was in and brought me to a city where for the first time in twenty years I'm happy and put me in a job where I amount to something and made it possible for me to earn a decent salary and have nice things like this apartment. Yes, sir, my friend, I'm very much indebted to Anton Lipp and I don't care what kind of a temper he has: I don't want anything to spoil my relationship with him or threaten what I have. Can you understand that?"

"Yes."

"Then you will be discreet?"

"Yes."

"Good. Now, if you don't mind, I'm getting a headache."

I stood up. "I'll let you know what Williams says."

Rasher nodded absent-mindedly. He remained seated. He suddenly seemed very tired.

I let myself out of the apartment.

Not everything he'd said sounded logical to me. But some of it did. And when I got back to the hotel I placed a call to Jack Williams.

31

• • • • • • • • •

"Unfortunately," said Dr. Chang, "I'm tied up this evening, but how about having lunch with me tomorrow? I'd like to show you my shop and the site I've picked for the new plant."

Which was what I'd had in mind. "I'd like to see them," I said.

"Good. Where are you staying?"

"At the Ritz."

"How about if I pick you up there at twelve-thirty?"

"Fine." My appointment with Williams was at ten.

Chang apologized again for being unable to take me to dinner, and we hung up.

I went to the window. There are larger parks than Boston's Public Garden, but I've never found one that's prettier. It was dusk. The shadows of the vast elms were long. The air seemed to have a purple cast. In the distance, on Beacon Hill, the gold dome of the capitol glittered in the last of the day's sunlight. I watched one of the swan boats being pedaled slowly around the lagoon.

For a moment nothing seemed urgent. Or even important.

The moment ended. I went back to the telephone and called Tom.

"Where the hell are you?" he said. "I called you at the Drake this afternoon, and they said you'd checked out."

I told him where I was. And explained why.

"Sounds like a waste of time to me," he said.

"Could be," I agreed. "I thought it'd be worth a try, though, as long as Williams doesn't object to talking to me."

"When will you be home?"

"I'm not sure. I have a date with Chang tomorrow afternoon. Since I'm in town, I thought, it wouldn't hurt to—"

"I made a date for you for Friday. Lunch."

"Who with?"

"Sir Archibald Beardsley."

"You talked to him?"

"Yes. And he's on his way over here. Coming in tomorrow, on his way to Washington."

"Did he tell you who the bank was acting for?"

"No. But from the way he spoke, I have the feeling that he might. He said we could discuss it when he got here. I fixed it up for the two of us to get together with him. That's what I wanted to tell you."

"I'll be there."

"O.K. So what's with Chicago?"

"I'm almost positive now that there really was a theft. All I need is enough proof so that I can ring the alarm bell. I'm hoping that Williams can point me in the right direction."

"Well, be careful. And I'll see you Friday at one at the St. Regis, if not before."

We said good-bye, and I placed a call to O'Brien. No point in antagonizing him further. But both he and Sestino were off duty. I left word as to my whereabouts. And decided to do the same with Irving.

He too had been trying to reach me in Chicago. He'd had a difficult afternoon. Calls had been coming in from customers as a result of the Tuesday letter, which most of them had just received. We'd taken Frankfurt Industries off our buy list, and the research department of Laird & West was contradicting us by recommending it. Those who did business with both of us were confused. Even the *Wall Street Journal* wanted an explanation.

175

"Stick to your guns," I said.

"I have been, but it's been tough."

"Have you heard from Harriet? I told her to talk to you if she couldn't locate me."

"That's why I was trying to find you, Brock. She called in about an hour ago. She says she has information for you. She seemed kind of excited."

My pulse quickened. "Where is she, Irv?"

"She said to tell you she isn't in Washington any longer. She's in Bangor, Maine." He paused. "Is she in some kind of trouble, Brock?"

"I hope not. Why?"

"Because she said she was calling from the police station."

"No, no. It's all right. What else did she say?"

"She said you were right about Jars. She said she was about to leave the police station. She's going to call me again at nine o'clock, in case I heard from you in the meantime."

"Great. I think we're finally getting someplace. Tell her to call me here at the Ritz in Boston tonight."

"O.K." He paused. "It may be premature to mention this, Brock, but I think you should know. I've been checking around. I haven't heard anything about Interlake or Computech but I did hear a rumor about Lipp personally. Someone said he was fooling around over in London a few months ago."

"Fooling around?"

"Silver futures. It's only a rumor, though."

"Thanks, Irv. Thanks very much."

We hung up, and I ordered dinner from room service. Then I settled down to wait for Harriet's call.

Silver futures. The Bristol Bank. John Patterson. And somewhere up in Maine a man named Clifford Jars.

The pieces were falling into place.

32

• • • • • • • • •

Harriet may have been excited before but she wasn't now. In fact, she was discouraged.

"I'm up against a stone wall," she declared.

"What happened?"

"It's terribly difficult to get anything out of the FBI, Brock. They just won't give. As a special favor—well, anyway, they do have something on Clifford Jars. Not Yars—Jars. He was part of a counterfeiting ring that was operating up here in Bangor about eight years ago. There were several men involved, and all of them were caught, except Jars. He got away. The FBI is still looking for him, they say—although I imagine they've sort of lost interest by now. At any rate, I learned that much and on the strength of it I flew up here this afternoon."

"Good girl."

"The FBI has an office here too, but it's just a little one, and nobody there would talk, so I went to the police. I thought they might have been in on the case—and they were. But they wouldn't tell me anything either. Officially, at least."

"Damn."

"It isn't as bad as all that. One of the men I talked to seemed to like me. He gave me the name of someone he said might know something. A policeman who was on the force then and who was on the case but who's retired now. I went to see him. He was very nice. He told me what he remembered, which wasn't all that much, but he did tell me that Jars had a daughter and that she still lives here, so I went to see her—and that's where I ran up against the stone wall. She says her father is dead. She says he's been dead for years."

"I don't believe it."

"You'd believe it even less if you talked to her, as I just did. I was at her house less than an hour ago. I'm positive that she's lying. I couldn't budge her, though, and finally she threw me out. Bodily, almost."

"You think she knows where her father is?"

"That's my feeling."

"Then you've got to keep trying, Harriet."

"I'll do anything you say, Brock, but I'm on the scene and you're not, and I tell you that I can stay here for a month and try three times a day and I still won't learn anything. Not from that woman."

I tried to think of an alternative course. I couldn't. "Maybe if I talked to her . . ."

"You're welcome to have a go at it. And I'll make another attempt myself. But my guess is that Geraldine Jars has been standing off the FBI and Lord knows who else for eight years and she's going to keep right on doing it."

"Where are you?"

"At the Holiday Inn. It's just outside of town."

"Stay there. I'll be in touch with you sometime tomorrow. I have a date in the morning with someone at the Federal Reserve who may be of some help."

"All right."

We talked for a few more minutes and then hung up. I began to pace the floor. How important was it to locate Clifford Jars? If it could be proved that the bonds were counterfeit, the identity of the counterfeiter was incidental—the fact that they were counterfeit was enough. But suppose that the counterfeit bonds had been used only temporarily. Suppose the real bonds had been used as collateral for a loan and counterfeit bonds substituted, to deceive the auditors, until the loan was repaid. Suppose the loan had already been repaid and the authentic bonds returned to the vault. In that event there'd be no proof of anything unless the counterfeiter could be found and made to talk.

If the loan had been repaid and the original bonds returned to the vault, would Wesley Harrington have been killed? Possibly. And would there have been an attempt to kill me too? Possibly.

I tried to reason it out. The fact that the original bonds had been returned to the vault didn't mean that a crime hadn't been committed. Or wouldn't be committed again—whenever Anton Lipp happened to need money.

Jars had to be traced.

Unless the Bristol Bank was the bank that had made the loan and had a record of the bonds which had been used as collateral. The chances of that were slim, though. The bonds on Harrington's list could have been borrowed against at any bank in the Western world.

The Jars girl had to be made to talk.

33

● ● ● ● ● ● ● ● ●

Williams had explained over the telephone that his office wasn't in the Federal Reserve Bank itself. The bank simply wasn't large enough to house all its employees, so the examiners had been relegated to the building at 201 Devonshire Street, a block away.

I walked there from the hotel. I'd been up since dawn and had more time than I knew what to do with. I strolled across the Public Garden and the Common, past the State House, the Park Street Church, King's Chapel, along Washington Street to the Old South Meeting House and then into the maze of narrow, crooked streets that crisscrossed the financial district.

Even with walking, I arrived forty minutes early. I looked around for a place to have coffee, but there was nothing of the sort in the building. It was, as office buildings go, an old one and not particularly large. The front entrance was on Devonshire Street, but there was another entrance on the street behind Devonshire, Arch Street. The lobby was a narrow arcade which connected the two entrances. At the Devonshire end of the arcade was a small newsstand, and I contented myself by buying a package of cheese crackers.

On the right side of the arcade were the elevators, and on the left was a glass wall with a door leading to the lobby of a branch of the New England Merchants National Bank. From the lobby of the bank a flight of stairs led down to the vault. I stood there, munching the crackers and gazing at the stairs to the vault. There was more wealth tucked away in the banks of Boston, I knew, than most people imagined. The first real fortunes in America had been made in Boston, and some of them had never left; they were still there, in vaults such as this, growing and compounding. The textile mills, the railroads, the electronics companies—what had been, and still were, some of the largest businesses in the United States were owned by unobtrusive families that kept their stocks and bonds in the safe-deposit boxes which were scattered about the few square blocks surrounding the building at 201 Devonshire Street. People can say all they want about the millionaires of Dallas, Houston and Los Angeles, but if you're looking for the genuine, centuries-old accumulation of money, go to Boston.

I finished the crackers and stepped into one of the elevators, hoping that Jack Williams would be able to see me before ten.

He couldn't.

So I sat in the waiting room for half an hour, and at exactly ten o'clock he ushered me into his office.

He was a chubby man with gray hair and blue eyes. The eyes were unusual. They managed to convey frostiness and friendliness at the same time. "I'm afraid," he said, "that I don't understand exactly what it is you want, Mr. Potter."

I gave him one of my business cards. He studied it for a moment and put it on his desk. "I'm head of our research department," I explained. "Wesley Harrington was an officer of Interlake General Insurance Company, a company that I'm studying."

"Was?"

"He's dead."

Williams was shocked. "I didn't know that. I'm very sorry."

"There are some questions surrounding his death. Mr. Rasher, the treasurer of Interlake, suggested that I talk to you."

"Questions?"

"Harrington was murdered."

Williams stared at me with disbelief. "Good Lord!"

"So while this sort of thing is kind of a side issue to what I'm really working on, I thought—for everyone's sake—an effort should be made to find out whether anything in his past might have caught up with him."

"Wesley murdered," Williams said, shaking his head as if he simply couldn't comprehend the fact. Then he pulled himself together. "I don't quite see why this Mr. Rasher should have involved you, Mr. Potter, but I don't suppose it matters—I'll be glad to tell you whatever I can." He shook his head some more. "Wesley Harrington murdered. Good Lord. I'm certainly sorry to hear that. I liked him. He was a fine young man."

"How long did you know him, Mr. Williams?"

"Ever since he started with us. Twelve years, I believe."

"Was he a bank examiner all that time?"

"Well, first he was a trainee, then he was promoted through several different grades."

"But he did make examinations of banks?"

"Yes."

"And, I'd imagine, from time to time he discovered irregularities."

"From time to time. All of us do." Williams explained that each bank that is a member of the Federal Reserve system is examined once a year. The examination is to determine the bank's solvency, its compliance with federal regulations and the quality of its management. Quite often the examiners find that the bank isn't up to snuff.

"What are some of the most common things you find wrong?" I asked.

"That'd be hard to say," Williams replied. "Bad loans, possibly. Improperly secured loans. Loans that should have been written off and aren't. Or links between the officers of the bank and corporations that the bank makes loans to."

"Can you recall any of the irregularities that Harrington turned up?"

Williams frowned. "That'd be rather difficult. Over a period of twelve years there are so many. But let me see. . . ." His frown deepened. He began to remember. And to recount various incidents.

The more he told me, the more I realized that Rasher was right: Harrington had been exposed to a great deal of wrongdoing. But there was no one case which from Williams' description of it stood out above the others. The First Federal Reserve District includes all the New England states, and at one time or another Harrington had been to every part of the district. He'd investigated large banks and small ones. He'd exposed all kinds of questionable practices. But he'd never been in on a case that was really sensational.

"Did he ever," I asked finally, "come up against any counterfeiting?"

The question seemed to surprise him. "Counterfeiting? What makes you ask that, Mr. Potter?"

"Just curious."

"Counterfeiting doesn't crop up much in our line of work. That's more within the province of the Treasury Department. Forgery, yes—forged notes, forged financial statements. But counterfeiting—I don't think I'd recognize a counterfeit document if I saw it, and my men wouldn't either, I'd venture to say. A good counterfeit bill or stock certificate is quite difficult to spot, you know. It takes expert examination—and the Federal Reserve doesn't have such experts. In fact, there aren't many such experts anywhere."

I was disappointed. "So Harrington, as far as you know, never ran across, say, a case where counterfeit securities were used as collateral for a loan or, say, where they were used to cover up a theft of the real securities?"

"I'm almost positive that he didn't."

"Was he ever in Bangor, Maine?"

"Certainly. Many times."

I thought for a moment. The Jars case had undoubtedly been

reported in the Bangor newspaper. If Harrington had been there at the time, he could have read about it. Or even met Jars. "What sort of memory did Harrington have?" I asked.

"An excellent memory. He was really quite an alert young man. And very personable."

"You never had any cause to be dissatisfied with him? He never had, say, a drinking problem?"

"No. In fact, I was sorry to see him go. And I don't think he would have gone, either, except that like so many of our people, the constant traveling began to get him down. And, of course, the job in Chicago did pay better."

I tried a different tack. "Tell me, Mr. Williams, did you ever hear of anyone named Clifford Jars?"

"Clifford Jars," he repeated thoughtfully. "I don't believe so. In what connection?"

"He was part of a counterfeiting ring that was operating in Bangor about eight years ago."

"And you think that there was some link between him and Wesley's—ah—murder?"

"I don't know. You say that Harrington used to visit Bangor. It's possible that the two of them got to know each other."

Williams didn't reply. I could see by his expression, however, that he didn't think it likely. And that the idea of a former associate of his being involved with criminals didn't sit well with him.

"Did you know Harrington's wife?" I asked.

"Vera? Certainly."

"What's your opinion of her?"

Williams smiled. His smile was like his eyes—agreeable but cool. "I've found it a good policy not to speculate too much on the wives of the men I work with. I'm almost always wrong about them." The smile vanished. "I'd say that she's a good woman. Possessive, maybe. She didn't like Wesley's being away from home as much as he was. And ambitious. I've the feeling that she's responsible for his accepting the job in Chicago. She was anxious for him to get ahead."

That seemed a reasonable assessment. I considered other questions but decided there was no point in asking them. Williams had told me about as much as he could. "Well, thank you," I said, getting up. "I appreciate your help."

He got up too. "I don't know how much help I've really been. Needless to say, I'm awfully sorry to learn of all this." We shook hands. "I'd like to know what happened, if and when you find out."

I promised to tell him, if and when. He walked me to the door. I continued on and rang for the elevator, feeling vaguely let down. Williams, I was certain, had done his best, but the interview hadn't been productive. Aside from the fact that he'd had a good education in the morality and immorality of bankers, I didn't know any more about Wesley Harrington than I'd known before. But perhaps that was all it was necessary to know. An ordinary man, intelligent and friendly, who traveled the length and breadth of New England, making sure that banks with national charters operated according to the rules. A man with an ambitious wife. A man who'd frequently been to Bangor and who may have had an opportunity to meet Clifford Jars. To meet him —and later to remember him.

The elevator came. I got in and pushed the button for the ground floor. There were no other passengers in it.

A waste of time, Tom had said. And that was what it had been. The answer to Harrington's death lay not in Boston but in Maine.

The elevator reached the ground floor. The door opened. I stepped out.

And for an instant everything in the world came to an utter halt.

Timothy Arco was leaning against the wall across from the newsstand. He was looking straight at me.

34

I couldn't move. Or think. Or speak. I couldn't even feel. I was a piece of stone.

There were other people in the arcade. I'd been aware of them when the elevator door opened, but I no longer was. And if there was sound I didn't hear it.

Arco. A single image. My mind had locked around it and could absorb no other.

One man, thirty feet away.

Two eyes, focused on me.

A pair of hands, sunk into the pockets of a pair of gray pants. In one of those hands, undoubtedly, a gun.

How long I remained like that I don't know. Two seconds. Three seconds. Five seconds. An eternity.

Someone jostled me. I returned to life. I took two steps backward. I was in the elevator again. The person who'd jostled me was a man. He pushed one of the buttons on the control panel. The door closed. The elevator rose.

I groaned. The other passenger looked at me but said nothing. I put my hand on the wall of the elevator to steady myself. I suddenly felt very weak.

The elevator stopped. The other passenger got out. I wanted to follow him, to grab him by the arm, to tell him that there was a man in the arcade who intended to kill me. But before I could get myself to do it, the door closed again. The elevator continued its ascent.

Go back to Williams' office, I thought. Have him call the police. Which floor was Williams' office on? I couldn't remember.

The elevator stoped again. A woman got on. She had a stack of envelopes in one hand. She pushed the button for the ground floor. The elevator started down.

No, I thought. I can't go back to the arcade.

I pushed the button marked three and when the elevator reached the third floor, I got out. Williams, I thought. Federal Reserve. Which floor? One of the lower ones. Not this one, though. This one is unfamiliar.

My mind began to clear. The first floor above the arcade, I remembered. The one that was called the mezzanine. But was Williams' office the place to go? Arco obviously knew I'd been there. That was the first place he'd look.

My mind cleared further. He wouldn't shoot me in front of witnesses. Not in a building such as this, in which the corridors were short and narrow—it would be too difficult for him to escape. In fact, he probably hadn't planned to kill me in the arcade either. Merely to follow me out onto the street, into the crowd. It would be easier for him there.

In Williams' office I'd be safe.

I looked around. There had to be a stairwell. The stairs would be better than an elevator. An elevator was like a trap.

The stairwell was behind a closed door on the Devonshire Street side of the building. Anyone who followed it to the ground floor would emerge near the newsstand.

I started down. Cautiously. Pausing every few steps to listen. Arco might still be waiting in the arcade or he might have decided to search the upper floors. There was, as far as I could tell, no way out of the building except through the entrances at each end of the arcade or through the bank. And the bank was one large open area, completely visible through the glass wall that

187

separated it from the arcade. A person standing opposite the elevators could keep an eye on the bank as well as the other two entrances.

Arco knew this, for he'd undoubtedly had ample time to reconnoiter. So he was probably waiting in the arcade. Yet I couldn't be sure.

I reached the floor below. The door to the corridor was closed. I opened it a few inches and peered out. There was no one in sight. But the arrangement of offices wasn't as I remembered it. Then I realized that the mezzanine must be down yet another flight from what was called the second floor. I quietly closed the door.

After two steps, however, I halted. Someone else had entered the stairwell. I flattened myself against the wall and held my breath, uncertain whether the sound had come from above or below.

Shoes scraped on a hard floor. The sound came from below. And whoever had made it was near.

I didn't wait. I spun around and in one stride was back on the second-floor landing. I threw open the door and raced into the corridor. I turned right and headed for an office—any office—but as I ran I caught sight of a man standing in front of the elevators, and a moment later one of them arrived. "Hold it!" I called, and raced across the corridor. I reached the elevator just as the door was beginning to close. I squeezed inside.

The elevator started down. I raised my hand to push the button for the mezzanine, but I noticed a button on the control panel that I hadn't paid attention to before. It was marked "V." Vault, I thought. I pushed it.

The elevator reached the ground floor. The other passenger got out. I pushed the "V" button again. The door closed. The elevator continued down.

I stepped out into a small carpeted lobby. It was directly under the arcade. On one side was the entrance to the safe-deposit boxes, on the other the stairway leading up to the ground floor of the bank. I hesitated, then started up the steps, hoping that if Arco was on the other side of the glass wall he wouldn't be looking in my direction.

I reached the ground floor. I didn't see Arco. I walked briskly across the floor to the revolving door that led to the street. And presently I was outside.

My heart pounding, I prayed that a taxi would come by. None did. I turned and moved swiftly to the corner. A sign told me that I was at the intersection of Arch and Franklin Streets. Fifty feet to my right was the Arch Street entrance to the arcade. A cream-colored sedan was parked at the curb opposite it. Someone was behind the wheel. I could only see the back of his head, but the picture of Paul Arco flashed through my mind. And if he was watching his rear-view mirror he could see me.

I hurried across the intersection. Two short blocks ahead was Washington Street. The foot traffic there was heavy. It would be easy to lose myself in the crowd. I quickened my pace and glanced over my shoulder. No one was following me.

But the cream-colored car had backed to the intersection and was turning into Franklin Street.

I began to run.

I didn't look back again. The first corner I came to was that of a narrow street, hardly more than an alley. On the far side of it were the rear entrances of the stores that faced Washington Street. I swung around the corner, ran across the pavement and yanked open the glass door that led into Woolworth's.

I was no longer reasoning. I was just running, a force in motion with no sense of direction. Down one aisle and across to another, not even aware of which way I was going. All I could think of was Tim Arco in the arcade of the building on Devonshire Street and the cream-colored car.

I jostled a stout woman who was reaching into her pocketbook. "Watch where you're going!" she snapped. The words brought me to my senses. I stopped. The panic subsided. Paul Arco couldn't be in the car and on foot at the same time. And his brother was still looking for me two blocks away.

I walked on, more slowly. I needed a place to rest, to work things out. The hotel might or might not be safe.

The exit to Washington Street was on my left. I went toward it and looked through the glass. There weren't as many people on the street as I'd imagined. Yet I couldn't remain in Woolworth's indefinitely.

I waited until a cluster of pedestrians passed the door, then went out and joined it. The people were walking north, toward Milk Street. I headed that way too, keeping as close to the buildings as possible. When I came to the corner I paused—and saw the cream-colored car. It was moving slowly down Milk Street, approaching Arch. It was too far away for the driver to see me. Nevertheless I backed against the wall of the building. At Arch Street the car turned. Evidently the driver intended to circle the area again.

I strode briskly across Milk Street. There was a taxi cruising east, past the Old South Meeting House. I tried to catch up with it, but the driver didn't see me and kept going. I glanced around. No other taxis. I walked a short distance farther and found myself in front of a Christian Science Reading Room. I went in.

There was a counter with books on it. An elderly man with a bow tie rose from his chair behind the counter and with a beatific smile said, "Good day." I nodded and kept going. On the other side of a glass door was a lounge. I entered it and dropped into a chair facing a long library table.

And suddenly the stream of adrenaline which had been squirting through my system dried up. I felt very tired. Let them find me, I thought. Let them kill me.

The possibility of their finding me was slim, however. There were too many shops in the neighborhood, with too many entrances and exits. They couldn't search every one. Besides, they wouldn't know that I was still *in* the neighborhood.

All they'd know was that I'd recognized them. By running I'd told them so. But would that stop them? No way.

I'd been lucky twice. I wouldn't be lucky the third time.

I sat there, breathing deeply, waiting for the return of energy. A worried-looking man with a bright green shirt and a brown necktie sat on the other side of the table, reading the Bible and moving his lips. He and a middle-aged woman, who was bolt upright in a wing-backed chair and had a shopping bag at her feet, were the only other people in the room. The woman was also reading. Except for the ticking of a large grandfather clock, the room was completely silent.

The thing to do was to get in touch not with the Boston police department but with O'Brien. Tell him everything and let him take over.

Would that solve my problem, though? As long as there were other killers available for hire, Lipp or Rasher could find replacements.

Anger swept over me. Anger at Rasher for his treachery. And at myself for my stupidity.

I looked at my watch. Twenty minutes past eleven. Was it safe to go back to the hotel? The Arco brothers had had all night to learn where I was staying. But then, if they'd wanted to ambush me outside the hotel they'd have done so.

What the hell, I thought. Ninety-nine and ninety-nine one-hundredths percent of the city of Boston is safe for me.

But the other one-hundredth of a percent—where was it?

I glanced around the room. The long tables, neatly arranged with books, reminded me of a school library. There were two books in front of me, held open with wire frames to the lesson of the day. One was the Bible. I picked up the other. The title was *Science and Health with Key to the Scriptures;* the author, Mary Baker Eddy. I glanced at the day's lesson. "Evil has no reality. It is neither person, place, nor thing, but is simply a belief, an illusion. . . ."

I thought of Jaime. I could actually feel the weight of him in my arms. I could see the stream of blood. I could hear the death rattle in his throat.

Evil was more than an illusion. Evil was what people sometimes did to other people.

I put the book back on the table. My strength and will began to return.

I sat in the Christian Science Reading Room until twelve-thirty, then placed a call to the Ritz-Carlton Hotel and asked to have David Chang paged.

Chang came to the telephone.

"I'm afraid I got tied up downtown," I said, "but I'm very much in need of a favor." And I told him what it was.

At ten minutes past one he picked me up at the reading room. He'd packed my bag and paid my bill at the hotel. He'd arranged for me to charter an airplane.

He drove me to the airport.

35

• • • • • • • • •

It was three-thirty when we landed in Bangor.

I told the pilot to stand by. Then I rented a car and drove the short distance from the airport to the Holiday Inn.

Harriet was in her room. The television set was on. And the *Wall Street Journal* was spread out on the bed, along with the latest issue of *Cosmopolitan,* a manicure set and a paperback edition of a book by Germaine Greer.

"I've been going out of my mind," Harriet said. "I've been sitting around here for five hours, waiting to hear from you."

"Sorry about that," I said, and turned off the television set. "Sit down."

She gave me a puzzled frown. "Is everything all right? You look angry." She sat down.

"I am angry," I said. "But not at you. Tell me about the Jars girl."

"There's not much more to tell. Her first name is Geraldine. She works at Freese's. That's a department store downtown. She sells dresses there. I tried to talk to her again. I went to the store first thing this morning. In fact, I was there before it opened. She remembered me, of course. She called the manager. Said I was harassing her. Threatened to call the police. I was asked to leave."

"I doubt that she'd have called the police."

"In any case, I didn't get anywhere."

"What kind of woman is she?"

"The kind who could curdle milk. No, that's not true. I don't know, Brock. She's had a rough time, I guess, and it's done things to her. She's quite young, really. No more than twenty-two or -three. But she looks older than that, because of her expression. She's bitter, and it shows on her face."

I'd often evaluated Harriet's work, but I hadn't in a long while evaluated her as a person. I did so now. She was a pretty woman, blond, small-boned, with large blue eyes—the kind of woman that any man would take a second look at. Yet I doubted that many did. Or that if one did he'd be tempted to start a conversation. For there was something about her—the way she carried herself, the way she returned your gaze—that discouraged intimacy.

"Why are you staring at me?" she asked.

"I'm sorry. I was just thinking. I'm going to have a go at her myself. But first I'd like to know everything you can tell me about her father."

"I can't add much to what I told you last night. He was a printer. He had a shop here in Bangor. How or when he got mixed up in counterfeiting I don't know. There were four other men who were involved with him. The printing business was evidently a legitimate operation, the counterfeiting a sideline. But it must have grown into a pretty big thing, because the FBI put in quite a bit of time tracking the gang down."

"What were they counterfeiting?"

"Money. I don't know what denominations."

"It doesn't matter. Go on."

"There isn't much more to say. The FBI finally got on the trail. They staged a raid on the shop. Eight years ago. The local police cooperated. Jars got away. No one seems to know just how. The policeman I talked to—the one up here who's retired—says he thinks he may have got out through a basement window."

"All the others were caught?"

"Two of them. The other two weren't there at the time. They were picked up later."

"But all four were convicted?"

"Yes. The only one who wasn't is Jars. They've never found him. They claim they're still looking, and maybe they are, but I doubt that they're looking very hard, what with all the other things they have to keep up with. And he wasn't the ringleader. That was someone named Sutton. Jars just owned the equipment that they used and was the one who made the plates. But the planning behind the whole thing and the passing of the money —that was Sutton."

"I see. Is Sutton still in jail?"

"I wasn't able to find out. You want me to keep trying?"

I shook my head. Sutton may have been the brains, but Jars had been the talent. "No. I want you to go back to New York."

She gave me another puzzled frown. "You *are* angry."

I realized that I'd spoken abruptly. I modified my tone. "You've done a good job, Harriet. I appreciate it. My being angry has nothing to do with you. I'm angry at myself. I walked into a trap this morning."

She said nothing.

"I should have been smarter," I added. I wondered whether to tell her what had happened in Boston. I couldn't tell her that without telling her everything else. And while I was deliberating, the telephone rang. "Who's that?" I asked.

"Probably the office," she replied. "No one else knows where I am."

"Answer it."

She did. And nodded confirmation. "Yes, Mr. Petacque," she said. "No, I'm still here. Yes, he got here a little while ago. You want to talk to him?" She handed the telephone to me. "It's Mr. Petacque."

"I had a hunch you might be up there," Tom said. "I tried to

195

reach you in Boston a couple of hours ago, and they said you'd checked out. I told Lieutenant Dodge you were probably in Bangor."

"Lieutenant Dodge?"

"From the Homicide Department. He wanted to know, and I thought I'd better tell him. But that's not the important thing. I spoke to Hardin Webster this afternoon. He knows you saw Patterson over the weekend."

"Good for him."

"Don't say it like that. It's made a difference. I was able to pump him. I learned something. He does have some inside information about Computech."

"Oh?"

"Lipp is planning to make another acquisition."

"Really? What's he planning to acquire?"

"Hardin wouldn't tell me. I doubt that he himself knows. Evidently it's something pretty big, though." Tom sounded excited.

"Nuts," I said.

"What's the matter with you, Brock? This is something you should find out more about."

"Nuts, Tom. I don't believe a goddamn word of it."

"Hardin wouldn't lie to me."

"Hardin wouldn't know. Hardin's doing what he's told."

"Sure, but Patterson'd know, if he and Lipp are so buddy-buddy. I think you ought to talk to Patterson."

"Forget it. And by the way, I'm not sure I'll be back in time to have lunch with you and Sir Archibald tomorrow. If I'm not, I'd like you to take Harriet instead."

"Sure. Anything you say. You're in a bad mood, I can tell that. What's the matter? Boston turn out to be a wild-goose chase?"

"Sort of."

"I told you so."

"Yes, you did. Anyway, thanks for the information. I'll be in touch." I hung up. I turned to Harriet. "How did Tom know you were here?"

"Irving told him, so somebody'd know where I was, because he himself was going to Detroit today. He called me around noon."

"Irving?"

"Mr. Petacque. Just to make sure I was all right. Irving had been worried about me, he said."

"Did you tell him what you were doing up here?"

"He didn't ask. He seemed to be in a hurry. He had another call waiting. Should I have?"

I considered. Someone had to know. And suddenly my thoughts took a nasty turn. "Is there a bar here?" I asked.

"Downstairs, by the dining room."

"Come on, I'll buy you a drink. I need one myself. But first call the airport. I want to make sure you get back to New York tonight. I want you to be in the office first thing in the morning."

Harriet made the call, and while she was making it my thoughts continued along the dark corridor they'd entered. Suppose I got killed—what then?

Harriet covered the mouthpiece with her hand. "I've missed the four o'clock," she said. "The only other one is at eight."

"Take it."

She made the reservation, and we went downstairs. The bar was a small dark room off the lobby. There were no other customers in it. I picked a table by the wall. We ordered. The waitress brought our drinks. I tried to force the idea of death from my mind, but it wouldn't budge. I knew that my death had been ordered and I'd faced the assassin—twice. But I hadn't yet thought of myself as being dead, and now I was doing it. A live Brockton Potter was viewing a dead Brockton Potter. And couldn't turn away from the sight.

"When you get to the office in the morning," I said finally, "I may be there or I may not. It depends upon how I make out with the Jars girl. If I'm not, I want you to call a little meeting. Irving will be back by then. I want you to get him together with Tom and Mark and tell them what you've been doing and what you've learned. But in order for you to do it properly I think I'd better tell you exactly what's been going on. Each of them knows part of the story, but none of them knows all of it."

I began with the telephone calls from Davis and gave her the details of everything that had happened up to and including my departure from Boston. She was a good listener. The dispassionate quality which might have been a drawback when she was with Geraldine Jars was an asset now. Whatever her feelings were, she kept them to herself, and I knew that if the occasion arose she'd present the facts exactly as I'd given them to her.

Her silence continued even after I stopped talking.

I finished my drink. "I could use another," I said.

She glanced at her own. She'd hardly touched it. "Not me," she said.

I got the waitress's attention and ordered a refill for myself.

At last Harriet spoke. "I can see what you mean about walking into a trap," she said.

"I should have known better," I said. "Rasher was being too helpful."

The waitress brought my second drink.

"You think he's the one who hired the Arco brothers?" Harriet asked.

"Not directly. I think he's the intermediary between Lipp and the man who actually did the hiring. That's the trouble with this whole thing. Even if one or both of the Arcos were caught, it would still be difficult to prove that Lipp is in back of the murders. There's always a danger when you go to hire a killer that the killer will someday point a finger at you. Lipp would know that. On the other hand, there's the other danger that if you involve too many people, one of the intermediaries will someday point a finger at you. What happened, I imagine, is that Lipp mentioned something, being careful not to be too direct, to Rasher, whom he trusted completely. And Rasher mentioned it to someone else whom *he* trusted completely. Who that person was we may never find out. But the idea originated with Lipp and was passed along by Rasher. I'm almost certain of that."

"So Lipp could never be blamed."

"Right."

"But the bonds . . ."

"That's something else again. If I'm able to locate Jars . . ."

"I'm sorry I wasn't able to be more helpful."

"I don't know that I'll be able to do any better with the Jars girl than you did, Harriet. But Jars is the key. Through him we may be able to prove fraud. Then the law could take over."

"You're convinced that the bonds were counterfeited?"

"Yes. Otherwise why the murders?"

"But the police or the Treasury Department—someone—could determine that, couldn't they?"

"Not if the counterfeit bonds have already been replaced."

She nodded. "And you think they have been?"

"I don't know. I think it's more likely that they haven't been. But I don't want to take any chances."

"But if the original bonds are back in the vault, how can you prove that the counterfeit bonds were ever used?"

"I can't. But at least there'd be something for the law to start with. And if Jars would talk, if he'd implicate someone at Inter-lake—Harrington, for instance—there'd be grounds for a thorough investigation."

"I just can't imagine that a man like Anton Lipp, with all his money, would resort to anything like that."

"A man like that is the only one who'd dare. And this is the point I want you to make tomorrow. All I have at the moment is a theory. I think it's the right theory, though. And if anything happens to me—if for any reason I shouldn't be able to continue working on it—I'd want the rest of you to carry on. I'm sure you would, and would eventually come to the same conclusions I have, but as a shortcut let me tell you what I believe.

"Building the kind of business Lipp has built requires certain qualities. You have to have a hell of a good head for figures and an eye that sees profit where others overlook it. You also have to be somewhat of a showman, a promoter, because you're constantly having to sell yourself. And you have to be a gambler. Lipp possesses all those qualities, plus the other essential: acquisitiveness. You have to want to keep on making money even after you've got more than you can spend."

"That's more or less the pattern," Harriet agreed. She lit a cigarette, although she rarely smoked.

"Well, I believe that somewhere along the line Lipp went a step too far. He overreached himself. He began speculating in silver futures, and you know how risky something like that can be. He must have taken a hell of a beating. And as the margin calls came up, instead of admitting he was wrong and getting out he kept putting up more money, waiting for a turnaround. He probably sold as much of his Computech stock as he dared without depressing the price—and still he needed more capital."

Harriet exhaled smoke. "So he dipped into the Interlake till."

"Exactly."

"But how much could he have lost?"

"Who knows? I read in the paper not long ago that one of the Texas oilmen is supposed to have made a quarter of a billion dollars in silver futures recently. And if one can make it another can lose it. I doubt that Lipp lost that much, but he probably lost plenty. Now he's trying to sell more Computech stock and in order to get the most for it he's spreading false rumors to people like John Patterson about the great things Computech is about to do."

A party of four men came into the bar. They appeared to be businessmen, the sort of middle-level executives who, along with vacationers, pour into the thousands of Holiday Inns and Quality Courts and Howard Johnson Motor Lodges on the outskirts of the small cities of America late every afternoon and check out again early the next morning. This group appeared to have had a few drinks already. They were in high spirits.

"You've got to use the whip on them," one said loudly as they passed our table. "It's the only thing that works."

"That's what I told Harry," said another.

Evidently there was a joke involved, because all four of them laughed.

I thought of Wesley Harrington and of all the other bank examiners who spent the better part of each week in cities such as this, drinking in motel bars, eating in motel dining rooms, whiling away the evenings in front of the television sets in motel bedrooms. It would be a lonely life. A local friend would be welcome company. A Rasher, a Jars—anyone.

"Where does Geraldine Jars live?" I asked.

Harriet took a small notebook from her pocketbook and gave me the address. It was on Broadway. She explained how to get there. Through the downtown business district, across the bridge, turn left at the top of the hill.

"Bridge?" I asked.

"There are a couple of rivers in town."

I finished my drink. "Do you need a ride to the airport?" I asked.

She glanced at her watch. "It's only six o'clock. But anyway I rented a car."

"Well, I'm going over there. I have to make some arrangements with the pilot. I'll probably spend the night here. Don't check out of your room. I'd like to use it—under your name."

More people came into the bar. I had a hard time attracting the waitress's attention, but finally she noticed me. I paid the check. Harriet and I walked into the lobby. We wished each other good luck.

"By the way," I asked, "do you happen to remember the date that the FBI staged the raid?"

"I didn't get the exact date," she replied, "but it was sometime . . ." She again took out the notebook and consulted it. "June is all I have."

"Thanks. That's all I need." We shook hands, and I walked out to the parking lot.

For a few moments I couldn't remember what my car looked

like or where I'd parked it. My mind was on something else: a river in Maine, in the month of June.

I checked the tag that was attached to the key ring, got the license number and found my car.

On the way to the airport I stopped at a gas station and picked up a map.

36

The plane was on the tarmac, where we'd left it. The pilot wasn't around. I finally found him in the coffee shop, perched on a stool at the counter, drinking coffee and reading *Penthouse*.

"Ready to go?" he asked, quickly closing the magazine.

"No," I said. "I'd like to stay here overnight. Can you arrange to stay too?"

He had to think it over. There was the time involved, he said, and his expenses.

I told him I'd pay for his time and his expenses.

There was no problem, then.

We went out to the plane, and he picked up a small kit that he carried for situations like this. I suggested that he have the plane refueled. He said he'd already done so.

I drove him to the motel, got him a room and left him to his own devices. I went up to Harriet's room. She'd gone. Except for the *Wall Street Journal,* which was neatly folded in the wastebasket, and an empty nail-polish bottle in the bathroom, there was no indication that she'd ever been there.

I sat down at the desk, opened the map and studied it. I came to the conclusion that I might be wrong about the river.

My thoughts turned to Geraldine Jars. To a girl who at fourteen or fifteen had suddenly been deserted by her father. Who at the same time had learned that he was a criminal, wanted by the

FBI. Who for eight years had been enduring the whispers and sidelong glances of her friends. Who had come to believe, because of the flaw in her background, that she herself was flawed.

I felt that I knew Geraldine Jars very well.

Around eight o'clock would be the best time, I decided. When she was relaxing after dinner.

If she was at home.

But she would be at home. A young woman like that seldom had dates.

I moved from the desk to the bed, and as I did so the image of Monica Lane crossed my mind. She was the other kind of woman —the kind who, instead of enduring pain, inflicts it. Just for kicks.

Monica Lane, Vera Harrington, Anton Lipp, Richard Rasher, Malcolm Davis—it had been a long trip in terms of people as well as miles. I was nearing the end of it, however. One more place, two more people.

Mrs. Ackroyd, Philip Quick, Jack Williams—the procession continued across the lens of my memory. Until O'Brien and Sestino appeared. At that point something in my subconscious registered. My thoughts briefly entered the same dark corridor they'd traversed before. But only for a short while. A dead Brock Potter, I assured myself, would be of no value to anyone.

I reached over and picked up the telephone.

O'Brien said it was a good thing I hadn't called any later, as he was just getting ready to go home. He'd received my message from Boston, he added.

"Well, as you probably know, I'm in Maine now."

"Maine? What the hell, Potter—"

"Bangor, Maine. Didn't Dodge tell you?"

"Dodge?"

I thanked the mechanism in my subconscious that had prompted me to make the call. For I knew what O'Brien was about to say.

I let him say it anyway, though.

There was no one named Dodge who was in any way interested in Jaime Ortega's murder or in me. There never had been.

37

• • • • • • • • •

A sign was nailed to a stake in the front lawn. It said: "HOUSE FOR SALE."

I could imagine someone wanting to sell the place but couldn't imagine anyone wanting to buy it. Weeds had sprouted through the cracks in the concrete walk that led to the front steps. One of the steps had a hole in it where someone had put his foot through a rotten plank. And the entire house listed to the left. A dying edifice in a dying neighborhood.

The door had a small glass panel. On the inside of the panel was a yellow lace curtain through which light was shining. I pushed the buzzer that was set into the doorframe, but nothing happened. The buzzer was broken. I knocked.

After a few moments the curtain was pushed aside and a face appeared. Wisps of hair dangling across a pale forehead. A narrow nose. Squinting eyes.

I smiled.

She opened the door.

"Miss Jars?" I said.

She said nothing. She was tall and painfully thin. The squint seemed to be permanent.

"My name is Brockton Potter," I said. "The name of my firm is Price, Potter and Petacque. We're stockbrokers, in New York. I'd like to talk to you for a little while if I may. Not about stocks." I gave her one of my business cards.

She didn't look at the card. She continued to look at me. "All right," she said finally. She stood aside to let me in and closed the door behind me.

The room to the right was a sort of parlor. I couldn't see much of what was in it. The only shapes I could distinguish were those of a round table and a lamp. The base of the lamp was of alabaster and seemed to glow in the reflected light from the hall. There was another room to the left, but the door to that was closed, and straight ahead was a stairway which led to the second floor. But the main source of light was at the back of the house, beyond the stairway: the kitchen.

"You want to know about my father," Geraldine said. "Like Miss Jensen."

I didn't ask how she knew. I guessed that the name of the company had given me away. I merely nodded.

"Come into the kitchen," she said.

The kitchen was evidently the room in which she spent most of her time. It was large enough to accommodate a table and four chairs as well as the usual appliances. Dishes were drying on a rubber rack beside the sink, a half-knitted sweater with yarn and knitting needles lay on the counter that abutted the stove, a dozen paperback books were stacked on the windowsill, and some African violets were doing their best to grow under the arm of a high-intensity reading lamp.

She'd been doing homework, I gathered. A textbook was open on the table, and there were notebook and pen beside it. The title of the textbook was *Accounting Made Easy*.

She seated herself on the chair in front of the open book and motioned for me to sit across from her. I did. So far so good, I thought. But then she said, quite flatly, "My father is dead, Mr. Potter."

I looked at her. Bitterness? I wondered. Not entirely. Rather, a tall and ungainly young woman with a near-sighted squint who'd never had any reason to believe she was desirable and who'd learned to reject others before they rejected her. "That's what Miss Jensen told me," I said. "When did he die?"

"What difference does it make?"

"A considerable difference, Miss Jars. A man in Chicago was killed recently, as was one of my staff. It's possible that their deaths were related in some way to your father."

She shook her head. "My father has been dead for years."

"I notice that this house is for sale."

She nodded.

"Are you the owner?"

She nodded again.

"Where do you plan to move to when you've sold it?"

Her chin went up, and she put her palms flat on the table. "That's no business of yours, Mr. Potter."

I smiled. "That's true enough. But don't get angry. I'm really not here to do you any harm, you know."

"My father is dead," she repeated. "I don't know why you're here or why Miss Jensen was here. I found her very objectionable and I don't think I like you either."

I kept smiling. "I can't say that I blame you. It must be very annoying, having people come around asking you about things you'd rather forget."

"I'm used to it. There've been plenty. Or there used to be. They finally stopped coming. But no, I don't like it. You wouldn't either. Now I think you'd better go." She got up.

I couldn't smile any longer. "Sit down," I said, "and tell me—if you didn't intend to talk to me, why did you invite me in?"

"I—"

"Never mind. I'll tell you. You live in hope. Alone, but in hope. Every time the doorbell rings—"

"Go, before I call the police."

"You're not going to call the police, and I'm not going to go."

"If you're not out of here in ten seconds, Mr. Potter—"

"Sit down and keep still, Miss Jars. If you call the police, I'll tell them why I'm here and what I know—that your father is alive and that you know where he is. And if you think you had people asking you questions before, just wait. There'll be more people knocking on your door, from more different agencies than you ever knew existed. And in case nobody's told you, withholding information as to the whereabouts of a wanted man is a very serious crime."

She went white. And clenched her fists. And glared at me. But she said no more about calling the police or about my leaving.

"I'm sorry," I said. "But I didn't come all this way to get lied to and thrown out. I don't mean to do you any harm, but I do want the answers to some questions."

She continued to glare at me.

"You're not planning to stay in Bangor, I take it. Once you sell the house, you're going to move away." I picked up the book on accounting. "And perhaps get a different kind of job."

She said nothing.

"Or else invest your money and live on the income. How much money do you have, Geraldine? Enough to live on for the rest of your life?"

Silence.

I perched on the table and let her go on glaring. "In case you don't know, the man who was killed in Chicago is Wesley Harrington. He was gunned down in his garage."

There was a flicker of something. Not much. Just a flicker. But she didn't speak.

I reached out and touched her shoulder. She cringed. "I can sympathize with you," I said. "I know what it's like. But I'll tell you something. Sooner or later you get over it. Do you smoke?"

She didn't indicate whether she did or not. But there was an ashtray on the countertop near the unfinished sweater, with a cigarette butt in it. I took a package of cigarettes from my pocket and held it out to her. She didn't respond. I took a cigarette for myself and lit it.

"Did you ever hear of Potter and Company?" I asked.

No answer.

"I don't suppose you did," I went on. "It was a pretty big company for its time. It dealt in mortgages—second mortgages, to be exact. My grandfather owned it. He made a lot of money from it. A couple of million dollars. And in those days a couple of million dollars was really a bundle."

She blinked and began to squint again.

"Well, anyway, along came the Depression, and second mortgages weren't worth very much. People couldn't pay their first mortgages, let alone their second. So between 1929 and 1932 my grandfather lost every dime he ever had. The company went broke, and he wound up with absolutely nothing. He had a heart attack a year later and died. My grandmother used to say he died of a broken heart and in a way maybe she was right, but at any rate he died, and not long after that my grandmother had a heart attack too. But she didn't die; she just became an invalid. I only remember her vaguely—she died when I was five—but I always think of her sitting up in bed or on the couch, because that was the way I knew her."

She nodded. In spite of herself.

"The one who got hurt more than anyone else, though, was my father. You see, he was only twenty when the company went bankrupt and he didn't know anything about making money. He'd had a pretty easy time up to that point and had never had to work and he was used to good things, and all of a sudden there he was with no money and no skill at a time when jobs were almost impossible to get, with an invalid mother on his hands and no brothers or sisters to share the burden. It was pretty tough."

I went across the room to get the ashtray. Geraldine followed me with her eyes.

"Some people were able to get back on their feet," I continued. "Others weren't. My father was one of the ones who wasn't. Eventually he got married, which in his case was a mistake, but I guess he thought he could handle it, and he and my mother had me, which was another mistake. But he was never able to make more than twenty dollars a week, and we all lived together in a three-room apartment in the basement of a building for which he was the janitor. They call them building engineers now but then they called them janitors, and they got free rent and a small salary. We were never cold and we were never hungry, but it was a long way down from the kind of life my father remembered—and eventually it got to him. He killed himself."

Geraldine made a sound. It was only a small sound, but it was quite audible.

"He hanged himself," I went on. "I came home from school one afternoon, and the fire department was there, and there were a lot of people standing around outside the door to our apartment, and one of them was the landlord, who lived in the building himself, and he took me and hustled me up to his apartment and kept me there, but I knew that something awfully bad had happened, and then later my mother came and got me and—well, that's all there was to it. But, you see, I'd always kind of liked my father—he seemed like a pretty nice guy to me—and for a long time I felt disappointed, like if he'd really cared about me he wouldn't have killed himself. I don't feel that way anymore, but it took years. So I guess I know how you must have felt, and probably still do. Right?"

I put the cigarette out. Geraldine watched me.

"May I have one?" she said finally.

I gave her a cigarette and lit it for her.

"Your father wasn't a criminal, though," she said presently.

"No," I agreed.

There was another silence. Geraldine broke it by saying, "My mother died of cancer. Two years ago."

I went back to the chair on the other side of the table.

"It took her a long time to die," she added.

I said nothing.

"I tried to look after her, but I also had to support us and toward the end . . ." She shook her head.

"You had no brothers or sisters, either."

She shook her head once more.

"Did your father have a boat?"

She gave me a startled glance. It told me all I needed to know.

"I've been thinking a lot about you the past couple of days," I said. "Even before we met I had the feeling that I knew you. Would you like to know some of the things I thought?"

"It was so hard," she said. "We had no money. Mother—"

"He took the money too? Well, let me tell you what I've been thinking. Correct me if I'm wrong. You thought your father was a pretty wonderful man, Geraldine, just as I thought mine was. You had no idea that he was mixed up in anything wrong. Then one day you came home from school, like I did, only instead of finding the fire department at your house you found the police, and a crowd outside wanting to know what was going on. The police searched the house and questioned your mother and maybe even questioned you—and that's the first you or your mother ever knew about what your father was up to. It was a hell of a shock."

Geraldine took a long drag on her cigarette, and as she exhaled the smoke a faint groan came with it.

"Nothing was the same after that. At school, at home—everything fell apart. And the situation never improved. If anything, it got worse. All because of what your father had done. Am I right?"

Half an inch of ash dropped from her cigarette to her lap, but she didn't notice. Her eyes were on me.

"All because of your father. And you began to hate him. Or at least part of you did. The other part of you missed him and kept hoping he'd come back. You knew he couldn't, but you kept hoping. And finally one day you heard from him."

She shook her head.

"You didn't?"

"Never."

"You went looking for him?"

She didn't answer.

"You knew where he was all along?"

She shook her head. "My aunt," she said.

"Your father's sister?"

She nodded. She took another long drag on the cigarette, then stubbed it out. She cleared her throat. "She and Mother never got along. But after Mother died I went to visit her. I thought she might have heard something. She lives in Canada, and I thought my father might have seen her. Either that or he was dead."

"You thought he might be dead?"

"I didn't know."

"Drowned?"

"You know about the boat, don't you?"

"No. It was just a guess. I thought of Canada, which was the logical place. New Brunswick is less than a hundred miles to the north, Quebec less than a hundred miles to the west, and Nova Scotia about the same distance to the east, across the Bay of Fundy. But I figured that if the FBI was going to raid the printing shop, one of the first things they'd do is notify the officials at the border, just as a precaution. If your father had tried to cross into Canada by car he would have been picked up, and since he wasn't I figured that he might have escaped some other way—by boat. He could go right down the river to the bay, then north along the coast to New Brunswick or east to Nova Scotia. The only thing that surprises me is that he wasn't picked up, going down the river. Is the river navigable?"

"The boat was in Bar Harbor."

"Ah." I tried to recall the map. "That isn't far from here."

"Fifty miles."

"And he drove to Bar Harbor?"

"He couldn't get to the car. A friend drove him. I didn't know

213

—he never told me. He never told me anything. I only found out a few months ago. This man—his friend—he told me."

"And the friend was Wesley Harrington?"

Geraldine nodded.

"The FBI didn't know about the boat?"

"Not until afterward. And it was never found."

"He probably scuttled it."

"I don't know. He didn't tell me. He didn't tell me anything. He —he's remarried. He remarried while Mother—he married this other woman six years ago. They have—two children. I have a little brother and a—a—a little sister. He—he—" Her voice broke.

Not only a counterfeiter, but also a bigamist.

Geraldine was rubbing her eyes with her knuckles. After God knew how much effort she'd finally, through her aunt, tracked her father down, only to find that she'd been replaced. And yet she hadn't turned him in. I wondered what I'd have done under those same circumstances. Probably the same thing, I decided. But the resentment I'd felt before would have been nothing compared to the resentment afterward.

She stopped rubbing her eyes. She swallowed. "I did wrong, didn't I?"

"Wrong?"

"I should have told the police where he was. I wanted to. I really wanted to. I couldn't, though. I just couldn't."

And Clifford Jars had undoubtedly counted on that. Nevertheless, seeing her must have given him quite a turn. "I'm not going to pass judgment on that," I said.

"Am I in trouble?"

"Not if nobody knows. And I don't expect to have to let the word out. But you did tell someone where your father is. You told Wesley Harrington. Didn't you?"

"He was a friend of Daddy's. He was the one who helped Daddy get away, he said. I didn't think he'd do Daddy any harm."

"And he didn't. He gave him a chance to make some money. He

also gave you money, didn't he? Quite a bit of money."

She looked away.

"It doesn't matter," I said. "That's water over the dam. But I too want to know where your father is. I want to talk to him. And I'm not going to offer you anything for the information; I'm simply going to ask for it. Where is your father, Geraldine?"

She drew herself up. A stubborn look came into her reddened eyes.

"You'd better tell me," I said. "Otherwise you aren't going to get a chance to enjoy that new life you're looking forward to, because even though I don't want to, I'll go to the police with everything you've said."

The stubborn look departed. Alarm appeared. "You said you wouldn't!"

"I said I didn't expect to. And if you help me I won't." It's not blackmail, I assured myself; it's an act of kindness. I wasn't sure, however.

"Oh, God."

"Don't go on hurting yourself," I said.

Her shoulders sagged.

I said nothing further.

But presently I walked out of the house with the knowledge that Clifford Jars was alive and well and living no more than a hundred and fifty miles away, in Yarmouth, Nova Scotia, and that under the name of Frederick Clark he was the owner of a company called Guardian Printing Ltd.

38

● ● ● ● ● ● ● ● ●

It took us longer than it should have to file our flight plan. The pilot had never flown to Canada. He wanted to make sure that the runway at the Yarmouth airport was hard-surface, that there were radio facilities and approach lights and that the octane content of the Canadian fuel was all right for his plane.

The flight also took longer than it should have. The thirty-mile-an-hour wind which was sweeping across the Bay of Fundy from the general direction of Newfoundland knocked the light plane about and made it difficult to stay on course. It was one-thirty in the morning when we finally landed.

Claude Goulet was waiting for us. He resembled a big brown bear that had somehow been fitted out with a plaid shirt and jeans. He grinned when he saw me and enveloped me in a hug that all but cracked a couple of my ribs. "This is a nice surprise—no?" he said.

I backed away and looked him over. He hadn't changed. There was a little more gray in his beard, perhaps, and the splayed lines at the corners of his eyes were a bit deeper, but the quizzical expression and general air of good will were still there, and if he considered it an imposition to have been asked to drive eighty miles in the middle of the night without having been given an explanation, he showed no sign of it. He'd even brought a thermos of hot coffee.

Because of the wind, the pilot felt that he should put the plane in a hangar, and while he made the arrangements I told Claude briefly why I'd come. I didn't give him much in the way of background. I merely said that I was trying to catch up with a man who'd once done some counterfeiting in the United States and was now, as Frederick Clark, up to his old tricks, in Yarmouth.

He regarded me with amusement. "You want to hire him?"

"No. To get an admission from him."

He continued to look amused. "You want him to confess what he's done?"

"Yes."

He laughed and clapped me on the knee. "You have a sword?"

I rubbed the knee he'd hit. "A sword?"

"A knight should have a sword, shouldn't he?"

I suggested that he break open the coffee.

The pilot returned presently, expressing awe over a new Lear jet he'd seen in the hangar, and we went out to Claude's station wagon.

The drive into town was a short one. The Grand Hotel was the best place to stay, Claude said, and that was where he took us. But when we arrived he refused to let me get out of the car. The pilot could stay at the hotel, he ruled, but I must come to his house.

"But that's on the other side of the province," I protested.

"Only eighty miles. I'll drive you there and back. It's better that way."

"But, Claude—"

"It's better that way," he repeated firmly.

He was right, I knew. And he'd evidently guessed at some of the things I hadn't told him. "Very well, then."

The pilot went into the hotel, and Claude and I drove off. We retraced our route to the airport, passed it and kept going. I recalled the map I'd studied in Bangor. Yarmouth was on the southwest coast of the peninsula, and Shelburne, where Claude was staying, was on the southeast coast. The distance between the two towns wasn't great as the crow flies, but the highway followed the irregularities of the coastline, which increased the mileage. The two-lane road curved and dipped, skirting bays and inlets, over a countryside which, in the high beam of the wagon's headlights, seemed mostly to be a forest of stubby evergreens. Fishing villages appeared suddenly and disappeared just as suddenly. A church, a cluster of houses, their yards piled high with unused lobster traps, a school—all dark—and then nothing.

After a while I began to doze. I'd been up for over twenty hours, but it seemed longer. The wild fear I'd experienced in the building on Devonshire and in the streets around it had taken something out of me. So had the encounter with Geraldine Jars. I was running out of steam.

I must have slept for a few minutes, for suddenly my body gave a convulsive jerk and I opened my eyes wide, positive that one of the Arco brothers had come up on each side of me and that they were forcing me into an automobile.

I looked around. Claude's profile, the swath of light ahead of us, the black shapes of trees brought me back to reality.

"You had a bad dream—no?" said Claude.

"I must have," I replied.

He said nothing for a while. I tried to shake off the uneasiness that the dream had produced. Finally he said, "You've become a detective, isn't that so?"

"You mean because I'm tracking down this Clifford Jars?"

"No. Because you found me."

"That was easy. Rodney Alpert gave me your address."

"Ah."

I glanced at him. Anyone else, I realized, would have asked immediately upon picking up the telephone how I'd known where he was, for under ordinary circumstances it would have been impossible to locate him—he was staying in a house that belonged to someone else. But Claude hadn't put the question to me until now, after he'd spent hours trying to figure it out for himself. "I bought one of the pictures you sent him," I said.

He grunted and asked which one. I told him. He said he was glad that I was the owner of the picture; he'd wondered into whose home it might go. Then he said, "I'd exhausted myself with people. I wanted something different. A seacoast. No?"

I recalled the day I'd bought the picture. Recalled the moment of Jaime's death. I sighed heavily and said, "I've about exhausted myself with people too."

"You are in trouble—no?"

I decided to tell him. "Yes. There's a contract on my life."

"A contract?" he asked, puzzled.

"Someone has ordered my assassination."

"That can be done?" He pondered for a moment. "Yes, that can be done."

I waited for him to ask who'd ordered the assassination and why.

He didn't. He merely said, after a moment, "Tomorrow I'll show you where I painted the picture. Perhaps the same gull will be there."

We drove on. There were no other cars on the highway. A town loomed ahead of us.

"Birchtown," Claude said. "Shelburne is next."

After a few more miles we came to a sign which announced that we were about to enter a limited-access highway. Another sign gave the distance to Halifax, which was where the highway led, and to Shelburne, which was down a side road to the right. Claude turned onto the side road, and presently we were passing through the outskirts of a town.

The houses were dark, the signs in the shopwindows were off. The community didn't appear to be a large one. The shape of the houses, the character of the businesses on the main street, gave me the feeling that I was in the midwestern part of the United States, in a town whose time had come and gone.

"They build ships here," Claude said. "Wooden ships. And they fish. The harbor is very good—no?"

We turned off the main street and went down a hill, and there the harbor was, a vast bay, black as ink. Almost at the water's edge the narrow street swung to the left. Claude followed it for a short distance, then pulled the wagon into a driveway. "At last," he said. "My house by the sea. Someday I hope to buy it."

I got out and looked at his house by the sea. It was old and tall and built of frame, with a steep roof. We went inside and Claude turned on the lights. He led me into the parlor. The house belonged to a woman named Anne Hardwick. Judging by the furniture, she was an elderly woman and she'd lived in the house for a long time. The room was crammed with heavy Victorian pieces which looked as if they might actually have been made during Queen Victoria's lifetime, with bric-a-brac, with plants. But Claude had made his presence felt also: the air smelled strongly of turpentine.

Miss Hardwick, Claude said, was eighty. She'd been a schoolteacher. She was now visiting her sister, who was eighty-five, in Vancouver. There was a possibility that she'd remain in Vancouver. "But you're tired, aren't you?" he added. "Let me take you upstairs."

I followed him up the narrow staircase and into a bedroom which faced the street. The odor of turpentine was even stronger on the second floor. The bedroom had a four-poster bed, a plush-covered armchair with crocheted antimacassars on the back and the arms, lace curtains and half a dozen trailing plants on the windowsills.

"You will sleep well in this room, I think," Claude said. "No?"

"Not too well, I hope," I replied. "I want to get an early start in the morning."

"Even a knight must sleep. Even a detective. No?"

"Even a stockbroker," I admitted, and sat down on the bed. It was very comfortable.

And I did sleep well in that room.

The sun was high and bright when I awoke. My watch said ten o'clock. Son of a bitch, I thought, and looked at the watch again.

There'd been a time change, I remembered, but I hadn't bothered with it. Nova Scotia was on Atlantic Daylight Time. Actually it was eleven o'clock.

"Claude!" I called.

There was no answer.

I went into the hall and looked around. I found the bedroom which Claude occupied. There were several unfinished canvases propped against the walls. The bed hadn't been made.

"Claude!" I called again. Receiving no answer, I went downstairs.

Claude was not on the first floor either. The thermos was on the kitchen table, along with a note. The note said, "The coffee is hot. Will return. C."

I opened the front door and looked outside. Claude wasn't in sight, and the station wagon was gone.

I closed the door. And sat down to wait.

He's a fool, I thought. He can't handle it. He'll get himself hurt.

39

· · · · · · · ·

I dressed and went up the hill to the main street of the town. I tried to rent a car. There was no place to rent one. I returned to the house, but didn't go inside. I stood in the front yard, looking at the driveway where the station wagon had been, thinking what a mistake I'd made by telling Claude anything about Jars and what a mistake Claude had made by involving himself.

After a while I turned away and walked slowly along the narrow street that separated the houses from the bay. A sign said that this was Dock Street. As I walked I attempted to convince myself that Claude hadn't driven back to Yarmouth. I considered other places he might have gone in the car, routine chores which might have taken him away from the house. He might even have driven to some spot outside town to get in some morning painting. But I couldn't bring myself to believe that under these particular circumstances, with my having popped unexpectedly into his life claiming that someone was out to murder me, he'd go calmly off to spend the morning at his easel. Not Claude. And I couldn't think of any routine chore that would keep him away from the house for more than half an hour. Furthermore, the fact that he hadn't mentioned in his note where he was going or when he'd be back indicated that he was up to something he felt would worry me.

I remembered a remark he'd once made. The reason he and I

got along, he'd said, was that both of us were romantics. I'd disagreed. Romantics didn't last long in the stockbrokerage business, I'd replied. But I'd thought that while he was wrong about me, he was right about himself. He was a romantic.

And romantics can't stay away from trouble. It attracts them.

Besides, Claude was a man with enormous confidence in himself. In some ways the confidence was justified. He'd had the will and the juices to develop from a poor, meagerly educated youngster into an artist of international repute. But in other ways it wasn't. He wasn't equipped to deal with someone like Clifford Jars.

There was a small park at the end of Dock Street. So small that it could barely accommodate the information kiosk and the commemorative plaque which stood on it. I stopped there. The kiosk was evidently used only during the summer tourist season; it was deserted now. I read the plaque. It explained that Shelburne was a Loyalist town. It had been founded by Americans who wanted to remain under British rule after the American Revolution. I recalled something I'd once heard: half the graduates of Harvard who were living at the time moved to Nova Scotia after the Revolution. I pictured a sailing ship anchored in the bay, and men rowing ashore with their families in small boats. Men like Claude Goulet—independent men. And men like Anton Lipp— for he too was independent.

I turned back toward Miss Hardwick's house. The bay, on my right, was a beautiful expanse of water, cobalt blue in the noon sunlight. A rowboat—perhaps the one Claude had painted— floated a few feet from shore, tied to a cleat. And beside the cleat a gull stood, watching another gull which was circling.

Counterfeiters aren't murderers, I told myself. Neither are bigamists. Men who are capable of certain crimes aren't capable of all crimes.

I wished that Claude would return, though.

It had taken us two hours to drive from Yarmouth to Shel-

223

burne. If Claude had left the house at seven o'clock, he'd had more than enough time to complete a round trip. But had he left the house at seven? I didn't know. He might have left at six or at nine. Even if he'd left at nine, though . . .

What could he have hoped to accomplish? I wasn't even sure that I could accomplish anything myself. But I had a weapon which he didn't have: information with which to threaten. There were a lot of facts I could throw at Mr. Jars-Clark which Claude knew nothing about.

I reached Miss Hardwick's house and kept going. There were only a few houses on the street, all of them, like hers, relics of a period when bricks were scarce and land was cheap. The house in the next block had a neat stack of lobster traps in the yard. So did some of the other houses. I walked until I came to a barnlike structure which was built over the water and had a sign that said "BRUCE'S WHARF." I looked inside. The place was a combination tavern and restaurant. I went up to the bar and ordered a beer.

A thought struck me. A person might not be able to rent a car in Shelburne, but he could certainly rent one in Yarmouth. And the pilot was in Yarmouth.

I left the beer untasted and hurried back to the house. The telephone was in the upstairs hall. I took the steps two at a time, grabbed the instrument and impatiently began to jiggle the disconnect lever. Nothing happened. Then I pulled myself together and dialed the operator. She was helpful. And presently someone said, "Grand Hotel."

The pilot was in his room. And angry. He'd expected to hear from me earlier, he said. What time were we going back to Boston? When I told him that I wasn't sure, he became even angrier. It was Friday, he said, and he had another trip lined up for Saturday morning. He'd agreed to fly me from Boston to Bangor, not over the whole damn Northeast. He didn't intend to stay in Nova Scotia one minute beyond four o'clock that afternoon. I explained that I was eighty miles from Yarmouth and couldn't possibly be ready to leave by four. I might even have to stay over another night. That was my tough luck, he said; if I wasn't at the airport by four he'd go without me. I reminded him that I hadn't yet paid him. To hell with that, he said; Dr. Chang had given him a credit card, which was good enough. "Four o'clock," he repeated, and abruptly hung up.

I put down the telephone and looked at my watch. Ten minutes past one, Nova Scotia time. Even if Claude were to return now, I couldn't be in Yarmouth before midafternoon.

Dark thoughts converged from all directions. I fought them off. Claude wouldn't do anything that was really reckless. Nothing had happened to him. He'd be pulling into the driveway momentarily. And it didn't matter whether I caught up with Jars a few hours sooner or later; the result would be the same either way. I'd get the information I wanted from him. I'd fly back to New York on a commercial flight, deliver myself to O'Brien, give him a complete account of the counterfeit bonds and my dealings with Interlake. I'd ask to be put under police protection until I could prepare my facts for the Insurance Commission—and this time I'd simultaneously notify the SEC. Everything was going to be fine.

I walked into the kitchen. The coffee in the thermos was still hot. I drank some. Then I went outside. I crossed the street and stood at the water's edge, gazing at the far shore of the bay. I imagined Clifford Jars sailing into a bay such as this, pulling the plugs from his boat, rowing ashore in a dinghy. A latter-day refugee. Refugee? No. Fugitive. The entire coastline of Nova Scotia and New Brunswick was like this; there were hundreds of natural harbors, many of them obscure. Jars would have had an easy time.

I imagined him traveling around Canada on the money he'd salvaged. He'd probably enjoyed every minute of it. I imagined him acquiring a new identity, a new wife, a new business, eventually even feeling confident enough to contact his sister. Strange that he'd chosen to settle down so close to the place he'd started from. Or maybe not so strange. The setting in southern Nova Scotia wasn't too different from what he'd always known; he probably felt more comfortable here than elsewhere. And with his new identity it didn't matter where he lived.

I anticipated our talk. There was no reason to suppose that I'd get from him the information I needed. Yet I was convinced that I would. Of all the encounters I'd had since learning of Harrington's death, it seemed to me that the one with Jars would be the least difficult. It was mostly gut reaction on my part—a hunch— but not entirely. Of the three men who'd made up the phony policies that Yankee Clipper had sold to other insurance companies, I'd persuaded each of them separately that it would be to his advantage to turn state's evidence. And I'd had less leverage with them than I had with Jars.

I moved away from the water's edge and started again toward the park. I took only a few steps in that direction, however, when I stopped. Claude's station wagon had come down the hill and turned into Dock Street. My heart leaped. I waved. Claude put his arm out of the window and waved back.

I ran across the street and was waiting for him when he brought the car to a stop in the driveway.

"My God!" I exclaimed as he got out. "Where've you been? I've been going crazy!"

"I went to Yarmouth," he replied calmly. He appeared to be none the worse for wear, but his expression was bemused. He had a book in his hand.

"I thought so!"

"There's big excitement there today." He took me by the arm. "Come into the house."

He led me into the kitchen and put the book on the table. It was a Yarmouth telephone directory. He unscrewed the cap of the thermos and put his hand over the opening to feel whether the coffee was still hot, then drank some. "I almost got into trouble," he said.

"I was afraid you might."

"I thought I'd make some inquiries, on your behalf—no?" He opened the telephone directory and flipped through the Yellow Pages. He found the listing he wanted. "This is the company you are looking for?"

I peered over his shoulder. The category was "PRINTERS." The box he was pointing to was a small advertisement. "GUARDIAN PRINTING LTD.," it said. "Commercial Printing—All kinds—Brochures, Labels, Photocopies, Booklets, Business Forms, Post Cards, Rubber Stamps." At the bottom of the advertisement was the address and telephone number. "That's the company," I replied.

He nodded. "That's what I thought." He sighed. "You no longer need a sword. The dragon isn't there."

"The owner—this Frederick Clark . . ."

"He's disappeared. The police are looking for him. They think it's possible that he was killed."

40

● ● ● ● ● ● ● ● ●

I stared at him. "Disappeared?"

Claude put his hand on my shoulder. "That's bad for you?"

I sat down. "Very."

Claude pushed the telephone directory aside and perched on the table. "It has created great excitement. Yarmouth is a small place. Only eight thousand people—no? News travels fast."

"Disappeared," I said. I'd considered many possibilities. But not that one. And I should have. Someone had tipped Jars off. Geraldine? Perhaps. More likely one of Lipp's people, though. The telephone call to my office. The information that I was in Maine. An assumption that I'd locate Geraldine. The fear that she might tell me where Jars was. They'd guessed—and guessed right.

Haltingly Claude explained that he'd looked in on me early that morning, but I'd been sleeping so soundly that he hadn't had the heart to wake me. He'd then taken it upon himself to make my job easier by locating the printer himself. He hadn't intended to speak to him—merely to learn where he was. He hadn't thought that it would be difficult, but he'd wanted to make sure.

In Yarmouth he'd studied the telephone directory. There were only a few printers listed. He gone to the first one and asked for Frederick Clark. He'd been told there that Mr. Clark had no connection with the company but was the owner of Guardian Printing. Whereupon Claude had gone to the Guardian office—and run into the police. They'd arrived only a short time before and were questioning the employees. They also questioned Claude. What was his interest in Frederick Clark, and when had he seen him last? Claude had answered that he didn't know Mr. Clark, he merely wanted to order some brochures. The police had let him go. But instead of returning home immediately, he'd stayed in Yarmouth, trying to learn what had happened. At first he hadn't found anyone who'd heard of the disappearance, but by eleven o'clock the news was all over town.

Claude still didn't know precisely what had happened, but the rumor was that Clark had received a telephone call at his house the evening before. He'd told his wife that he was going out to meet some men on business. When he hadn't returned by midnight, she'd become alarmed and called the police. The police had located his car in the parking lot of the shopping center near the airport. They hadn't found Jars himself, however. Which led them to believe that he might have been kidnapped or even murdered.

"The jet," I said.

"Jet?"

"The private plane that my pilot saw in the hangar last night —it might have been sent here to pick him up. I wonder if the police know about it."

Claude frowned. "He received the telephone call early in the evening. The jet was still at the airport long after midnight—no? Besides, it would have been impossible for him to have passed through the airport unnoticed."

I recalled the layout of the airport. The hangar was quite a distance from the passenger terminal. It wouldn't have been too difficult for Jars to board the plane without being seen. But Claude was right about the time interval. If Jars was going to make a getaway, why would he have waited?

"Is it possible," Claude asked, "that the police are right—that he has been kidnapped or murdered?"

"I don't know," I replied. "All I can say is, I hope not." I got up. "Let's go."

"Go?"

"Into Yarmouth."

Claude nodded and got off the table. We went out to the station wagon.

My initial disappointment was wearing off, and as we sped out of town toward the main highway my mind began to work rapidly. The fact that Jars' automobile had been found in the parking lot didn't mean that he hadn't got away by car; it meant only that he'd had help. And possibly he'd gone no farther than Halifax. That was the nearest city, and it was large enough for a man to hide out in. It was unlikely that he was dead. He was part of Lipp's team, and Lipp might want to use him again in the future.

We reached the highway and turned toward Yarmouth. Claude put more weight on the accelerator.

Jars would eventually be found. But perhaps not for weeks or even months. Meanwhile I still needed to know about the bonds.

The countryside seemed quite different by day. The stubby evergreens, the bays and coves, the villages with their wooden churches and small schools, the fishing boats—nothing had changed, but at night with limited visibility everything had appeared small and compact, and in the bright sunshine the impression I got was just the opposite. This was a vast area—thousands of square miles of timberland and rolling hills, thinly populated. Properly equipped, a man could remain hidden for a long while. But on the other hand, a stranger coming into one of the small towns would be easily noticed. Jars had been lucky once. Would he be lucky twice?

Claude's thoughts were evidently similar to mine. "In a small place like Yarmouth," he said, "there's more safety than in a city, wouldn't you say?"

I didn't answer. It would be more difficult to attack someone on the street in a small town and get away with it. During the day, at least. But at night, I wasn't so sure.

Claude seemed to have reached the same conclusion, for he said, "You must continue to stay with me."

"I can't stay here indefinitely, Claude. I may be safe, but I have a business to run."

For a while he said nothing. There was more traffic now than there had been at night, and passing on the two-lane road was difficult. He had to concentrate. We were making good time, though. The little towns flew by. Barrington, Shag Harbour, Woods Harbour, Lower East Pubnico.

He hadn't dismissed the matter from his mind, however. For eventually he asked, "What are you going to do, then?"

"What the police were doing this morning. Question the employees."

He gave me a startled look.

"Unless Jars had a secret printing press somewhere, which I doubt, he must have used the equipment in his shop. Even if he made the plates himself—and I imagine he did—there must be someone in the place who knew what he was up to. And it's even possible that the plates are still there—if not in the shop, at his house or in his garage—somewhere. He may not have wanted to destroy them." I paused, and went a step further. "I wouldn't be too surprised, as a matter of fact, if he was working on new plates." Depending upon how badly Lipp needed money.

Claude guided the station wagon smoothly around a pickup truck that was carrying a large winch. "That may be. But what makes you think the employee would tell you?"

"In the past I've been fairly successful in getting people to tell me things that at first they didn't want to—by explaining how it'd be to their own self-interest to do so."

Claude grunted. "And if this time it doesn't work?"

"Then I'll go to the police—and hope that the plates haven't been destroyed." But it was liable to take the police a long time. And during the interval Lipp would be able to cover his tracks.

Claude grunted again, and sped around a car that had two bicycles lashed to the roof.

Lower Argyle, Central Argyle, Tusket—we were approaching Yarmouth. The highway widened. In the distance I could see the airport.

"Do you want to stop and find out about the jet?" Claude asked.

I looked at my watch. Five minutes past four. "Not now," I said. "Maybe later." The private jet, if it was still there, was less important than getting to the printing shop.

But as we drove along the field I saw a small plane taxiing down the runway. It was the plane I'd hired. No matter what happened now, I was going to have to stay in Nova Scotia for another night.

We passed the shopping center beyond the airport. "That's where the car was found," Claude said. He slowed the station wagon. I glanced at the cars parked in the lot and wondered whether the one belonging to Jars was still there.

Traffic was quite heavy now. It wasn't the bumper-to-bumper traffic of a large city, but there were stop signs and intersections at which it was necessary to wait behind cars that were attempting to turn.

I looked around. The town was really smaller than I'd imagined. There was only one main street. I admitted to myself that Claude was right: a place like this was safer than a large city. It would have been impossible for Jaime to have been murdered here as he had been in New York and the killers to have got away.

We passed the Grand Hotel and stopped for a red light.

"The shop is two blocks down," Claude said, "and around the corner."

The light changed. We moved forward.

"Don't come in with me," I said. "This is the sort of thing that I can do best by myself."

Claude cocked his head skeptically, but said nothing.

We came to the next stoplight. It was green. Claude turned the car onto a side street. He slowed our speed. "There it is," he said, pointing.

I wasn't prepared for anything so small. It was a dilapidated red brick building, two stories high, with two windows on the ground floor and three windows on the floor above. A hand-painted wooden sign over the door said "GUARDIAN PRINTING LTD."

"The police car has gone," Claude said.

I nodded. It wouldn't have taken long to question the few employees of a shop such as this. I doubted that there were more than four or five of them. Which would make my own job easier. "Let me off, and park," I said.

Claude applied the brake. He indicated the narrow driveway which ran along the side of the building. A small van was parked at the far end of it. "I'll be there, if you need me."

I crossed the sidewalk. The windows on the ground floor of the shop were covered from the inside with a pegboard which had samples of Guardian's work thumbtacked to them. Various kinds of stationery, calling cards and business forms. And there were a couple of posters which had nothing to do with the printing business. One was an advertisement for the Fun-Time Water Cruiser and Fishing Charter service, and the other called attention to Tuna Festival Week.

I backed away and took another look at the building. It seemed almost incredible that in a place as insignificant as this twenty-three million dollars' worth of bonds had been counterfeited to save the fortune of a man who was known in financial circles all over the world. But they had been; I was positive of it. I felt a quickening of excitement as I stepped up to the front door and turned the knob.

The front door was locked.

I glanced at my watch. Four twenty-five. The shop couldn't have closed so early.

I knocked. And thought I heard a movement inside.

The door opened.

A gun appeared.

"Come in," said the man who was holding the gun.

I'd never heard him speak before, but his face was all too familiar. He was Tim Arco. And Malcolm Davis was standing behind him.

41

• • • • • • • •

"Move," Davis said impatiently.

The muzzle of the gun was less than a yard from my chest. And seemed very wide. I came forward into the shop, and as I did so the two of them stepped backward. But the gun didn't waver a fraction of an inch.

Davis closed the door and locked it. "It took you long enough to get here," he said.

I managed to tear my eyes away from the gun. Davis was paler than I'd ever seen him. His expression was that of a man under great strain. Arco, on the other hand, appeared utterly calm.

I said a fervent prayer: Go for help, Claude.

Arco intercepted the prayer. "What about the other one?" he asked Davis.

"Where's your friend?" Davis asked me.

I had to swallow twice before I could speak. "He's gone."

"It's a blue station wagon," Arco told Davis. "See where it is."

The front of the shop was a small office. It was separated from the presses and typesetting benches by a waist-high partition. At the far end was a stairway. Davis left us and went up the stairs.

I looked at Arco. He was standing perfectly still, not even blinking, and the gun was like an extension of his hand. I looked beyond him, at the work area on the other side of the partition. There were three presses. All of them were idle. But a man was working beside the middle one. He was tying rope around a package. There were other packages, already tied, on the floor around him. He finished making the knots and put the newly tied package with the others. He came through the swinging door in the partition and sat down at one of the two battered desks in the office. He regarded me with mild curiosity. I'd never seen him before. I knew he wasn't Jars, though; he was too young. He said nothing.

I listened for sounds. The only ones I could hear were Davis's footsteps.

And presently Davis returned. "The wagon's parked in the driveway. The man's in it."

"Get him," Arco ordered. "Tell him Potter wants to see him."

Go, Claude. Go while you can.

Davis nodded. Arco motioned me away from the door. I didn't move. Arco brought the muzzle of the gun a few inches closer to my chest. I moved. Davis unlocked the door and went outside.

Don't believe him, Claude. Start the engine and go for the police. He's not armed. And he's lying.

One minute passed. Two minutes. I began to sweat. Then Davis came back. Claude was with him.

Claude saw the gun and raised his hands. He didn't speak. Davis locked the door again.

"Over there," Arco said to Claude. "Hands on the desk. You too," he said to me.

We obeyed. My face as I bent over the desk was only a foot from that of the man who'd been tying the package. Although he was young he had jowls and a double chin. And beard stubble indicated that he hadn't shaved that morning. Or, if the bloodshot eyes meant anything, slept the night before. But he was smiling.

"Frisk them," Arco said.

Davis patted us down, clumsily but thoroughly. "Nothing," he reported.

"Get the car keys," Arco said.

Davis went through Claude's pockets. "He hasn't got them."

"Look in the car," Arco said.

Davis went outside for the second time, closing the door behind him.

"You got any masking tape?" Arco asked the man on the other side of the desk.

The man got up, went through the swinging door to the back of the shop and began rummaging around.

And suddenly, in one swift movement, Claude spun around and lunged at Arco. I turned too.

Arco fired the gun.

Claude dropped to his knees and swiped at the gun with his hand. He missed. Then he went over on his side, blood trickling from his thigh, just above the knee.

"Son of a bitch," Arco said, and kicked him.

The other man came running from the back of the shop.

"Get the goddamn tape," Arco spat at him, and kicked Claude again.

Claude groaned.

I started to kneel beside him.

Arco kicked me too. The blow caught me on the shin. "Get back there," he said angrily.

Eying the gun, I retreated. My leg hurt like hell.

The other man returned to his search for the masking tape.

Davis came in, holding the keys to the station wagon. He saw Claude on the floor. The blood which was seeping from Claude's wound had formed a small pool on the linoleum. "Not here, you fool," he said to Arco.

"Shut up," Arco said. "Start loading the junk. Use the back door."

Davis stared at Claude a moment longer. Then, pocketing the keys, he went to where the packages were and picked up two of them. He carried them to the back of the shop, where there was a small door.

Claude groaned again and uttered an oath.

I looked at him. He was grimacing in pain.

Arco ignored him. He was watching me. The gun was again pointed at my chest.

I glanced once more at Davis. He'd put the packages down and was unlocking the back door. When the door was open he picked up the packages and took them outside. Junk? I thought. No way. Plates. The plates that had been used to print the bonds.

The other man came through the swinging door with a roll of tape.

"Their mouths," Arco instructed him.

The man nodded. He tore off a piece of tape and knelt beside Claude. Claude turned his head. The man pulled it around and slapped the tape on Claude's mouth. Claude made a stifled sound. The man put a second piece of tape over the first.

Davis reentered the building and picked up two more of the packages.

The other man noticed the pool of blood. "I'll have to clean that up," he said.

"You've got time," Arco said. "You told the others not to come back until Monday, didn't you?"

"Yes, but one of them might anyway."

Arco grunted.

The other man got up and came toward me with the roll of tape. He ripped off a piece and stuck it across my face from one cheek to the other. I tried to separate my lips but couldn't. Nevertheless, he reinforced the first strip with another.

"Now get some of that rope," Arco told him.

The other man put the roll of tape on the desk and started toward the swinging door, but paused beside Claude. "We'll have to carry him," he said.

"So we'll carry him. We've got four of us."

Four? Where was the fourth? I thought of the van. The younger Arco brother, or someone else? The younger Arco, I guessed. Behind the wheel of the getaway car, as usual.

The man with the jowls went through the swinging door.

"And tell Davis to move the wagon," Tim Arco said. "It's probably blocking the driveway."

"Right."

Davis returned. The man spoke to him.

"Paul's moving it now," Davis called to Arco. He picked up two more packages and carried them out.

I wondered where they were planning to dispose of us. Somewhere out in the country, no doubt. Where we wouldn't be found for days, if ever.

The man with the jowls stooped to pick up a length of rope from the floor beside the press. He coiled it around his hand and reached for something else. A knife.

I glanced at the gun. It looked as deadly as ever. I was getting used to it, though. Arco's eyes were shifting back and forth between Claude and me, so that he could fire at whichever of us made an unexpected move. But they focused on me longer, because Claude was out of action, his eyes screwed almost closed, muffled sounds coming from deep in his throat.

The other man came back with the rope and the knife.

"Tape their hands in back of them," Arco instructed him. "Then run rope all the way around them where their elbows are. Pull it tight as you can. I'm not taking any chances. Potter first."

The man stepped behind me. "Your hands," he said.

Arco frowned as he concentrated on what was about to happen. "Tight," he said.

"Your hands," the other man repeated.

But at that moment Claude unscrewed his eyes and reached out.

Arco caught the movement with the corner of his eye and spun around. Not quickly enough, though. Claude had gripped one of Arco's ankles. Arco fired the gun.

I threw myself against him, grabbing his wrist as both of us staggered and tripped over Claude. We went down against the partition. The second bullet had evidently hit Claude somewhere, for he was writhing on the floor, making dreadful strangled noises.

Arco tried to free his gun hand but he was squeezed between me and the partition, and I managed to hang on with one hand, forcing the gun out to the side. His confederate cowered for a moment beside the desk, but when he saw that the gun wasn't pointed at him he picked up the knife.

Arco squeezed the trigger. Wood splintered on the other side of the room. With my free hand I ripped the tape from my mouth and sank my teeth into Arco's wrist. He yelled. I tasted blood. I bit again and felt bone. The gun dropped to the floor. The other man had the knife poised. I snatched the gun and fired in his general direction. He doubled up, clutching his stomach, and went down, still holding the knife.

Arco kept trying to get out from under me. Blood was pouring from his wrist. I guessed that I'd punctured the artery. I aimed the gun at his head, hesitated a moment as I heard footsteps pounding across the shop, then pulled the trigger.

Arco died more quickly than Jaime had. More quickly than Harrington too, perhaps.

The footsteps stopped.

I stood up, the gun in my hand. Davis was staring at me, bug-eyed, ashen. He opened his mouth. No sound came out.

"Lie down on the floor," I said, pointing the gun at him, "and put your hands behind you."

He got down on his hands and knees and was about to stretch out when a figure appeared at the back door. I fired at it. Davis screamed and went down on his face, thinking that I'd fired at him.

The figure disappeared from the doorway. A moment later an engine roared.

I took my time taping Davis's wrists. And closed the back door very cautiously. Then I examined Claude. In addition to the wound in his left thigh, he had one in his right shoulder. But he was conscious.

I knelt beside him. "Thank you," I said.

And right after that I called the police.

42

• • • • • • • • •

The Canadian police were in no hurry to release me. They held me for three days and then made me stay in Yarmouth several days longer while they continued the search for Jars and for Paul Arco.

Arco was picked up on the fourth day when he attempted to cross the border into the United States at Niagara Falls. He'd got rid of the Guardian Printing van by then and was traveling in a car which he'd rented with a fake driver's license and a fake credit card in Halifax.

Jars hasn't been found yet and may never be found. From Davis the authorities learned how he'd escaped. The Fun-Time Water Cruiser and Fishing Charter service, which consisted of one thirty-six-foot sport fisherman, belonged to him, and he'd got away in the boat.

But some of the plates used to print the bonds were still in the shop, along with a supply of the kind of paper on which such documents are printed. These were impounded and would be sufficient evidence of the counterfeiting operation, in case I needed them. It was doubtful that I would.

Claude corroborated my story. So did Malcolm Davis. In fact, one of the reasons I had to stay in Canada so long was that Davis wouldn't stop talking. He went on and on. Partly because he was trying to convince the Canadian police and the FBI, whose representatives had arrived on the second day after Davis's capture, that he was an innocent victim of a scheme which hadn't been his idea in the first place—that he was merely carrying out orders. And partly, I think, because he simply had to get everything off his chest. At any rate, by the time he'd finished he'd told more than anyone really wanted to know, including things which I'd guessed at but hadn't been certain of.

On certain matters he lied and then told the truth later. On others he lied and stuck to his lies. But mostly he told the truth without hesitation. Including the key fact that the counterfeit bonds were still in the vault at the Monroe National Bank.

According to him, he didn't know about the counterfeit bonds until Harrington told him. Harrington had been approached by Rasher, who in a roundabout way had brought up the subject of counterfeiting and the counterfeiter from Maine whom Harrington had once mentioned to him, and before long Harrington had been engaged in an attempt to track the man down and hire him. For this Harrington had been paid fifty thousand dollars. Later, as the examination by the Illinois Insurance Commission approached, Harrington had become frightened that the examiners would discover the bonds to be counterfeit and that he'd be implicated. Furthermore, his conscience had begun to bother him. He wanted the truth to come out, but in such a way as to clear himself. He'd conceived the idea of contacting me, for he'd read about my role in the Yankee Clipper case.

He'd made the mistake, though, of confiding his thoughts to Davis. He'd done it when they were drunk, but Davis had remembered and brought the subject up when they were sober. Harrington had admitted his plan. Davis had then informed Rasher.

The way Davis told the story, his own motives had been pure. He'd merely wanted to save the company from a situation which would be harmful to it. In this I felt he was lying. He'd been afraid of losing his job because of his drinking, in my opinion, and wanted to ingratiate himself with Rasher. Not long after

243

that, Rasher came to him and hinted that it might be a good thing for someone to "speak" to Harrington. The manner in which Rasher said it made it plain that he intended something drastic. One word led to another, and presently Davis found himself in touch with Tim Arco. He'd heard of Arco from his friend Jerry Stone, the bartender at the Pillbox, and Jerry was the one who made the contact.

Davis insisted that he didn't know that Harrington was to be killed, that he thought Arco was only going to put a scare into him. In this he was obviously not telling the truth. Any more than he was telling the truth when he denied that he'd set Harrington up that Sunday night, and when he said that Arco hadn't been instructed to kill me but merely to frighten me into discontinuing my investigation.

What I found hardest to understand were Davis's motives in making the three telephone calls to me. He admitted making them. He claimed that Harrington talked him into it and that he himself saw no harm in doing so, since by then he knew I'd never see Harrington anyway. To me that didn't make sense. My own belief was that he never expected me to learn of Harrington's death and that he had a duplicate list of the missing bonds; that he intended to see me himself and sell me the list; but that he'd lost his nerve. I couldn't prove it, though.

Paul Arco, if he ever talks, may implicate Davis further. Or Rasher may. Rasher was picked up two days after Davis's arrest, in Mexico City. He might have got beyond Mexico, but the flight had been too much for him. He'd had a slight stroke in his room at the María Isabel-Sheraton and had been hospitalized.

At any rate, Davis will go to jail. So will Rasher, if he lives through the trial.

The only one who got away was the man who was the moving force behind the whole conspiracy: Anton Lipp. If you can call it getting away. He's in Brazil, safe from extradition. But by the time all the agencies that are going to investigate his affairs are through, he'll be broke. Or at least I hope he will. With a man like that, you never know how much money he has tucked away in numbered accounts. I suspect, though, that most of that hidden money was used to cover his losses in silver futures, which according to Sir Archibald Beardsley were enormous. And if he ever returns to the United States, he'll be arrested. For there's evidence to link him to the Arco brothers: it was his jet that flew them from Boston to Yarmouth, while Davis traveled on commercial planes via Toronto and Halifax. Besides, Rasher will blame as much on Lipp as he possibly can. The chain of command which worked in one direction—Lipp to Rasher to Davis —will work in reverse.

The day I left Yarmouth it rained. In fact, it rained so hard that there was a question as to whether the plane would be able to take off. It did, however, and once we were above the clouds the flight was a smooth one. Tom was with me. Both he and Mark had come to Canada immediately, to help extricate me from the grip of the Canadian authorities. Mark had already returned to New York, though, to make sure that nobody was stealing any of the office furniture or using the telephones to make personal calls.

I'd been to see Claude in the hospital the night before. His leg wound wasn't serious, but a bone in his shoulder had been chipped, and there was doubt at first that he'd be able to use his right arm freely. But now the doctors were certain that the arm would be fine. He was cheerful, but impatient to get back to work. He'd been doing some thinking, he said, and he had a new concept which he was anxious to experiment with. I didn't entirely understand it, but it had to do with the admixture of good and evil. He felt that in the past he hadn't probed deeply enough into the duality of all nature.

I understood the concept better, however, as I talked to Tom on the plane. For he was cheerful too, after we'd passed through the storm zone. He kidded me about getting us into trouble again with the SEC. I assured him that I wouldn't. I'd already made my appointment to see them on the same day that I had my appointment with the Insurance Commission. Furthermore, I'd instructed Irving to say nothing to any of our customers about either Computech or Interlake.

"It seems too bad in a way," he observed ruefully, "that we should know something and not be able to pass it on to the people who depend on us to give them information."

"They'll still be the first to know," I promised.

"Be careful," he said. "I don't want you to do anything that even borders on the illegal." And then, in the very next breath, he said, "It wouldn't be a bad idea if we sold short some Interlake and Computech ourselves."

"Tom!"

"Both stocks are bound to drop. We could make at least a quarter of a million."

"Under the circumstances that would be an out-and-out criminal act."

"We could do it through another brokerage house and have the stock held in street names. No one would know." He sighed. "But I suppose you're right. It would be a wrong thing to do." He smiled. "Well, anyway, it won't be the first good opportunity we've had to pass up."

"And it won't be the last."

"A lot of stockholders are going to get hurt anyway."

"I know. But Interlake is a damn good company. And Computech is basically all right too. Both stocks will eventually recover."

He smiled again. "You're a fine one to talk about criminal acts. You killed two men."

"Purely in self-defense." Arco's death didn't bother me. But I felt bad about the other man. He'd died on the way to the hospital. His name was Ian Gordon, and according to Davis he'd been Jars' assistant and confederate in the counterfeiting operation. I wished that he'd lived, for the sake of the case and for the sake of my conscience.

Neither of us spoke for a while. Finally, as the plane began to circle over JFK Airport, Tom broke the silence by suggesting that we get together the following Saturday for a few games of squash.

I accepted.

A few minutes later we were on the ground.

I hadn't expected a reception committee, but there was one: Detectives O'Brien and Sestino. The Canadian police had alerted them that we were coming.

There were, it seemed, a number of things they wanted me to explain.

And they weren't the only ones waiting, for as I came out of Customs I heard someone call my name.

I looked around and saw Carol.

Mark had told her I was coming in, she said. She wanted me to know how relieved she was that I was all right. In fact, she added, she was so relieved that she'd even decided to forgive me for not having called to tell her that I couldn't take her to see *Summer Song.*

Tom went home in a taxi. O'Brien and Sestino drove me to my house in their car, and Carol came with us.

The detectives remained with me in the den until after ten o'clock. They insisted that Carol not be present while we talked, so she'd left the room.

She hadn't left the house, though, for as I accompanied the detectives to the door I heard music coming from the bedroom, and when I went upstairs I found Carol on my bed with a book on her lap and my portable radio beside her.

We had something to talk about, she said, and before I could ask her what it was she told me. She wanted to know exactly what it was about her that I didn't like.

I said that there was nothing about her that I didn't like.

Well, then, she asked, why couldn't we still be friends?

I assured her that we still were friends.

But I suspected that what she had in mind was something more than friendship.

And, as I presently found out, I was right.

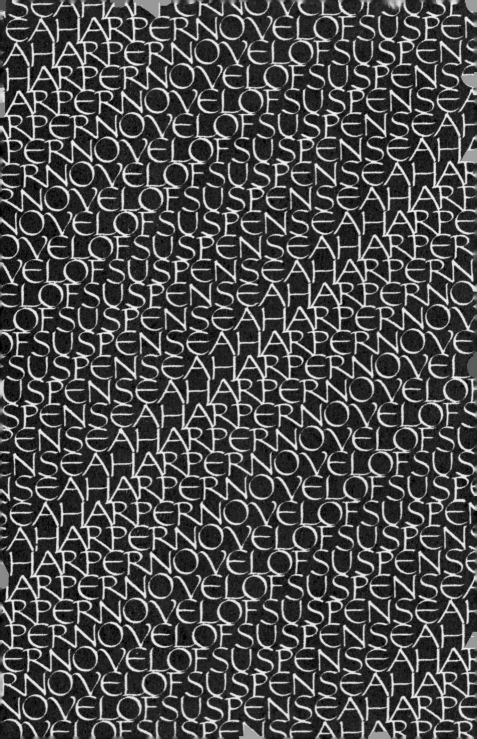